Never Love An Outlaw

Deadly Pistols MC Romance

Nicole Snow

Published in the United States of America.
First published in October, 2015.

Disclaimer: The following book is a work of fiction. Any resemblance characters in this story may have to real people is only coincidental.

Cover Design - Kevin McGrath - Kevin Does Art.
Photo by Allan Spiers Photography
Formatting –Polgarus Studio

Description

I'M FALLING FOR AN OUTLAW I HATE…

MEGAN

I wasn't supposed to end up in an outlaw biker's bed. I wasn't supposed to love it. I definitely wasn't supposed to crave his fiery kisses, beg for his touch, or ache to know the man behind the evil looking ink and scarred smirk.

I was the good girl. He was the monster. Then everything changed.

I became a prisoner. I prayed for Skin to save me. He did – and he kept me for himself.

He's no saint, and I'm no angel. They've already taken so much from me. I'm scared he'll take what's left.

Never love an outlaw, they said. I believed it. So why can't I stop myself from falling for this bad boy so hard I break?

SKIN

I went psycho when I saw her in that dirty whorehouse. She's everything I never wanted, a spitfire with a body meant for claiming.

Then she told me her secret, and I almost needed a straitjacket. I saved her life instead. I gave her a second chance.

I know she's a marked woman, caught between my club and the b*stards I killed. Damn if I won't make her wear my name, even if she's trouble on two long legs I can't stop picturing wrapped around me.

I'll brand her, bed her, own her, no matter how much hell I'll pay. Outlaws love like ticking time bombs, and I'm gonna blow Meg's world apart 'til she's begging for more…

The Outlaw Love books are stand alone romance novels featuring unique lovers and happy endings. No cliffhangers! This is Skin and Megan's story in the Deadly Pistols MC series.

I: Smothered in Shadows (Megan)

I couldn't remember my own name sometimes.

When you're so shocked, so broken, so completely sick at heart, the ego dies in every breath, and mine died fast.

My pimp kept me chained up like a dog when I wasn't being used. *Fresh,* he called me, the only name I responded to because Megan was so far away.

Megan was my name in another life. Megan was what they called me when I smiled and laughed, before I spent every waking minute in a nightmare.

"Fresh, baby, wake the fuck up." Ricky grabbed me by the hair and pulled me off my cot, breaking a beautiful sleep where I almost believed I wasn't trapped in this hellhole. "You've got business."

He grinned, showing his dirty teeth. Maybe I couldn't settle on a name or identity anymore, but I knew his.

Ricky the bastard was my judge, jury, and executioner for every day I managed to stay alive in this place.

"Okay, Ricky. Just give me a minute."

He nodded, satisfied, and then pulled the tarnished key out of his jeans. His coarse hands grazed my throat as he unlocked my collar. It was always too tight. I reached up and rubbed the tender, raw impression left by that damned collar like I always did.

Another day. Another John. Another chapter as Fresh, rather than Megan.

"The crew coming in means business for you and Bell," he growled, shoving a small plastic bin of soap, shampoo, and a towel in my face. "Get cleaned up. We're a little light today. Cherry Anne says she's sick, and I'm looking for you and Bell to pick up the slack. These guys aren't our regular big rig cocks. They're tough, mean, and they like to fuck *hard.* You'd better be ready to work for every red cent."

"Always, Ricky. Always."

I flashed him that soft, dead look that always seemed to make him shut up. I learned a long time ago not to negotiate, not to even speak to this man in anything resembling complete sentences. Saying more than I needed to got me into trouble, and sometimes planted nasty ideas in his brain, too.

He'd used me before, and it was always worse than the other Johns. The faceless men who came and went, paying for sex, rarely put any emotion into it. But when Ricky pushed my mouth over his cock, the pimp reminded me who held all the power here, and that I'd be his slave until the day he decided to sell me off to someone else.

Holding my breath, I squeezed the towel, almost ready to turn and head for the small bathroom attached to my room. I winced when I felt his fingers on my skin.

The pimp chuckled, running a fat hand all the way down my back, stopping in my inner thigh. He liked to pinch, and this time, he did it hard. I closed my eyes and let out a whimper.

"Fucking whore. You're the best one here, and you know it, don't you?" His dark eyes beamed down on mine, proud, sick, and demanding. "You're goddamned lucky I only let these boys have one hole. You'd think I was giving them the moon when they throw money at me for your hot little mouth. I can't wait to see what the rest of you earns someday soon. We're close to a buyer, baby. I just know it. I've got a couple bites."

His hand slid around my legs. Cupping my mound through my panties, he squeezed. My fingers twitched. I hadn't had to fight the urge to slap him, bite him, gouge his fucking eyes out for a long time.

But I did just then, praying he'd be done soon. I suppressed a shudder, holding in everything until he finally pulled his hand away.

"Go shower now, girl. These guys aren't the real patient type. I'll be watching today, keeping you safe, so no worries. You never know what these biker assholes can do."

Keeping me safe? It was so sick I wanted to laugh.

Bikers? Ugh. I remembered the last time I had to service them, the hard, vicious men from the Deadhands MC.

Their VP, Big Vic, was the only man who managed to scare me besides Ricky. The bastard grinned the entire time as he slammed my face into his crotch, hard enough to leave me sore for a couple days. Once, he leaned down and cursed in my ear between his ragged breaths, told me how much he'd like to shoot Ricky in the head and take me away forever.

I feared the day he'd actually come back and do it. The pimp was bad, but there were bigger bastards than him in this world, and that included everyone with a Deadhands' patch on their leather cut.

Ricky hit me with his dead-eyed *what-the-fuck-are-you-waiting-for?* stare.

I gave him another fake little smile, a nod, and then retreated into the bathroom. I heard my cot creek outside as he settled into it, humming lullabies to himself while he flipped his gun in his hands.

Those tunes made me think he had a soul once. The first few times I'd heard them, I thought maybe I could convince him to let me go once he was done with me. Maybe this was just business to him, money, and he didn't really want to hurt me unless he needed to.

Of course, the real Ricky wasn't like that at all. It was the ultimate wishful thinking. I had too many bruises and scars to prove it, too many nightmares that broke the only peace I got from hard labor in this miserable trucker whorehouse.

How many months has it been? I wondered, leaning into the shower to clean myself, loving the way the hissing shower head temporarily drowned out the horror of my life.

I couldn't figure out how much time had passed since my first day here, and I doubted I ever would. It had to be months, maybe years.

My reflection told the full story. The beautiful, confident, playful girl who used to stare back at me in the mirror turned into a dead-eyed whore with sunken cheeks, one I hated to even acknowledge.

Megan the socialite, the flirt, the dreamer, was dead. Long live the whore.

"Hey, Fresh! Hurry your sweet ass up! Don't bother with the fucking fishnets." He yelled it so loud I could practically feel the tremor in the tile underneath my feet.

Wincing, I dried myself quickly, and then slipped into a fresh change of clothes he'd laid out the day before. Calling it an outfit would be generous.

The purple lace bra was too damned tight. The Johns who managed to break them open always did me a favor, lending some relief to my poor boobs. Not that it mattered.

He had a near endless supply of the same cheap, suffocating lingerie for all the girls, including me.

"Yo, lady, hurry the fuck up!" This time, he slapped the wall. "I wanna get this show on the road. We don't got no time to dilly-dally, bitch, you hear me?"

"One more minute, Ricky. Almost ready. I promise."

The nervous bite in his voice made me smile. It never took much to upset him, really, and nothing did more than dealing with the Deadhands MC.

I couldn't completely blame the bastard for being

worried. Hell, I wondered if this would be the day they decided to burn this place down and take the girls for themselves, including me. My heart pumped terror every time I remembered Big Vic's big, ugly grin, the nose ring in the middle of his fat face twitching every time he roared some new humiliation.

Bitch! Cunt! Whore!

Ricky called me all the same names as the biker, but he didn't have a tenth of the wicked outlaw's hateful energy when he said them.

Shimmying my panties up one more time, I slid into my heels, and stepped outside. Ricky leaned on the frame leading into the hall, making hushed words with some man I couldn't see.

"Look, buddy, you can have her tongue any way you want. Grab her hair and fuck her 'til she gags. If you haven't heard our Fresh is the best little cocksucker this side of the mountains, then you've been living under a rock. But I need to be there for security."

"Security." A low, dark voice repeated the word, dripping sarcasm. "What the fuck do I look like, pimp? Some chump who's going to stand there getting sucked off while you watch?"

"It's not like that, mister. I'm just hanging out to protect my property. Hell, I'll put my eyes on the ground. You pay up, and you can do anything you want to her –"

"And I'm telling you I want some goddamned privacy. Don't make us turn this place upside down more than we already are, asshole." My jaw dropped as I watched two huge tattooed arms shove Ricky against the wall. "You're a clueless little shit, aren't you, pimp? There's a lot you don't get if you're not following what's going down here today. I fuck the way I want and take whatever I need, and so does every other man in this club. Yeah, yeah, I know you've got Deadhands' protection. Your first mistake was thinking any of us gave a shit the minute we walked in here."

They scuffled again, spilling their noise into the hallway.

"Hey!" Ricky let out a yelp and desperately grabbed for the man. The biker ripped his gun out of his hands first.

I backed into a corner, my mouth still hanging open, watching as the stranger's hands flung Ricky's handgun around like a toy.

"Play nice. Go mop the toilets or some shit like a good little boy, and maybe you can have this back. Give all the brothers some peace and quiet, stay the fuck outta our way, and you'll walk outta here today without a hole in your head."

"Skin, you're making a big mistake. I didn't know this was a fucking shakedown. I thought you guys were just here for the regional fees or some shit. We can work this out. Just let me talk to your chief and explain –"

The sickening slap of metal on thin skin cut him off. I pinched my eyes shut, wondering if this was just another bad dream.

No, of course not, I'd never been so lucky. Not since this became my life. Ricky whimpered, staggering in the narrow hallway in a circle, the same way he sometimes did when he got really drunk. Except this time there was pain glowing in his eyes, hurt and terror, something I'd never seen before on his nasty face.

Why does that look make me feel so excited and scared simultaneously?

"Get the fuck outside, Ricky," the stranger growled. "Stop crying and listen. I don't waste my time saying the same thing twice. Next time you give me any bullshit, pretending you've got everything under control and we're just here for a tea party, I'll break your fucking jaw. You'll lose teeth. Now, outta my damned way."

Ricky hit the wall again with a loud thud. Other sinister sounding male voices filled the hallway, just as a huge shadow stepped into the doorway.

My heart came to a total stop when I stared at him. It was dark and dingy, the only dull light coming through the blinds, turning my world into a canvass of shadows.

Tall, dark, and handsome didn't begin to describe the giant about to enter my world, and probably my body too.

Shit, *tall* didn't do him a bit of justice.

He was so big he had to duck when he finally stepped through the frame, into my room. Instinct forced me to walk backwards, pressed me against the wall. I froze, running my eyes across his leather vest for telltale signs of the demon red lettering and severed hand symbols the MC always wore.

But he didn't have that at all. His cut looked…cleaner, somehow. I didn't recognize the symbols either. Smoking guns, skulls, and neon yellow one-percent signs plastered his chest, flanking the patch with his name.

I looked and looked, and I couldn't believe what I was seeing. This was another club, another man, another dangerous predator ready to rip me to shreds.

The fear and shock broke my protective wall. We locked eyes, and I trembled, saying his name.

"Skin? Seriously?" I instantly regretted the words.

I lost my smart mouth the first few times Ricky slapped me across the face. I couldn't comprehend why it suddenly came back the second I was staring at a man ten times as dark and powerful as my brutal pimp.

He stopped less than a foot away from me, painfully close. His smile distorted the long scar across his cheek. All I could think about while I watched it was how it complimented his warrior look, like he'd just walked into the real world from the Norse legends I read about in college.

His huge, tattooed arm rose up to his chest, and he tapped the name patch with two fingers. "That's what they all call me, babe. Don't wear it out before I fuck you ragged."

Oh, God. My brain shut down. I couldn't understand why he was here anymore. Skin was too vicious, too strange, too devilishly good-looking to be in a whorehouse like this one.

I knew I'd just met my ruin.

Six Months Ago

Becky laughed in the driver's seat, taking the mountain curves way too fast. I was too drunk to care that we might go careening off into the nearest ravine, right through the flimsy guard rails.

Tonight was ours. We were out to conquer a new set of boys like we always did and drink ourselves stupid.

If only those damned heels would've stopped digging into my ankles…

"You fighting with your shoes again, girl?" my best friend said with a laugh. "You try way too hard when you flirt!"

"Whatever, it's not like they'll be staying on for long anyway," I said. "Crawford's been texting me all week. Pretty funny, really. I thought the son of the biggest real estate mogul in Knoxville would be knee-deep in pussy…he seems kinda desperate."

"Oh, please, they're all like that. Awkward rich boys." Becky spun the wheel in her hands. My stomach lurched as we took the next hard turn.

"Hey, at least he's cute. If he isn't a total dud tonight, maybe we'll be onto something."

"*Psssht.* We're too young to go hubby hunting, and you know it! This party's going to be packed with hot guys, Meg. Don't get in too deep having the hots for Craw-daddy. He wants in your panties and he's a heart breaker."

I rolled my eyes. She'd always been the perfect foil for all my wild intentions, and sometimes a bigger party slut than me.

Too bad. Becky wouldn't put the brakes on my fun tonight, and I wasn't buying her carefree attitude for once.

Lately, I'd been thinking a lot about growing up. Something about being twenty-two without a man, maybe, or else the fact that Daddy was getting more frustrated with me by the day, having me around the house.

I barely went to the Wilder Corp offices, even though I had an internship there through his strings. What did it matter? I had the same sweet trust fund that had gotten me through college. My salary rolled in like clockwork, whether I went in and answered a few phones each week, or slept off my latest hangover.

I'd plowed through college last spring and walked out with my Communications degree. Good for setting me up as the public face of Daddy's company after he decided to retire. And honestly, as long as I had my fun and landed a good husband, I didn't really care.

I was born a Wilder, and that meant living life on easy mode. I had the money and the name to be whoever I wanted.

It wasn't a sin to be figuring that out in my early twenties, right?

Sure, the future mattered, but I didn't have to think too hard. I didn't have to settle tonight. I just wanted to *explore,* have some fun with Crawford, and see if he was more than fuck buddy material.

I'd drink with Becky and the guys. Then we'd have the

best skinny dip of our young lives, cooling off in the private mountain pools, the perfect way to end a long, muggy September day.

The next mountain bend twisted my ankle as I dug my heel into the car's floor for support. *Fuck.*

Hiccuping, I reached down, fixing my strap. Becky laughed harder, snickering the whole time.

"You know, Meg, you could use some of that big family fortune to go to Nashville and have some fancy-schmacy designer there make you heels worth walking on. Last summer, when I went, I found this awesome little place where…"

Blah, blah, blah. I zoned out, too drunk and eager for fun to care about Becky lecturing me on fashion. My core tingled, excited for the night to come.

I lived for the chase, the first time with someone new. I'd never found anything better than taking on a new man, feeling his face and his hands all over my pussy. Despite my wild streak, I'd stayed a good girl.

I wouldn't give any man my cherry until he put a ring on my finger. I'd fuck him every other way, and feel his tongue all over me, but I wouldn't give *that* up.

Time was on my side, after all. I didn't care if I needed to suck off half of Eastern Tennessee before I found a man worthy of claiming me as his wife.

Becky was still blathering on about some fashion crap while I nodded and purred agreement. The car pulled onto Crawford family land, and we spied about a dozen other vehicles lined up on the side of the mountain.

For a second, I worried Becky was too trashed to parallel park without plowing into someone, but she managed. She always did.

As soon as the emergency brake was on, I popped my door, and staggered out, straightening my white summer dress. The slope leading up to the little party hut next to the mountain pools was hell on my legs, but I appreciated the warm-up.

I'd need it for all the fun I knew we'd have tonight. There'd be flirting, necking, and maybe finding a little love.

It was just another carefree Smoky Mountain night, the kind I lived for. What could possibly go wrong?

"Crawford, I don't know..."

"Aw, come on, baby. We've got this side of the waterfall all to ourselves. You're a lovely lady tonight, and I'm a hot blooded man, both of us rich as Midas. Stop fighting this thing we're both feeling. Let me be the first man to give it to you like nobody else ever will."

His hard cock moved against my leg. I laughed as he dove for my neck again.

Crawford was nice, lean, and strong, but he was either the clumsiest kisser I'd ever been with, or I was more drunk than I thought.

"Wait, wait. Let's not get carried away. I want to take this slow, Craw." I pushed against his chest until he rocked back.

His eyebrows furrowed. "You? Slow? Shit, that's not

the Meg Willow Wilder everybody knows. They all said you'd have your lips wrapped around me by now…"

I froze up, staring at him like he'd just punched me in the face. Hot, drunken anger burned my cheeks, so sultry they'd rage like furnaces if I reached up and touched them.

Okay, sure, I knew I had a reputation. But he was calling me a slut to my face, and expecting me to act like one. Consider me blindsided.

"You've been talking to other guys about me?"

Crawford's turn to blush. "Meg, come on, it's not like that. I just mean I thought you'd want to have some fun tonight, that's all. I didn't know you'd become a good girl overnight. Baby, who do I look like?"

Smiling, he inched towards me, throwing an arm around my shoulder. "You don't have to use your mouth with me for anything but a warm-up. Your friends talk a lot. I know you're still a virgin in one way, Meg. I know I'm good enough to fuck you. Why are you fighting this so hard, baby? Give me what I want tonight, and I'll give you all kinds of things that'll make you scream."

This couldn't be happening. Was he seriously bribing me? Trying to buy me off with some sick quid pro quo? Hell, with the way he'd been talking, he probably just wanted to bang me and brag about it to his friends.

My eyes bugged out as I fought him off, pushing through the cool mountain pool, covering my boobs with one arm.

I'd heard enough. I turned my back to him, swam several strokes to the rocky wall lining the pool, and clambered out. Crawford yelled something after me, but I barely heard him over the burbling waterfall next to us.

"Meg, wait! We can talk this out. I'm sorry, I got carried away. Come back!"

I couldn't believe it. Just when I wanted to get my life together, this asshole rubbed my reputation in my face, acting like he expected me to suck him off just because I'd been a total slut in the past.

Well, those days were over. I found my dress and towel laying on the nearby cooler where I'd placed them. I quickly dried myself off and dressed.

I didn't want him to follow. If he had another chance to talk to me later, it'd only be after I cooled off.

Maybe I'd whored myself to too many men. That was my mistake. But *nobody* treated me like they were entitled to my body or my family name, and I wasn't going to let Crawford be the first.

I didn't care if his family was a little richer than mine. Being a Wilder gave me all the wealth I'd ever need. It also meant I wasn't backing down for anyone who came after my ego, whether or not they had some truth behind it.

I stomped into the forest, heading onto a half-overgrown path. The clear night stars shone overhead, complemented by a huge summer moon. A walk would clear my head, take the edge off his stupid comments. I'd return in an hour or two and go from there, depending on how I felt.

I knew Becky would be screwing around with Tim Yates for a few more hours. I expected to stumble across her in some corner of the forest, rolling in the dirt with her latest dirty talking pump and dump crush.

They never lasted long. I could say the same, and the old Meg would've just shut up and went along with Crawford for the night, if only he were a better kisser.

I hated getting older. Thinking about my career, my family, finding my future husband just brought more anxiety. But nothing made me more anxious than thinking about the party lifestyle forever.

I couldn't creep toward thirty still acting like I was twenty-one. No fucking way.

When I came into a cool, dark clearing, I stopped to admire the view. The moonlight came down through the break in the trees. I walked over to the smoothest mountain boulder and sat, feeling the dew veil against my legs.

God, what a beautiful night. So, why was it becoming so ugly?

Soft, transparent mist swirled low on the ground. They didn't call them the Smoky Mountains for nothing.

I was busy focusing on the beauty when I heard something snap nearby. I spun and saw a figure coming through the darkness. Figuring it was Crawford, I bolted up, folding my arms, ready to hear his pathetic apologies.

"Look, before you start, I'm not in the mood for excuses."

"Excuses? My, my, girl. I'd say you're right out of a dream, standing here in the dark up in these mountains, but you're too angry to be a fantasy." His voice was older, too arrogant and gravely to be Craw's.

I whipped around and faced a tall, rugged looking man with a cap pulled tight over his eyes. He wore tight jeans and an open shirt. He looked like he'd just wandered out of a lumber mill or something.

Great. Running into weirdos up here in the boonies was exactly what I needed.

"Sorry. I…I thought you were somebody else." I looked him up and down, sizing him up. "What're you doing out here?"

He smiled, raising an eyebrow. "I could ask you the same thing. Seems you've gone a long way from the party happening down by the springs."

Crap. How did he know? We must've been really noisy, or else he just knew his turf that well.

Better than me, if I had to run.

Shuffling my feet uncomfortably, I tried not to think about how fucked I really was. I didn't know this man, nor his intentions.

Nobody except Crawford knew I'd run off – and knowing how much of a bitter wimp he was, he wouldn't be coming to my rescue. I could only hold my ground, and hope to God this was just some eccentric mountain man wanting to make friendly conversation.

"Too noisy for me," I lied. "I wanted to get away and enjoy the forest beauty while I'm up here. I don't get out to the Smokies as often as I'd like."

His thin smile widened, and he took a step closer. I was about to bolt when he flopped down on the boulder next to me, spreading his arms wide, staring up at the sky.

"It's a gorgeous fucking night, ain't it? My name's Richard, by the way." He tilted his head up and shot me a wink. He reached into his pocket.

I couldn't help but smile and feel a little more ease creep in when he drew out a small silver flask.

"Care for a swig? It's our very own moonshine. My grandpa's recipe."

I shook my head. Okay, maybe he wasn't the danger I'd feared at first.

Just a big, drunken mountain goof. I hoped. I'd seen his type before out hiking, and they never did any harm.

Friendly or not, there was no way I'd share a flask with a stranger.

"Suit yourself, princess." He popped the cap and took a long pull, then emptied the rest on the ground. "I was bullshitting you about the moonshine. It's just plain ol' Jack."

"Decent choice. Do you come here often, or maybe live nearby?" I decided to make small talk, taking my place several rocks away, fixing my eyes on the same distant stares filling his eyes.

"I'm a hiker. Nothing builds a man up like a bull better than taking these mountains one step at a time. It's always an adventure up here. You ever see the abandoned ghost towns tucked back in these mountains? People worked and lived and died in these parts for generations before they flew the coop, leaving their homes and a few old tractors behind. There's something charming about that. It takes you back, away from all this shit in our lives, you know? Simpler times. I like 'em."

I nodded glumly. Redneck or not, he was nice, and eerily in touch with my own feelings tonight.

Just then, I'd have given anything to get away from all my frustrations. Sure, I could hop a flight to Europe or the Caribbean next week, like I'd done on my summers off from college, but those getaways never lasted forever.

"Tell me more about your adventures again. Sometimes I think I could use some of that."

He tucked the flask back in his pocket, then sat up and smiled. "I do a lot of trucking when I'm away from home. It's hell half the time, honestly, driving down the Florida panhandle or all the way out to Cali-fucking-fornia with some boss riding my ass. But there's always a new experience every route, and that's what keeps me working more than just the money. New faces, new things, new thrills. You haven't been living 'til you've been through Wyoming in the winter and almost felt the wind blow your rig over."

"Sounds scary," I said, warming up more than I really should. A lot of it was the alcohol, a delayed buzz in my veins, but his tone sounded so honest, authentic in a way all the rich boys and girls I always hung around with couldn't be.

"You'd better believe it. The shitty parts of LA will make you feel alive too, when some gangbanger decides to take potshots at your truck just for sport. It's funny how being on the open road and putting up with so much shit makes a man appreciate the quiet more."

He stood up and walked out into the clearing, stretching toward the sky. I believed him.

"You said you don't come out here often? Well, hell, neither do I. And that's what makes me love it when I do. When you're busy dealing with crowded cities and traffic jams half the time like I am, these mountains are a slice of heaven. I wouldn't trade my adventures for nothing, even the shitty parts, because they make home what it is." He turned, his eyes narrowed. "Don't tell me this is as wild as you get? Skipping out on your friends and looking like you're about to freak the second some stranger says 'hello?'"

Christ, was it really that obvious? I smiled uneasily, shaking my head.

"Sorry. I'm a little on edge tonight. Like I said, I don't come up here often. You never know what a strange man might want out in the boonies."

"What if he just wants to give you a good time?" He paused, just long enough to feel my heart sink, while tension roiled my belly. "I'm not talking about fucking, girl."

That caught me off guard. I twisted my head, stood up, creeping closer as he extended a hand.

"You're too pretty for me anyway. Let's be friends for the night. I'll take you out for a burger and a malt." His smile grew, and I watched him reach into his pocket, this time taking out a pack of cigarettes.

I didn't know what the hell to think. He was offering

me a chance to leave my comfort zone behind. I had a weird feeling he could give me something authentic too, if only for an evening. He wasn't really my type – even for a fling – but if he really didn't care about that…

"No, Richard, I really shouldn't. I don't know you. My friends are waiting."

"Aw, come on. What's your name?"

"Megan."

His hand shot out, taking mine in his after I'd turned him down before, giving my fingers a tight, over-friendly squeeze.

"There. Now that we know each other, what do you say? You're a local, aren't you? We'll go get some grub and keep this conversation going. Then I'll drop you off before midnight. I know you want to get outta here, I can see it in your face. What've you got to lose?"

His soft, whimsical tone held a challenge. I hated being taunted, and he wasn't even doing it openly.

He shrugged impatiently. "Go tell your girlfriends if you need to. Let 'em know you're going out with Richard for a bite. That's all this is, babe, I promise. What do you think's gonna happen? You'll wind up on some late night murder mystery show with your eyes blacked out and duct tape on your mouth?"

Laughter belted out his gut, echoing through the shadowy forest. His laugh was high, sharp, and so unexpected I couldn't stop myself from giggling too.

"Okay, you win. You don't look like a killer or a rapist."

He began walking me down the path, the one leading further and further into the Smokies, away from Crawford's private property.

One more wink was all I needed to let him lead me along like a stupid schoolgirl.

If only I'd done something then. I could've run, yelled, screamed bloody murder, or at least re-awakened my old instinct to sober up and ask myself why the *hell* I decided to walk through the eerie mountains to a total stranger's pickup truck.

But he never made a move, not even when I was securely in his passenger seat, and we headed down the lonesome highway. He had to lure me deeper first.

I flipped the greasy burger over in my hands. I was hungry, yeah, but the deserted diner offered up some serious crap. I couldn't finish it.

The conversation wasn't going much better. Richard kept talking about his ex, some woman who walked out on him when he was my age, which must've been over a decade ago just looking at him.

I wasn't in the mood for lonely, stupid men tonight, however nice they might be. Whatever, at least it was better than hanging around, waiting for Crawford's awkward apologies. I reached into my purse for my phone at one point, only to realize I'd stupidly left it somewhere near the pool.

"Fuck," I sputtered, choking down a sickeningly sweet sip of strawberry milkshake.

"Yeah, I thought so too, baby doll. They always love you and leave you real fast, the bitches. If she'd stuck around, I'm sure my life would've been a lot more exciting by now. I wouldn't have to work my ass off every day and take these mountain hikes. Hell, I'd probably have a family, maybe a house, instead of renting a studio apartment above that goddamned forsaken place."

I blinked, barely even paying attention to his long, rambling life story anymore. "Hang on. I need to hit the restroom."

I headed in and splashed cool water over my face, looking for a pay phone on the way out. There had been one – I could see the faint gray outline where it used to attach to the wall, now ripped out, leaving a shadow like a relic from another time.

A cab ride home sounded awfully good right now. Unfortunately, short of asking the restaurant to make a call on their business phone, it wasn't looking like an option.

Richard was weird and needy, but he'd kept me company, and he didn't seem like a total creeper. Besides, I was getting more tired by the second, and what harm would there be in one more ride home?

If he was really going to ambush me, he'd have done it in the mountains.

I'd let him drop me off in my neighborhood so I could stumble home. He didn't need to see my parents' huge house and get his hopes up about doing favors for a woman who was richer and prettier than he'd ever be.

Total bitch? Yeah, sure. And also a *very* tired one.

Jesus, I was drained. It must've been the mountain walk. By the time I got back to the table, I could barely make my knees work, and I covered a brutal yawn with my hand.

I wanted to go to sleep right there. Luckily, he settled our bill with a waitress who was probably bored out of her skull. She didn't even stop to laugh at his wise cracks.

Closing my eyes for a second took what felt like five minutes. When I opened them again, Richard stood over me, pushing his hand into mine.

"Damn, girl. You're crashing on me, ain't you? We'd better get you home. Come on."

"I can stand," I moaned weakly.

No, no, I couldn't.

The instant I tried, my knees buckled, and I slumped into his arms. He scooped me up like a sleepy kitten and carried me outside, pushing me into the passenger seat, complete with a ratty old pillow he'd fished out of the back.

"Hold up, I need to give you my address," I said, struggling to remember the numbers in my own head as another jaw-popping yawn conquered me. "It's…uh…it's…"

"Don't think too hard, baby," he growled, starting up his truck. "I already know where you live. Just go to sleep. You'll need that energy for tomorrow."

What the fuck was this man talking about? Tomorrow? How did he know anything about me?

"Tomorrow? Huh?"

It felt like an entire hour slipped by before he answered me.

"That's the day you find out you fucked up bad tonight. I haven't picked up a new girl since Loretta left me when I was still a sad, broken little man, trying to make an honest living. That shit I told you at the diner tonight was true, but you didn't care. Nobody ever gives a fucking shit about some asshole hauling loads across the country. Whatever, baby, it's not your fault. You're a stuck up, rich little cunt, and I'm gonna give you something to care about."

I tried to jerk up, tried to scream, but I couldn't seem to move anything except my eyes. What happened to me? I hadn't been alone with him in the diner at all, except when I used the bathroom twice.

Twice. Goddamn it.

The first time, I'd come back, and our food was waiting for us. That had to be when he did it, slipped something into my food or drink, springing the trap he'd set from the very beginning.

The one I'd been too stupid and drunk to see.

"You...you lied."

His high, shrill laughter split the night, and everything in my head started spinning. "What? Were you expecting hugs and kisses and free meals from strange men in the woods? I don't know what kind of stupid bitch you are, but you're *mine* now. Sleep tight, little girl. And by the way, the name's Ricky. It fits me now. You ever heard of a pimp named Richard?"

Ricky. The last coherent thought before the blackness swallowed me up was knowing that I'd probably hate that name forever.

Oh, how right I'd been. I knew it the next day, when he splashed ice cold water in my face, and I realized I was completely naked.

He had my driver's license in his hand, twirling it around like a wild card in some poker game he'd just won.

"Jeeesus H. Christ, woman! I think you've just made me the happiest man in the world."

I glared at him, saying nothing. If it wasn't for the fear constantly churning in my stomach, I would've spit in his face. I hated his arrogance, his treachery, and my own stupidity, but I hated his cruel joy more than anything else.

"Let me go, Richard. It's not too late to pull back. You can drop me off with the cops, my family, I don't care. I just want to go home. I won't even press charges."

Yeah, right. He saw right through my hollow promises. Next thing I knew, his palm slapped me across the face, so sharp and sudden my whole head spun.

"It's Ricky, bitch. Get used to it. I'll let you off light because you're something else." He paused and sniffed, staring excitedly at my license again. "You know, I really thought I'd hit the jackpot when I got myself a pretty mountain girl, all doped up and goddamned beautiful. But shit, you should've told me you were a Wilder girl sooner.

Your pussy might make me retire early!"

Bastard. I swallowed the hard, hateful lump in my throat and forced myself to look at him, ignoring the fiery sting on my cheek.

"You're going to ransom me, then? Let me talk to Daddy. I can get you the money faster than if you do it alone, I swear, he'll –"

Ricky cut me off with his nasty, shrill laughter again. "Oh, please. You really think I'd give you up for a few bags of cash, only to have a SWAT team storm in here and tear this place apart? I've got better plans for you, little princess. You're gonna make some rich, twisted motherfucker *very* fucking happy. I just gotta spread the news through the grapevine and find myself a buyer."

My heart started pounding. I stood up, only to feel him throw me back down against the shitty bed, the flimsy mattress snapping against my spine.

"Don't do this, asshole! You have no idea who you're dealing with. You *will* pay, one way or another. My family won't let me go. My friends know where I disappeared. We can't be that far from town, somebody'll come looking and then you'll regret the night you saw me in that forest."

He rolled his eyes. "Yeah, yeah, you're not the first bitch to say that, trust me. You're just the richest little cunt I've ever had in here."

The richest? For the first time I lifted my head up and took a good look around.

The door to the small room was cracked. Ricky sensed my hesitation, and he marched over, flinging it open.

Across the hall, there was another room, also with its door wide open.

A dead-eyed, gray-faced woman sat on a bed, wearing nothing but cheap heels and torn stockings. She took a long look at me, pushing her long greasy hair behind one ear, and then turned back to her arm as if seeing a beautiful young woman with hot tears running down her face was completely normal here.

That passive, defeated look told me everything about the hellhole I'd fallen into. So did the rubber band around her arm. And so did the syringe she stabbed into her vein a second later, pushing it deep, until the junk hit her system and she let out a loud, heavenly moan.

"You starting to understand? A girl like you must have a fancy education. You're not stupid. Take a good, long look, bitch. That's your future. Only I ain't letting you have none of that junk. Gotta keep you happy and healthy for top dollar."

I lost it. I couldn't bear to take another look at the miserable woman, holed up just like me, and I couldn't stand for the pimp to see me cry either. I buried my face in my hands, letting the hot tears come, until he pinched my shoulder so hard I looked up.

"Stop crying, beautiful. I won't let you get hooked on shit. You're too valuable to me. Shit, I'm gonna make every boy who comes in here use rubbers too. I'm not letting anybody fuck you up with damage, drugs, or disease while you're working off your rent. You'll be treated like a queen compared to these other junkie whores."

I shook my head again. His cruel words blurred together, becoming incomprehensible. What the *fuck* was he getting at?

"What is this place?" My heart dropped another inch as I said it.

Deep down, I already knew.

Ricky stepped forward, wearing the same serpent smile I'd come to know too well, the one that strangled me, poisoned me, killed the woman named Megan.

"You kidding? Haven't you ever seen our billboards? Or are you one of those bitches who pays more attention to texting on her phone than the damned road when she's going down the highway?"

He reached into his pocket and pulled out a crumpled piece of paper. He slammed it against the wall, smoothing it out before he pressed it into my shaking hands.

It took everything not to retch when I saw the outrageous, neon letters and overdone whore with her lips pursed on the cover.

LONG HAUL? COME UNWIND AT THE BIGGEST, BADDEST, HOTTEST TRUCKER SPA IN EAST TENNESSEE!

A trucker spa. A dirty, ditzy fucking whorehouse. And now that I was on the inside, it was even more miserable and soul crushing than I'd ever imagined.

"Jesus…help me." It was the last thing I whispered before I took off running, flying into the cramped little bathroom attached to the beat up room.

Ricky held me like he actually cared while I spat out

my guts. He reached over me when I was finished, flushing the bile down, a loud, harsh sound like the end of my life.

"There, there, baby girl. Be good for me. Get it all out of your system. Your first clients are coming this afternoon. I need those pretty lips clean and healthy for their dicks. I'll bet you suck a mean cock."

I wanted to vomit again, but there was nothing left in my system. "Don't do this. *Please.* I'm a virgin."

That got his attention. Ricky's eyes flickered, and the nasty smile he wore disappeared. He crouched next to me on one knee, grabbed my head, and pulled me close, until I was only inches from his evil face.

"You gotta be shitting me. A rich party cunt like you?"

I nodded, feeling my whole body shake. I didn't know if I was making another huge mistake, or telling him the only thing that might save me, but I was way past caring.

I had to get out of this. I didn't belong here. Megan Willow Wilder wasn't ever supposed to be reduced to sucking off strangers in a creepy fucking trucker's spa.

If only I could delay him, trigger some mercy deep inside him…

But when I opened my eyes again and looked at him, his eyes were small and black. Cold, cruel, lifeless as coal.

"If I find out you're lying to me, bitch, I'll fuck you myself. I swear it." He reached for my chin, digging his fingers in so hard I could feel him on bone. "Last chance. You telling me the truth, or are you just fucking around?"

"It's true," I muttered, my voice cracking as more hot

tears came.

"Fuck. I never believed in miracles before, but I'm starting to think somebody up there loves me." His sick smile reappeared, and he looked right through the ceiling, before turning back to me with the same vacant expression as before.

"Okay, Meg, here's what we're gonna do – you'll put those lips to work like a good little girl and earn me some money to keep you fed, clothed, and sheltered. In the meantime, I'll do my damnedest to land you a permanent home. It's out of my control the day I've got a buyer, but as long as you're here, I promise it'll be sane, sweet, and easy."

Sane, sweet, and easy. It wouldn't be the first time he used that phrase.

I'd hear it over and over again, almost every fucking day, whenever I was washing my mouth out with baking soda and water, trying to forget the foul taste of latex and cherry flavored lube.

"Take a couple minutes to yourself, baby. I'll bring you some breakfast, leave you alone to get your head straight. You haven't figured out why you're here yet, and that's okay. Give it a few more weeks, a month or two, and you'll understand." His rough palm patted my cheek, and I slumped down, holding myself in a fetal position until I heard the door close behind him.

Alone. Defeated. Confused.

I didn't believe him then. It didn't seem like it was possible for me to ever understand anything again.

Six months showed me how wrong I was. They showed me I didn't even know who or what I was. I'd been stripped down, rebuilt, recreated in sorrow and shame and dozens of anonymous cocks.

My ego, my self, my mind disappeared in a haze of sweat and smoke. My pimp gave me food, shelter, and weed. I'd never been much of a pot head before, but I smoked up without hesitation.

I used the stuff to take the edge off, to take me away from this hell for a few blissful hours. I took the only escape he offered.

Ricky kept his word. Greed held the bastard to his promises, the only thing that saved me from the wretched existence of the other girls I shared a brothel with.

He carefully controlled the men who used me, and he even went so far to test me each week, steering the roughest, dirtiest truckers and thugs to his other girls – all of them except the Deadhands he feared. I became the golden girl again, the same thing I'd always been, but this time there was no glamor or pride.

I was still a whore, a prisoner, and completely broken.

Every day I stumbled awake and rubbed my sore eyes, I wondered if I was dreaming this demented fairy tale. Ricky wasn't the only demon here.

The bigger ones showed up just a few weeks in, the first time the bikers came to the whorehouse. I learned not to stick my head out of my room and stare at the men from the Deadhands MC too long. Whenever I did, they started to ask Ricky uncomfortable questions about his 'hot, new piece of ass.'

The first time Big Vic came after me, the brute shoved his gun in Ricky's face, told him he wouldn't hesitate to kill everybody here if he tried to get in the way. The pimp caved, pleading for his life, and begging them not to ruin his pet project – me.

I realized I wasn't the only one here forced into prostitution. Ricky groveled to the bikers. He feared them.

One day, he warned me point-blank, told me that if they ever wanted more, he couldn't protect me anymore. They'd take my virginity and whatever else they wanted, and he'd let them, since the alternative was ending up in a shallow grave.

These were the monsters in my story, my life, an endless parade of them. Some days, they were all I saw. I wondered about the yin to my yang, all the joy bled from my life.

It wasn't fair. There wasn't any balance.

Where was my prince? Where was my happy ending?

There had to be more to my life than working for this grubby, cruel man who smiled like a crocodile and never paid me a single cent for my slavery. There had to be another way out besides ending up with a sicker, richer, more brutal stranger, right?

I hoped and prayed. The months wore on, long and cold and brutal. The police didn't find me.

Life in the whorehouse became such business as usual that I wondered if I'd ever known anything else, or if my life in the big ranch on the hill had been a dream. Only the faded white summer dress hanging in my closet told me the truth.

Some nights, I held it close, trying not to stain it with more tears, my only reminder that another world was possible. I'd had it once, and had it stolen away.

"Don't forget," I'd whisper to myself. "There's a whole, wide world beyond this place."

Yes, there was. I'd known it once. Mountains, grand family picnics, and beer fueled laughter with friends and soft, playful men. Times with girlfriends and lovers who laughed at the gaudy billboards along the highways, who'd never dream of stepping foot into a trucker's spa with the sticky floors and hallow-eyed women.

I thought about Becky, Crawford, and my parents the most. Too bad they weren't as easy to hold onto as my dress, the last thing I'd worn as a free woman.

Lately, I couldn't even cry about them anymore, and I wondered why they felt so empty. My memories were fading with my mind, perhaps. He'd already taken away my name, depersonalized me the second week, when he started calling me Fresh.

Fresh, as in Fresh Meat. At first, I despised it, but little by little, it wore me down, until I forgot what it even felt like to be called by anything that wasn't fit for a low budget whore.

I accepted my name. It fit this hell, and most anything else I could imagine.

Sooner or later, I had to stop waiting, wondering, hoping. I had to accept my fate.

There were no heroes in this story, and there wouldn't be a happy ending. I was going to be Ricky's until the bitter end.

And if I wanted to stay alive, I had to be dead inside to the man who took me next. Strangers used my lips, my tongue every single day, and giving up more of my body didn't bother me anymore.

But I wouldn't give them any joy, any spark, any life. I had none left to give.

Meg died. Fresh lived.

I swore I'd go to my grave with that name, and if any filthy bastard who touched me ever called me anything else, he'd have to strangle me to make me stop tearing pieces out of his flesh.

The pimp killed Meg without a fight. Fresh wouldn't go down so easy.

She wouldn't wait for her knight or her happy ending. She'd pick up the shattered pieces of herself and wield them like broken glass.

II: IOU (Skin)

Twenty-four Hours Earlier

The worst part about the club being flat out broke? No fucking pussy.

When I heard the Prez wanted us to shakedown the trucker spas toward Knoxville, I could've ripped out my nine millimeter and shot it through the ceiling, screaming like an idiot.

I rolled out of bed early, showered and dressed, threw on a clean shirt and my cut. I took a second to study myself in the cracked mirror, a morning ritual I'd started the day I earned my prospect patch.

The colors on this leather had changed a lot over the years, but what it meant hadn't. Everything here was *earned,* just like a soldier's medals, the story of my entire adult life writ in blood and fire.

My fingers trailed up cold leather, grazing the skull with the one-percent sign etched into its head. I got that the first time I went away for the club after a bar fight. I could still feel myself gripping a pool cue, slamming it across the disrespectful motherfucker's head, the smartass who'd pushed the Veep and called our club *piss.*

I'd slowly filled my cut with skulls and pistols after that, patches I'd earned for killing more disrespectful fucks and finishing runs for the club. I turned around in the mirror, glancing at the backside, which told all the rest.

Everything I'd ever die for appeared in the blood red smoking pistols and the skull sewn into the back. DEADLY PISTOLS MC, TENNESSEE, surrounded it.

Seeing my colors sent hot, angry blood flowing through my fists.

Some men had careers that kept them running like fucking hamsters, and other boys had families. This club was my job, my blood, my whole life.

I didn't do cubicles, and I damned sure didn't do love. That gun with the smoke pouring out of it reminded me of my place in the world every day – the only place I'd ever belonged.

The club had been good to me, and always would be. She might be in dire straits now, but fuck if I'd go limp and walk away. When I got patched in as a full voting member, I vowed my life, and now I was trying every day to stop the MC's lifeblood from bleeding through my hands as Treasurer.

We needed money, and lots of it. Collecting our tribute from the Deadhands' network of shitty whorehouses would tide us over for a while, but we were really after a treasure map.

I was putting on my helmet when the brothers filed

out, one by one, everybody heading for their bikes.

The Veep, Joker, wore the same deadpan rip-your-arms-out-of-their-sockets expression he always did. The two prospects, Tinman and Lion, walked with him, and they all started their engines, holding position for the Prez.

"You remember the plan, Skin? Or did you forget last night while you were beating off to cable porn?" Firefly got on his bike next to me and shot me a sharp look, a fresh smoke in his mouth, blowing contrails over his bars.

"Fuck you, man. You know I'm more in love with the ladies than the bottle. Sorry all that sweet Jack makes it so hard to get your dick up."

He grunted and laughed, then blew a long stream of smoke toward me. I ducked, wondering if there was some truth to the shit I flung at him.

Yeah, I'd been jerking off last night. What red blooded man with hurricane force testosterone and no pussy in sight wouldn't? I thought about the last girl I had under me while I pumped the volume up so high it must've disrupted our Enforcer's beauty sleep.

Her name was Stockings. Or at least that was the nickname I gave her. She was too drunk to mumble out her name, and I didn't fucking care. She looked a lot like the whore on the screen I beat my cock to last night.

One hard night with my face and cock buried in her pussy taught her mine. They *always* remembered Skin. And they always fell hard and fast too, coming back to find me in a bar or at the clubhouse with those big doe eyes.

I had to turn 'em down. I rarely fucked the same chick twice, and never when they were expecting something.

Too many wanted to bag themselves a biker boy and turn into proper old ladies when times were better. Ever since our budget dived into the red, the real sluts didn't come around no more. They gave it up for easy, free flowing booze or bud, and that shit was the first to go when I delivered the financials last month, and the Prez laid down the law.

Speaking of the Prez…shit, he stomped through the garage looking like he had a fire breathing dragon crawling underneath his skin. Every man who heard his name before they saw him expected someone older, weaker, a stallion put out to pasture.

But Dust had been running this club since my balls dropped. He'd ridden with my old man and squeezed my shoulder at Dad's funeral. He'd given me my prospect patch and my bottom rocker. He'd killed more sonsofbitches than all of us combined.

Fun wasn't this man's specialty. He was all business, all the fucking time, and he looked more intense than ever today, slowing his walk as he stepped past us, hitting us with those dark gray eyes like a commander inspecting his troops.

He fit the part. And he left Crawl and Sixty mumbling apologies as they swung their legs over their bikes, making excuses about being late because they had a call, or the coffeepot was broken or some shit.

I rolled my eyes. Firefly pulled his helmet down and

stubbed out his cigarette, flashing me an energetic look that said it was about to get all too real.

"All right, boys, you know the drill! The Prez, the Veep, and the prospects are gonna hit the little cock stops on the edge of town, and fan out toward Tri Cities today. As for the rest of us, we're taking on the big one run by that goddamned viper, Ricky McNumbnuts or whatever the fuck his name is."

The brothers laughed. Even I cracked a smile, not that the dirtiest pimp in the county was a laughing matter.

"Any questions? Hit 'em now or I'll hit all you sorry fucks later for not asking me or the Prez."

We waited about ten seconds, and nobody had anything. The Prez pulled up on his bike and the VP followed, everyone filing into formation, before we split into two groups on the highway.

Attack mode. We'd done this drill before. I'd been through it a couple dozen times over the years, and it still got the adrenaline flowing, which meant more testosterone and more raging hard-ons if shit got heated enough.

Fuck. I regretted not beating off a few more times last night, or trying to track down that Stockings chick to fuck and dump again.

"Ya'll heard the man," Dust growled, stopping at our open gate and looking over his shoulder. "Shut those shitholes down for a day. Don't come back 'til you do. They're human toilets, and we've let 'em troll for the Deadhands for too damned long in our own backyard. They ought to be paying us for the privilege of operating in our territory. They owe us big for hosting our enemies on our turf, and we're not walking away 'til they pay up. You know what we accept – talk, blood, or cold hard cash."

Men cheered. I just nodded, having a funny feeling the last one excited the Prez the most.

"Remember, boys – forever deadly, forever pistols." With our battle cry, the Prez surged ahead, and we all rode out behind him, a flock of roaring motorcycles gunning into the mountains.

We split into two teams several miles down the road, our group heading for the massive trucker spa. A man couldn't miss the damned place – the billboards only got closer together and more outrageous the closer we came.

I'd never stepped foot inside it before. I looked up at the plastic-looking models on the billboards and clenched my teeth, unsure whether to laugh or rage.

I'd bet my left nut there wouldn't be a single chick there half that good-looking. I'd heard all about these places before. They were nasty little rat nests full of greasy pimps and desperate girls, usually chicks being paid in booze, crystal, or smack, while the shitheads controlling them pocketed all the money.

Some guys said Ricky's joint had women there unwillingly. He'd have his day of reckoning one way or another, if that was true, but the club couldn't bring him down while we were flat out broke.

We needed to rattle the bastard first. Scope the place out, see how well armed he was or how much he'd let his guard down. The Deads taking him under their wing couldn't fly either.

We should've run the fuckers outta our territory the first time we caught a whiff of them coming across the state line. But the club was distracted then, putting its fingers into too many projects in a desperate shot at going legit.

Dust had two auto chop shops, a strip club, and a bar going. Everything except our main garage went bust in less than a year. I knew it better than anybody, handling the financials as the club's Treasurer.

Talk about a goddamned train wreck. Nobody blamed the Prez for trying. We had to find something after Dust's old man decided to wind down the drug trade before passing the gavel to his son, and we did our damnedest to keep ourselves clean.

Naturally, it didn't work, and now the only path open to us was guns. Too bad we were lined in by enemies like the Deadhands, and we'd have to fight our way through them to the coast if we ever wanted a shot at trading with the bigger, more powerful clubs out West. The Prairie Devils and Grizzlies wouldn't give us the time of day unless they respected us – and right now we ended up in fistfights at Sturgis because the other bastards didn't even know our name.

I watched Firefly make a sharp turn in front of me, going down the exit. I held onto my bike and gunned it, feeling the Harley's comforting growl between my legs. The ride gave everything below my waist the most excitement I was likely to see all week – unless the whorehouse had even one fuckable woman worth paying for.

We pulled into the cracked parking lot. Sixty whistled, pulled off his helmet, and squinted at me, stroking his goatee.

"Fuck a duck. Am I the only one who expected this place to look like a carnival on the inside only?"

Crawl and I both snorted. He wasn't wrong.

The outside walls were flaking neon pink paint. The entrance was flanked with four big circus poles painted barber shop red-white-and-blue. Didn't notice they were round at the top like dicks 'til we got off our bikes and started heading for the door.

I pushed my way in first, hand at my hip. The entryway looked like a run down lobby, and I rang the bell, taking a careful look to make sure we hadn't missed any girls or Johns loitering out front.

When we did this housecleaning shit, we put everybody on lockdown. No stragglers.

"Hey, gents. You here as a group, or are you looking for some one-on-one action?"

A thin, wiry man came walking up. Skinny, ugly, and too damned young to be working in a shithole like this.

Didn't mean he wasn't dangerous. I reached for the nine millimeter on my hip and drew. All three of my brothers pulled their guns too, and I heard them click behind me, aiming all our firepower at the gawky-looking asshole who came up to the front desk.

"Hands in front of you where we can see 'em," I growled, locking my eyes on his wrists.

"Whoa!" The snake looked like he was about to shit. He listened, though, and that was all that mattered. "Can I *help* you guys? I'm real sorry, I don't recognize your patches...you're not with the Deadhands, are you?"

"No." Firefly stepped in front of me, lowering his gun and slapping the counter. "Get your boss, Ricky, out here right fucking now. We've got business."

The man licked his pale lips. "Uh, mind if I ask what it's all about?"

"We're not asking you again!" I snarled. "If you don't get his ass out here in the next thirty seconds, we're gonna be talking to you. Oh, and make sure he comes out with his hands up. Wouldn't want any misunderstandings, you dig?"

We waited. Our guns went up the second Ricky came trotting in. Bastard was tall, pot-bellied, and weaselly as ever. I'd only seen the pimp a couple times, back when he'd come to our clubhouse, fishing for protection.

The club didn't owe him shit. He owed us for pushing pussy in our territory, and now he'd wound up on our bad side by hosting our fiercest enemies.

"Hold up, pimp." I pointed my gun at his head, freezing him in his tracks. "Don't even think about reaching under your belt."

"What? Not even for a condom?" The pimp gave us a crooked smile. "I'm happy to have you boys as customers or –"

"Shut the fuck up. We're not here for pleasure." Firefly stepped up, pulled out his phone, and thumbed the camera lens on it.

Crawl cleared his throat. "Well, Prez didn't say anything about sampling the goods while we're taking inventory..."

Ricky laughed. My heart throbbed. Goddammit.

My horny, older brother was just as hard up as everybody else for pussy since our parties dried up and the girls stopped coming to the clubhouse. Only difference was he'd fuck anything that moved, and I'd always had high standards.

"My house is your house, boys. Anything you want. Neighborly discount. Just, come on, put the guns down, guys." Ricky's voice trembled.

"We'll think about it once we've decided you're not storing shit for the Deads." Firefly moved his gun down to Ricky's chest and spat at the floor, before he turned to me. "Skin, take this sorry sonofabitch in the back and make sure he doesn't get smart. The rest of us are gonna comb through these rooms and hit his office. We'll save the red meat on paper for you to dig through later."

"You got it, Sarge." I walked up and shoved the barrel of my gun into the pimp's skin. "Start walking, asshole. I wanna see your whores and make sure there's nobody else hiding out in those dirty rooms. You'd better be honest, starting right now. If I find anything I shouldn't, I fucking swear to God..."

I stopped, pushing the gun harder into his scrawny

back, 'til the metal rubbed on bone. Ricky jerked forward, throwing his arms up in the air.

"Okay, okay! Christ, man. Cut me some fucking slack. It's not like I expected any of this shit today. If you'd given me some kinda heads-up, I'd have –"

"Bite your damned tongue and walk. I don't have time for these bullshit excuses."

He led me forward. The place was big, but it wasn't half the size I'd expected. If this truly was the biggest trucker spa on this side of the state, it made me wonder what ugly little sewers the rest of them were.

The first two rooms we walked through were about what I expected. Girls in cheap, torn hose and ratty fishnets, slumped on even cheaper beds. They barely cracked their eyes when he opened their doors and smiled at them.

They gave their boss a look like he'd just told them the whorehouse was going clean. One of them moaned, something soft and incoherent about being a good girl for good ice. She looked at me and licked her pale lips.

"My, you're a mean-looking one. Why don't you come in here and let my tongue do the talking, sugar? Shit, I bet you pay in that nice, pure stuff too, don't ya? Listen, if you've got any of that on you, I don't even need cash. I'll do anything and everything for a few more hits of heaven."

Fuck. If only I could've put a bag with holes over her head and pray my dick didn't fall out after I screwed her mouth. She had a sexy voice, but that body was thin, blotchy, clammy.

My sex deprived dick stopped right in its tracks. I'd had a long dry spell, but I wasn't *that* fucking desperate.

"Shut your whore mouth, Hazel," Ricky snapped, turning to me with nervous shame in his eyes. "She's had a slow week. I'm sorry about that, you can take a lap around if you wanna make sure there's no guns and shit inside. I'm going across the hall, just for a second…next girl's a softie. Scares easy. She needs a little prepping before you barge in. She's the best I've got."

I ignored the whore, Hazel, and did exactly that. Kept my eye on the pimp outside the door, wondering why the fuck he was bent on giving so much special attention to this new chick, when he'd shown all the others nothing but scorn.

Ricky's girls barely seemed to own anything. I looked for telltale signs of chains, handcuffs, anything that might tell me they were slaves. I had a serious urge to unchain any whores there being kept prisoner.

Not because I wanted to play hero. No, I wanted to spite the miserable piece of shit for prowling around underneath our noses, spite this whole fucking place for teasing me with sex when I hadn't gotten my cock soaked and sucked for at least a solid month.

But I didn't see any slave girls. I started to doubt the rumors were even true.

The sluts in the other rooms whined or buried their faces in their pillows. They were miserable, but only because I wasn't bringing them drugs. They wanted business – not freedom.

Soon as I saw there wasn't any contraband hidden for the Deads, I stepped out into the hallway, just as that greasy little prick came walking toward me again.

"If you're here for pussy, I'm down with that, but you've got to be careful with this girl."

"Careful?" I cocked my head.

My gut told me this fuck was hiding something. I didn't come here looking for a hot, warm hole – especially after I'd seen the run down tramps this asshole had on market.

"Yeah," Ricky clucked anxiously. "Just...don't be too hard on her. You can only have her mouth. Everything below the waist is off limits with this bitch. Her choice, not mine, and I respect it. Use a condom too."

Bullshit, I thought, studying his face.

Okay, now I was totally convinced. The way that smirk disappeared when he talked about her told me something was up.

He was feeding me a steaming load of crap, and I decided there was no good reason I couldn't do the same.

"Outta my way," I growled, shoving my hand into his chest so hard he flew back and slapped the wall.

"Wait, Skin! You can't go in there without me. Wait, wait, wait..."

I let him catch up before I looked him dead in the eyes. "You've got five seconds. Hearing you flapping your gums just makes me want to fuck her even harder. I'll have her, and I'll do it alone. You think I give a fuck about your roles, you're flat out wrong."

He winced. The pimp's nervousness doubled, and he started giving me some shit about how he had to hang out and watch, for 'security' purposes, telling me again I could use her mouth, but not anything else.

I'd had enough.

I reached for his gun and slammed him into the wall so fucking hard his teeth rattled. Music to my ears, and I wanted more.

"Play nice. Go mop the toilets or some shit like a good little boy, and maybe you can have this back."

I must've been speaking a different language. The fuck whined about us, pretended he didn't know this was a 'shakedown.'

He couldn't be that fucking stupid. *Of course* we weren't here for tea, we were here to bust his ass for info, guns, money, and to flush this viper's nest clean of any poison. I held on tight to his greasy gun and pistol whipped his ugly face so hard his head slammed into the wall.

One. Two. Three.

The third time, I almost busted out his teeth. I realized my cock was hard, and it wasn't just due to the power struggle here.

I was honestly starting to get my hopes up that maybe the girl in the other room wasn't just another piece of half-starved druggie meat.

Maybe she'd look halfway decent. Maybe I'd actually want to fuck her.

What then?

Ricky whined some shit I didn't pay attention to, wiping the blood off his lip. I stuffed his gun into my pants and turned, giving him one last push against the wall as I told him to get the fuck outside and out of my sight.

I'd do this alone, or I'd knock him out cold and pop half the teeth in his mouth like popcorn kernels.

The blows to the face must've knocked some sense into him. He didn't follow when I walked into the chick's dark room and slammed the door behind me.

She huddled in a corner, and I caught a flash of bright blue eyes in the darkness. Awesome blue eyes, the color of hot gas flames ready to ignite the world.

Shit. She was pretty.

No, fuck pretty. Compared to all the other bitches here, maybe even most chicks I'd seen in my life, this girl left them all in the stinking dust.

She had three times the curves on her slender body the other whores had. Her skin looked more pristine with every step I took closer. She looked healthy, sexy. She looked like the first thing in a long time that truly caused my cock to bolt up.

My dick begged me to slam her against the nearest wall. The fucking hair stood up on the back of my neck when I looked at her, imagining those blue eyes rippling like pools while I slammed myself into her, snarling like a devil and filling her cunt with my come.

The young brunette looked scared out of her wits, and she couldn't stop running her eyes up and down my cut, like she already wanted me. Or else she wanted to figure out what the fuck I was doing standing there.

What the hell? She had to have seen a biker bastard like me before. She'd probably taken about a dozen cocks from the Deads, not to mention a few hundred truckers, but damn if she didn't look like a virgin.

My cock hammered like mad in my pants by the time I was close enough to speak. Fire churned hot in my balls, sending pure hellfire into my blood. My brain still wanted me to talk like a sensible man, but everything below the waist decided then and there that I *had* to fuck this girl.

My boot scraped something on the ground – a scrap of leather and metal. I realized it was a chain, like something for a dog.

Fuck me. What kinda kinky shit did that twisted little shit have her doing?

Her eyes locked onto my name patch. I was about to reach for her sweet, sexy face and take what my cock commanded me to when her plump lips opened, too plush and healthy for any Tennessee whore I'd ever known.

"Skin? Seriously?"

Fuck, maybe she was actually half as innocent as she looked. I smiled, reached up, and pounded my fist on my chest.

"That's what they all call me, babe. Don't wear it out before I fuck you ragged." My dick throbbed again, harder every time.

I hated fighting the unruly bastard. I seriously wanted to do everything I said, but I didn't come here to fuck whores. I just had to make her believe it.

Her cheeks flushed. Turned honest-to-God red, like some prom girl on a date letting a man see her panties for the first time.

"You got a name? Or at least a sexy nickname from your jackass pimp?"

"Fresh." She paused. "You know...like fresh meat."

I threw my head back and laughed. It was cruel, absurd, and downright fucking stupid. That couldn't be the name I'd call her by. Not a fuckin' chance.

I reached for her face, cupped her chin, and squeezed. Leave it to Ricky to give the most beautiful woman I'd seen in this place the stupidest goddamned name on the planet.

"Seriously, what the fuck's going on here?" I gestured to the limp leash with the chain on the floor. "You don't seem as whacked out as all the other girls. I know you get special treatment. The bastard was all nervous before I came in here, begged me not to see you alone. Why does he chain you up if he's so hell-bent on selling your mouth to strangers?"

My eyes fell to her lips. Fuck, they were moneymakers, if I ever saw any. Sweet, glossy and vibrant. Just the kinda lips I liked to imagine wrapped around every inch of me, pulling on my balls, stamping wet kisses up and down my body before I claimed the wet heat between her legs and shook her 'til she screamed.

"Because I'm Ricky's favorite. His prisoner." The minute she said it, she spun around, refusing to face me.

I watched her little hand cover her mouth. *Prisoner,*

huh?

Now, we were getting to some meat and bones. My arm went around her waist and I pulled her tight, slamming her into me, making me gasp 'til she met my eyes.

"Start talking. I knew he was sweeping something under the rug."

"I can't," she whispered, wiping the long, hot tear sliding down her cheek. "Please, just let me do my job. I shouldn't be telling you any of this. This is what you're here for, right?"

She jerked toward the nightstand, bending in my arms. A drawer popped open, revealing the biggest stash of condoms I'd ever seen.

Blood rushed to my dick. For a second, I seriously considered letting her gag on my cock if she didn't want to talk. Too bad I was born with a conscience, and all the violence and dirty deals in the MC hadn't beaten it outta me yet.

She turned gently, wearing a shaky smile, tearing at the foil with her teeth. My fingers darted out and I flicked the condom out of her grip. It hit the floor with a loud bounce.

Surprise shone in those perfect blue eyes. But it wasn't half of what I saw a second later, when I picked her up and moved her across the room, flattening her against the nearest wall. She gasped, so sharp and sudden I wanted to hear it a hundred more times, preferably naked and moaning.

"What do you want? I thought you'd rather have me on my knees," she sputtered, shock crinkling her face.

"I want you to sing. I'm not here to fuck. My brothers and I hit this dump to see what Ricky's been up to, and you're the first interesting thing I've found. Who are you? Really?"

She cracked. I loosened my grip as more hot tears fell down her face. I ran my fingers through her chestnut hair, noticeably cleaner and softer than the other girls I'd seen. They couldn't compare.

"Megan Willow Wilder," she hissed, soft and harsh in my ear.

"The fuck?" That was a fancy name for a place where the girls were supposed to have stupid names like Honey, Cherry Anne, or Fresh.

She shook her head, tightening her face like she couldn't believe I'd never heard the name.

"Spill it, babe," I growled. "You're not supposed to be here, and I need to know why."

"I was kidnapped. He drugged me, brought me here, chained me up. Ricky pimps me out to cover my upkeep, but he really wants to find me a buyer for bigger bucks. I'm a virgin."

I had to catch another laugh tearing at my throat. No fucking way.

Did she really expect me to believe this? A virgin in a trucker spa, sucking off guys and wearing a kink chain? For all I knew, she was Ricky's favorite, the pimp's personal slut that he used to unwind after a long day of work. Some of the bastards had them, after all.

"I'm Eric and Judy Wilder's daughter. Look them up, please." She sounded desperate. Probably noticed the skepticism lining my smirk. "You have to believe me. We're rich, my dad owns three businesses all over the state, just do a search and you'll see. You have to get me out of here, Skin. Please. Get me out, before Ricky gets what he wants. I don't want to die a fucking slave!"

That did it. My fingers smoothed their way through her hair, and then I pulled it tight. I forced her to look at me through the tears.

I had an incredible ear for bullshit. Always had.

This chick's story sounded like a drugged out fairy tale, but damn if she didn't put up a good act. "It's not too late, Skin. Take me with you. I'll do anything to get out of here."

Her tongue flicked across her lips. Her small, soft hands pushed against my chest. Those palms traveled downward, and I saw lightning in her eyes when she moved them over my abs.

My cock screamed, begging me to take her, to do the one crazy thing I couldn't. Not today, anyway.

Not after the shit she'd just told me. I wasn't gonna fuck an honest-to-God slave, no matter how hot she looked in that cheap getup. Not unless she surrendered willingly with nothing more than unbridled lust.

No bullshit. No quid pro quo. No bargaining.

Fuck. I grabbed both her wrists and pushed her away, putting some sorely needed space between us.

A man can't think rationally when he's been without a woman this long. Especially a man who's used to getting what he wants, fucking women with ease, feeling them fall all over him just because he's got the right patch and a hard, inked body underneath it.

"I can't do it," I growled, eyeing the disappointment in her face. "There's no way to know you're not putting up a smokescreen 'til I check you out. I get it, I asked, but what the fuck do you think I'm supposed to do with a question like that? Throw you on the back of my bike and ride off into the sunset after I shoot the pimp in the gut and leave him here to bleed like a stuck fuckin' pig?"

Her eyes shined hopefully. Damn if it didn't sound good to me, too, but I'd been in this lifestyle long enough to know it was too simple. Too convenient. We couldn't be reckless – not when the Deads were certain to come sniffing around a dead pimp under their protection.

Dust and Joker would give me hell if it went off like that too. I had to go back, check this woman out, and clear it with my brothers. If rescue was in the cards, then I needed backup. There wasn't another way, not if I wanted to keep my sanity and make sure we all stayed alive.

"If you gave a shit, you would," she said coldly.

I narrowed my eyes, wondering what kind of sexy, strange little thing I was really dealing with. Challenges didn't scare me away, but damn if she wasn't asking for the impossible.

I had to prove her wrong. I had to get her the fuck out of here, and trash the dirty pimp keeping these drugged out chicks chained up like dogs.

"I'll look you up, Meg, and I'll be back." She shuddered as I grabbed her, jerked her close, pinned her in my embrace.

"Bullshit. I shouldn't have said anything." She sighed, her voice straining with more sadness. "You men are all the same. You're the first one I thought might be decent enough to save me, and I told you everything. I can't believe what a *fucking idiot* I am."

My fingers pinched her cheeks, hard enough to shut her the hell up. Then I folded my hands behind her soft, fragile neck and pulled the heavy silver loop off my ringer finger.

My eyes pierced hers. I'd let her keep clucking about how bad I was. Didn't give a shit if she thought I was the devil himself.

"I slipped up," she whimpered. "Go ahead. Leave me here. Pretend you didn't hear anything."

Just a few more days. She'd see how flat out wrong she was.

"I'm telling you, I'm coming back. Take this and stuff it somewhere he won't find it," I said, pressing my ring into her hands. "You'll give it back to me when I break you outta here for good. This is a club ring and a family heirloom of sorts. My brothers tugged this thing off my old man's dead, cold fingers. It's all I've got. If you think I'm gonna abandon ship, then you'd better take a good, hard look at who you're dealing with. That ring's mine, babe, and so are you. I'm not leaving either one of 'em to rot in this shithole."

I fist-thumped my chest, right across my name tag. I wanted to burn my name into her brain every waking minute.

She'd better get used to hearing, thinking, seeing *Skin,* and nothing else. That was the name she'd be calling her savior soon, the one she'd be begging with those lush little lips, the only name she'd be screaming when I threw her into bed and fucked her so hard I wiped away every last trace of the dirty, violent bastards she'd served in this place.

"Give me a couple days or so. I'll be right back here for you, baby, and next time you'll be coming with me. I promise."

Her lips pursed sourly. For a second, I thought she meant to give me more sass, more of her ridiculous doubts. But she squeezed her palm around my dad's club ring and brushed away more tears.

"I need to go. He'll start wondering what the fuck we're doing in here if I linger too long." I gave her a sharp look. "Keep that thing safe. I'm counting on it. Anytime you start to doubt, think you're meant to be here forever, you pick it up and fold your hand around it just like that. Hold on 'til it burns your skin. You don't belong here, Meg, and I'm not letting you spend a second longer in this fucked up cage the instant I get my brothers on board."

I put one arm over her shoulder, guiding her to the bed. Tears rolled down her face in steady, hot rivulets. I brushed away as many as I could, feeling her jerk softly each time I touched her face.

Fuck, that face.

For a whore, she really was beautiful. It wasn't just the lighting or my own imagination. Hell no.

The woman was real, every damned inch of her. Prettier than the vapid party girls who normally sucked and fucked every inch of me. They came to ride cock and put their lips on a biker boy when their dirty mouths weren't on the bottle, or some weaker man.

Yeah, the girl in front of me had sucked off too many strangers to count, and the only thing I saw on her lips was a rough desire for freedom. Something about that struck a cord, making me finger the gun near my holster.

Who the hell knew irony could be so sexy?

I kissed her on the forehead and turned, before the urge to walk out and blow the pimp's brains against the wall became too much to resist. The rat bastard stood in the hall, waiting for me like an impatient hall monitor, when I stepped out and gently pushed the door shut behind me.

"Well? Did you enjoy yourself?" The cut on his bottom lip was starting to dry, but he'd have a lot more swelling soon.

Good. It was the first punch of many the asshole deserved if even half of what she'd told me was true.

I didn't say shit. His scorned ass didn't deserve an answer. I walked right past him, heading for the beat up lobby, and found the rest of my brothers waiting there. Firefly gave me a look like he'd been waiting forever, wondering what the hell I was up to.

I pulled Ricky's gun out of my belt and jerked the clip off, then passed the empty shell to the pimp. "Just making sure you don't do anything stupid before we leave. Thanks for the bullets and the bitches, pimp. Are we ready, boys?"

"Yeah, we got what we came for." Sixty winked and held up a black leather bag, flexing his arm, causing the flaming dice tattooed all over it to bulge.

I looked at Ricky. The seething look on the pimp's face told me we'd emptied every last penny we could find in this hole.

I nodded, motioned to Sixty and Crawl, and pushed open the door. Firefly lingered behind a second longer, and I heard his gravely voice warning the pimp on our way out.

"You keep this between us now, asshole. The Prez is letting you off light. If it were up to me, I'd charge you interest on top of your licensing fees. Consider yourself lucky, and don't breathe a word about this to the Deads, or you'll be seeing us again real soon. And next time, we'll bring our shovels."

The pimp swore. He probably pissed himself at the thought of us digging his grave.

The boys laughed as the flimsy door slapped shut. I watched our Sergeant at Arms inside, shoving a shitty looking club card into his hands, the only evidence we'd ever been there.

We didn't worry about him showing our rivals anything. Hell, I hoped he fucked up and did it. Then I'd have all the excuse in the world to kick his ass before I put a bullet in his head.

My brothers smoked and traded bawdy jokes while we waited for Firefly. Just before the Enforcer came stomping out and signaled us to get on our bikes, Crawl ribbed me, flashing his big, bright smile.

"Did you really get head from any of those bitches? Everyone I looked at was too damned greasy and run down for my liking, but shit, if their tongues make up the difference..."

"None of your damned business, brother. You know I don't kiss and tell."

Sixty snorted. "Aw, shit. That's our Skin – silent and sensitive as a baby. It's okay, bro, if you don't wanna tell us how some chick tripped out on crystal gagged on your dick, I don't need to imagine it. Just hope you wrapped it up, or else you're smart enough to get a shot to make sure that shit doesn't fall off."

He pointed between my legs. I reached over and elbowed him in the ribs. Both guys were still laughing when Firefly climbed on his bike and whistled, so loud and sharp it nearly burst my damned eardrums.

"Let's get the hell home, boys. No time to dilly-dally. Prez'll want the loot in the vault by sundown. We've got bills to pay. We didn't come here to drink and do stand-up comedy."

Word. I climbed on my Harley and strapped on my helmet. A few minutes later, we roared into the mountains, satisfied that the club would live to fight another day with the dirty cash infusion.

I couldn't stop thinking about Meg, chained up in that grimy little room. This whole operation was about second chances. The MC deserved another chance, and so did she.

God willing, I'd give her one. And I never let anybody down on my word.

Back at the clubhouse, I crashed in my room with a beer, and lingered there 'til about midnight. I needed the break after I'd hit my laptop and looked her up.

Megan Willow Wilder. Heiress to a multi-fucking-millionaire. One time prom queen. Missing person.

Everything she told me was the honest-to-God truth. I knew it from the dark edge in her voice, the desperation, but hearing it and seeing it on my glowing screen were two different things.

I ranged. I fought the urge to pick my computer up and smash it against the wall, then ride back to Ricky's dump and get her the fuck out all on my own.

I shouldn't have waited another minute to blow the pimp's rotten brains out and take her home.

She'd been the number one missing person's case east of Nashville 'til the story got buried with time.

Her parents were as rich as she said – business barons with the cash to offer a quarter million dollar reward for any intel leading to her recovery.

That was a goddamned golden hoard for anybody short on cash. I thought about the reward money, but mostly I thought about her crying, hurting, sucking off nasty motherfuckers for the pimp.

No woman captivated me like she did. It wasn't just my sex starved dick talking either.

I had to bust her out, and I needed help to do it. I'd lean on the greed motive, whatever it took to get my brothers on board, maybe even the Prez himself.

Any talk about money brought Dust out of his hole these days. I expected him to come rapping on my door in a couple hours anyway, and I'd have a late night ahead of me talking to him about the club's bleak financials.

I got up, exited my room, and crushed the beer can into a nearby trashcan next to Dust's office. I heard him in there, shuffling around, agitated and deep in thought.

The rest of the boys were at the bar, minus Joker, who was probably off laying on a bed of needles or something.

Our Veep's road name was the most ironic one in the club. He'd never been anything but a stiff, deadpan, fish-eyed motherfucker from the moment I'd been patched in. Having him out for the evening always eased tension in the clubhouse.

Crawl and Sixty looked up at me as I reached over the bar for a bottle of…what the fuck?

"Smoky Mountain Bronze? What is this shit?" I popped the cap on the half empty bottle, took a long whiff, and instantly recoiled.

"Fuck me. Doesn't smell like any whiskey I know."

Truthfully, the shit smelled like bootleg, brewed in some empty farmhouse.

Sixty smiled. "Shut up and drink it, brother. It's all right if you mix it with something…fuck do I miss drinking the good stuff straight."

Bad sign. The bastard was still sober. That's what told me the booze was really sour.

Crawl suppressed a hiccup as I sat between them, reconsidering the shots I'd planned to nurse while we huddled. Screw it, I was better off sober for this talk anyway.

If I wanted Meg out ASAP, then I had to be reasonable. I had to whip them into line and convince them to ride with me on this crazy ass mission underneath the leadership's nose.

"I gotta talk to you guys about something," I began, lowering my voice and looking back and forth to make sure they were paying attention. "You gave me shit about seeing a whore, and I shrugged it off. Well, truth is, I did see one in the back – but she wasn't a drugged out ice queen like all the others."

"Shit, I knew you were too damned wound up not to have gotten your dick wet," Crawl growled, the stink of that cheap whiskey on his breath. He shrugged. "Where are you going with this, brother? We got what we came for. Prez is counting it out right now."

"Listen good. Both of you." I paused, ready to put my hands around their throats if I had to. "I didn't fuck her. This girl's no ordinary whore. She's a prisoner. She's a virgin. And that bastard, Ricky, wants to auction her off to the highest bidder."

Sixty's face twisted and his loud, rowdy laughter burst out. I gave him the death stare.

"Holy fucking shit. Sorry, bro. But you're expecting us to believe you bought this fairy tale?" He snorted, pulling on his goatee in amusement. "Girl must've been hooked on some wild shit. How many teeth was she missing? The more space there is in her mouth, the more she's got in her head, and it sounds like she fed you some fucking crazy off her junk."

"That's the funny thing about having a brain in your skull – it makes you double-check the facts. Everything this chick said checks out. She's Megan Willow Wilder – some rich kid from Knoxville – and there's a fat reward for bringing her ass to safety." Both my hands shot up, silencing them before they could give me any more crap. "I know, I know. You're gonna tell me she's not our problem, that she's some rich bitch who probably wound up in the wrong place at the wrong time. You think she's just another whore, feeding me lies. I'm telling you right now I don't give a single fuck. I want this girl *out*, brothers, and I'm counting on your help."

"You've lost your damned mind, Skin." Crawl slicked back his dark hair, wearing the same look I'd seen on him the night we killed three dirty drug dealers trying to fuck with our club because we cut their supply route down to Johnson City.

Typical Crawl. My eyes darted to Sixty. He stared down at his glass. The man hated disappointing me because we were so tight, and I could see it in his eyes, gathering his thoughts for a few seconds before he finally looked up.

"Crawl's right. This isn't our damned problem. Hell, this club's got one too many on its plate. We're trying to un-fuck ourselves and get back to the times where we could have a little fun, remember? Don't see how playing hero to pull this whore outta the fire's gonna change that. She ain't club business, and there's no reason to make her any."

"I'm not doing this for charity," I snapped, jerking their drinks away from them and standing up.

Both men shouted, ready to fight. I had a point to make.

"Come on, guys, we don't wear this patch because we're here to fuck and booze, or even to stack up cash. It used to mean something, back before the old timers got lazy and then passed the torch. You think my old man would've even let a snake like Ricky operate in this territory?"

"Doesn't matter, bro. Things change. We've barely got the funds to keep our own asses sheltered and fed. We can't go gallivanting off after girls."

Crawl smiled. "I'd wax Ricky in a heartbeat. Piece of shit deserves it. Trouble is, he's in with the Deads, and if he doesn't go whining to them about our little visit today, I'll be surprised. He'll wind up dead sooner or later anyway – what the fuck's the hurry? It's not worth going behind Dust and Joker. Even if we wanted to help you bust this chick who's got your dick in a knot outta her hellhole, we'd all get whipped raw for going behind their backs. You know that."

"Not if we give the Prez what he wants most, and what this club desperately needs. I mentioned the reward for taking this chick home to her loving parents. A quarter million, easy." I looked at both men, watching the defiant expressions on their faces melt. "You don't have to crunch the numbers all fucking day like me to have some idea what that kinda money'll do for us. Far more than knocking off a few thousand from these trucker spas."

That shut them up. My brothers both looked past me, considering.

"It's still too dangerous without the Prez's approval," Crawl said finally. "You want the three of us to go alone, you'll be making a big mistake. What if we run into the Deads? Fuckers always outnumber us if they come full force. We'll wind up prisoners ourselves, maybe worse."

"Not if we go tomorrow. We won't waste any time pulling her out. Let's talk about how we wanna handle Ricky. Hell, the greedy bastard probably hasn't even told the Deads about his hostage because he'll want to keep all the proceeds to himself when he sells her. She's just another whore to them. Nobody'll come looking."

Sixty sucked in his cheeks like he was chewing tobacco. I watched him shuffle several steps to the bar, reach behind the counter, and return with a ratty old notepad.

"We do this for you, brother, you owe us big."

"Of course I do." I walked up and slapped him on the shoulder, motioning for Crawl to join us. "You think I'd ever let any of you guys down? Fuck, we earned our bottom rockers just months apart. You two kept me sane when Dad left us. You're brothers to me in every sense of the word, and that's never gonna change. I'm just asking for one last favor – the only one I'll ever be asking you for."

Fuck, what am I saying? I seriously wondered as I watched Sixty tear two pages from the notebook, looking into my eyes.

Meg touched something deeper in me than I liked to admit. I'd never dived into this hero crap before. I didn't know shit about her, and I sure as fuck shouldn't care about anything besides the reward money.

But I did. When she looked at me with those sad, blue, puppy dog eyes, I saw someone who didn't belong, someone who needed my help. And no, it didn't help that she was the most beautiful pussy I'd seen in months, everything I dreamed about laying flat and pounding into the nearest surface.

"We're gonna make you keep your word on that," Crawl said, caving at last. He knew exactly what Sixty had in mind, and so did I.

I reached to my belt, and pulled out the switchblade we only used for slicing shit up and close combat. They both watched closely while I pressed the blade to my pointer finger and cut a neat line through my fingertip.

I soaked each sheet of paper in blood, scrawling the letters I.O.U. as neatly as I could.

I had their backs forever, and they had mine. Now, all I needed to do was find out if Meg was really worth all the trouble.

III: Drag Me Down (Megan)

I couldn't stop looking at Skin's ring. I held it in my hand until I nearly fell asleep, remembering to tuck it into the little drawer on my nightstand at the last second.

He said he'd save me. I wanted to believe him. For all I knew, the heavy, deadly looking ring with the claw holding onto the pistol might be nothing more than a gimmick.

Whatever they'd said and done to Ricky wasn't just an act, though. The pimp didn't bother me all night. They'd hurt him, rattled him, bad.

I'd expected him to be pissed off and take it out on me. I was ready to drop to my knees and suck him off so he wouldn't hit me again. But the bastard never came, never even knocked on my door that night, too busy shuffling around with an icepack pressed to his jaw.

When I heard his truck rumble and drive off in the parking lot, I knew I was safe.

Safe to sleep. Safe to live another day. Safe to believe that maybe, just maybe, I'd find my way out of this living nightmare, if only Skin was as good as his word.

"Wake the fuck up, bitch." Ricky's sharp hand impacting my face woke me up before his cruel voice.

"What the hell?" I bolted up, scurrying into the corner, as far as the chain would let me, covering the sting on my cheek.

His lips smiled, but his dark eyes shined with explosive rage. "You're a lucky girl. It's your big day, and believe me when I say I'm a little sad I can't rough you up and feel those lips wrapped around my cock one more time."

I shook my head, wondering what he meant.

"You've got yourself a buyer."

My heart sank. I felt the color draining from my face. My eyes flicked instinctively to the drawer, where I hid my secret, my hope, all smashed to pieces in those five terrible words.

Skin couldn't save me now. His ring wouldn't comfort me. Not when I was ready to be carted off to hell's lowest tier.

"Get your little ass in the shower and freshen up. My buyer's guy just dropped off my advance, and I'm counting the dollars. I'll get the rest once you're safely at his place." Ricky paused, and then brought his hands together in a resounding clap, so fierce I jumped. "Come on! Move, bitch."

I did, just to get him out of my sight.

A minute later, the cold shower poured over my shoulders, freezing the hot tears raining down my cheeks. The chance encounter with the Pistols yesterday was like a sick joke.

For one brief night, I'd had hope. I shouldn't have counted on it. Should've known it would be taken away like this, and the only direction my life would ever go was down, down, down.

I lingered in the shower as long as I could, until I heard his fist pounding on the door. I mouthed something angry and flippant back. I didn't care anymore.

Maybe I could finally give the pimp a few barbs before he shipped me away.

He wouldn't hurt me now. Not seriously. I couldn't show up at the new man's place beat up and bruised.

I toweled myself off and slipped into a cheap white skirt and tank top. The skirt was slightly better than the crap he normally gave us to wear. Too bad the color made me think about the elegant summer dress decaying in my closet, the thing I'd have to leave behind today forever, the last piece of my old, happy life.

"Your purse is on the bed, Fresh. Pack your shit up. I threw in a bag of pretzels to hold you over. Sounds like it's gonna be a long ride to Charlotte for you, but you'll have friends to keep you company."

Pushing past him, I dug into my purse, ripped the shitty snack bag out, and threw it on the floor at his feet.

"I don't want your fucking sympathy, Ricky. You know what the best part about today is? I'll never have to see you or your crusty, yellow balls again."

For a second, he stared at the bag, his eyes bulging. I watched him lift a boot and slam it down, crunching everything to smithereens.

He pointed a shaking finger at me. "Don't get smart with me, you vicious cunt!"

"Why? Are you going to beat me up again? Maybe shove your puny cock down my throat?" I started shaking as I said the words, but they felt so good, so empowering, even if I was risking the idiot flying into a fit of range and blowing his deal just to hurt me.

I had to fight. I had to distract him. I eyed my nightstand, and knew I couldn't walk out of here without taking the only thing anyone had given me that ever mattered – even if it couldn't save me anymore.

"You think you're pretty smart, don't you, girl?" He stepped forward and chuckled. I could smell the stink of whiskey on his breath, probably an early celebration over the sale. "The bastard who bought you is a friend to the Deads, and he's a pretty sick, rich motherfucker from everything I hear. Give it a couple weeks. You'll *wish* to high heaven you were dealing with me again. I really treated you nice, Megan. The least you could give me is a sweet goodbye."

Hearing my real name on his lips made me cringe.

The demon eyed my breasts, the cleavage peaking out of my tank top. I couldn't control it.

I lunged forward and spat in his face. He stood there, stunned, before slowly raising a hand and wiping away the mist I'd spattered over his nose and eyes.

"You're goddamned lucky you're down to your last hour here," he growled. "I'll let you throw a fucking tantrum and leave you to settle the hell down for a couple minutes. I'm Mister Nice guy compared to what your new owner's gonna do."

He kept saying that, and I didn't care. Not one bit.

"Oh, and don't try any of this shit on the boys I hired to transport you. They won't take kindly to it like I will."

I slumped on the bed and watched him step out, slamming the door behind him. Thank God.

The second I was by myself, I ripped the drawer open and gathered up the trinkets inside. Some lipstick, a small mirror, a half empty packet of birth control pills.

I'd gotten it by trading the loose change Ricky sometimes missed to the other whores for a steady supply. I took them religiously, my only defense to make sure I'd be protected from some monster's kid if Ricky ever went back on his word about blowjobs only, or if he couldn't control one of the Johns.

I picked up Skin's ring and held it up for a moment, admiring the heavy, elegantly engraved metal. I knew it was hopeless, but it didn't feel that way when I held it.

The ring took me away from this. It gave me faith, hope, an alternative to the new impending doom breathing down my throat.

My mind went to stupid places. I couldn't stop thinking that maybe somehow, someway, he'd find me again. The ring would draw him like something out of a fairy tale, and I'd never be alone forever, just as long as I held onto this precious thing he'd given me for comfort. I'd give it back to him one day, just like I promised, and he'd give me a second chance.

I slipped it onto my finger. Way too big. But it didn't matter, I clasped it to my chest anyway, remembering the unmistakable touch of the only man who'd treated me kindly since I'd shown up here.

With a sigh, I pulled it off and stuffed it into my purse, shoving it in a little side compartment where I hoped nobody would find it.

Maybe my new owner would be as sloppy as Ricky, especially when he let his lust or rage take over. I'd learned a thing or two about working men over when I could, but I hadn't figured out how to use my charms to buy my freedom.

Someday, I promised myself. I zoned out for what must've been a half hour, clutching my purse when the door burst open.

Ricky walked in with three huge men behind him. I'd seen them before, a trio of dark-eyed, evil-looking bastards who'd visited the whorehouse before, all of them wearing Deadhands MC cuts.

Big Vic wasn't with them, the only saving grace.

"Careful now, boys," Ricky said nervously. "Please don't rough her up. Big Vic doesn't get his cut if you hand her over bruised, and the guy on the other end notices. He was very specific about wanting undamaged goods, if ya'll know what I mean. I told her not to get smart with you."

"Yeah, yeah, whatever, pimp." An older man with a salt and pepper handlebar mustache motioned to the others. "Chaps, get this bitch on your bike and find her a helmet.

Spiny, let's make sure this cocksucker shows us the money. Up front. All of it."

A nasty, muscular man wearing a PROSPECT patch stepped forward and grabbed my arm. "Let's go, girly. I'll make sure you're all taken care of."

I gasped on the way out, feeling his hand run up my skirt. It was looking extremely unlikely these brutes were going to treat me nicely while they did their job.

The worst part? There was absolutely nothing I could do about it. Not even Ricky could object now, not when he had his eyes totally focused on the money, and bikers of any sort seemed to be his personal nightmare.

We'd be roaring over the mountains toward North Carolina nonstop. If I tried to run, tried to wave to anyone in traffic and show them what was happening, I'd be a dead girl in a matter of minutes. Jesus, I'd probably get other people killed.

I had to play along. I had to numb all my feelings and just get through this.

If I could survive the trip, see what I was dealing with on the other side, I could plan my next move. Everyone had a weakness, even this new buyer. If I could find it, exploit it, and use it to get in touch with Skin, then I still had hope.

I wouldn't give up. I promised myself I'd stay true, stay strong, stay –

"Fuck me raw." Chaps put his hand on my shoulder as he pushed me onto his bike. "It's gonna be pure hell having your hands inches from my dick on this long haul.

Sure hope the Prez gives the okay for a little fun before we drop you off with your new daddy."

I looked away, refusing to give him the satisfaction. His eyes clung to me for a few more seconds, and then snorted and turned away, lighting up a smelly, cheap cigarette.

I had to take myself away from all this. My mind turned over, working to find that numb, vacant space I'd gone to before to survive this nightmare.

Peace never came easy. I was still searching for it, trying to put myself in that rare zen space I'd found a few times before, when the other men came storming out.

Ricky hovered behind the door, looking out the dirty back window, his eyes on me. I wouldn't look at him, too busy eyeballing the harsh, nasty men who got on their bikes. Mustache Man signaled the younger ones, and we took off with a roar.

I hated having to hold onto the bastard driving. My eyes focused on his pal in the mirror, the one called Spiny. He drove strangely, kissed the back of our bike with his front wheel several times on the highway. I saw something smoking in his hand, too fat to be a cigarette.

"Oh my God. Is he stoned?" The fear raging in my chest made me want another one of Ricky's joints, the only thing I'd ever had at the whorehouse to temporarily put me out of my misery.

"Shut your pretty mouth and relax, princess, or I'll fucking make you," the biker in front of me growled. "You're safe. Just trust us. Now, squeeze me tighter. I'm looking for an excuse to shove both those little hands on my cock, and you'll give me a good one if you don't close your mouth."

I did. I bit my tongue for several more miles, watching as the other Prospect drove like he was drunk. My heart filled with hope and terror when I saw a squad car about to pass us on the other side.

This could be it.

If the policeman noticed Spiny's crappy driving, maybe he'd pull them over, and then I'd find my way out of this. Assuming it didn't end in a shootout…

I started to count my heartbeats as the car drew nearer, so heavy and tense they made me want to pass out. The policeman passed, didn't even slow down, and a second later he disappeared behind the latest mountain bend.

Fuck. Disappointed again. Why did I ever expect anything else?

It took forever to cross the state line into North Carolina. Far longer than it should've.

The men kept getting lost in the mountains, and I realized Mustache Man was just as fucked up as his Prospects.

My driver, Chaps, swore repeatedly. Then the storm hit, and ice cold rain buried his curses.

Freezing bullets pounded everything, so torrential and sudden and loud it should've been terrifying. We couldn't see. The bikes skidded down the hills just when I thought we were about to wreck, into some nameless little town with pale yellow lights blurred by the small ocean dumping down on us.

I was officially numb now. Ready for whatever was going to happen, even my own death.

The men screamed at each other as we rolled into a cheap motel. At first, I thought it was to fill up, but the gas pumps outside were just as derelict as the little shack next to it with the broken windows.

Our bike jerked to a stop. I watched Chaps jump off and go stomping toward his comrades, all of them pissed off and yelling.

"We'd better spend the fucking night, Lock. No way are we gonna get to Charlotte and make this chick presentable in this kinda weather."

"The pimp said no delays, asshole. We'll take a few hours and keep going, whatever we need for this shit to blow over. Veep's got us on a tight schedule. Big Vic'll choke our sorry asses out personally if we don't keep moving." Mustache man pushed the prospect, and I watched Chaps stagger back, a hatred he couldn't reciprocate glowing in his eyes. "Fuck you both. Get your own rooms. If you're just gonna stand there, I'll take care of this cunt myself. She owes me extra for all the trouble."

I barely had time to blink or wipe the latest cold rain from my eyes. His huge hand practically ripped me off the bike, and soon we were heading for the dingy motel office.

I stood like a zombie, listening as he made arrangements with the bored looking man working in the run-down place. The dumpy owner didn't see anything out of the ordinary. He mistook my tears for rain, if he noticed at all.

Cash and keys were exchanged. The gorilla's hand seized my wrist again, pulling me out, toward a small white door with its paint flaking off.

My stupor didn't lift until I realized he was about to push me inside, alone with him.

Oh, God. He reeked booze and motor oil up close. The way his eyes wandered while he fumbled with the key told me he wasn't sober. Small miracle we hadn't all died on the way here.

His reckless expression told me he had even less incentive to hand me over untouched. He wanted me before I reached my buyer, and the demon was obviously too stoned to care about the consequences.

The door popped open and he flipped me around. I hit the wall hard, his body pressed against mine, too clumsy and horny to even close the door.

"I've had my good eyes on you this whole time, bitch. Fuck, I can see why that bastard in Charlotte paid a pretty penny for you. The pimp said you'd never been fucked before. Is that true?"

He didn't wait for my answer, and I wasn't giving him one. Both his sick hands fondled my breasts, squeezed them so hard I wanted to yelp.

I had to keep my guard up against my instinct to fight. If I made any move to push him, to kick him in the balls, he'd probably kill me.

Christ. Why was it so hard to get back to that numb, detached place I'd found in the storm?

"It'll be our little secret tonight, baby girl. Just you and me. The fuckhead buying you won't know shit about what I do to you tonight. I'll leave you something sweet to remember when his floppy old cock's busy fucking you. I hear he's an impotent piece of shit – likes to rough his girls up and get foot jobs." He stood up straight, a tremor in his hands, his overgrown mustache twitching. "Never understood that shit. Tonight, little girl, the only shit I'll be doing with your feet is holding them over your head 'til you fucking scream."

I opened my eyes, ready for the horror.

But he wasn't looking at me. I thought he was about to put his filthy lips on mine, but he stood straight up, listening to the deafening growl outside our door.

Bikes. Lots of them.

"Shit!" he snarled, jerking away from me and reaching for the gun tucked into his belt. "If those boys got themselves in a skirmish with some other smartass fuckers, I swear I'll wring their fucking necks."

His boot hit the door and it swung open. I screamed when he flew back a second later and hit the ground.

The bastard went down. He hit the floor with a resounding thud and didn't move. It wasn't until I saw the hole in his chest that I realized he'd taken several bullets, and my knees gave out.

I ducked, flattened myself against the ground, as several more shots went off outside. Men swore, talked in hushed voices, and then there were boots on the pavement outside.

At first, I thought the man who stepped through the door was one of the Deadhands' prospects. I whimpered and pinched my eyes shut, only opening them when his hand wrapped around my wrist like a vise.

"Get up, babe. Hope you've got my ring. I swore I'd be back for you."

No way. It couldn't be!

But it was.

Skin, standing in the flesh, with several men I didn't recognize at his side. They all shared the same patches. It must've been safe, or else he wouldn't be tugging me outside to his bike.

"Come on. Hurry up. We have to get away from this place right fucking now." He helped me onto his bike and quickly fixed my helmet, throwing his on as he started the engine.

There wasn't time to ask any questions. What happened here was written in the bloody trails left outside from the two dead bodies. All the Deads were...well, dead. And I was safe, plucked from certain hell by this magnificent, mysterious biker man.

We went roaring into the rain, lighter than before. I didn't relish having more freezing mountain water splashed on my back, but it was a small price to pay for sweet freedom.

I clutched my purse between us, and held onto him tight. Skin didn't make me recoil the way that disgusting prospect did. Having my hands on him felt oddly natural.

I squeezed his body, marveling how easily he made me

feel safe. Alive. Free.

With Skin's rock hard abs underneath my hands, I didn't need to search for the numb, black void that prevented me from going totally insane. I just leaned on his shoulder and breathed deep, taking slow, gradual breaths, inhaling his scent.

He oozed masculinity. Danger seeped out his veins like fine cologne. His scent conjured goosebumps, caused my heart to skip a few beats, sent thoughts into my head that I hadn't had since the night I screwed around with Crawford, before I was disappointed, abused, destroyed…

What the hell is he doing to me? I wondered.

My brain didn't want to think too hard. Riding with Skin put me into a trance. The rain tapered off. We rode at least an hour and a half in a heartbeat, back over the mountains, his brothers driving steadily behind us.

Their bikes never wobbled and they didn't shout. None of these men acted crazed or drugged up like the Deadhands, but I wasn't ready to let my guard down for anyone. I'd never seen a clean motorcycle club yet.

Maybe Skin was a rare gem in a cesspool, a man with a heart in a world that wasn't supposed to have one. My eyes traced the edges of the patch on the back of the cut, the skull perched between two guns with smoke curling outta them.

God willing, I'd be out of this world soon, and I'd never have to worry about dealing with bikers again. I let the comforting roar of his engine and his warmth wash over me.

I must've dozed, because the trip seemed like it was over in the blink of an eye. Next thing I knew, we were past the state line, rumbling through Newport, on our way toward Knoxville as the sun came up.

Smiling, I leaned into him, just as we pulled into a gas station. As soon as he parked the bike to fill up, I reached into my purse, found his ring, and presented it to him like a soldier receiving a well-earned medal.

"I kept it safe. I just can't believe you kept your promise, Skin. How did you find me?" He gently took the ring.

I watched his strong hands move as he pushed it onto his finger, back in its rightful place. Just then, I swore those hands could've conquered the entire world, could've owned me – and I wouldn't resist.

"Wasn't hard after we caught up with that piece of shit, Ricky," he rumbled.

My breath caught. Holy shit. Had he killed the pimp?

"Is he…?" I couldn't bring myself to say it.

Imagining Ricky dead excited me, but it was also like having a savage chapter in my life slammed shut. Far too soon for me to process.

"No. This is our home turf. We can't just go around snuffing people out like fire ants. Shit, I'd have loved to finish him myself, but not in front of the other girls there. We didn't have time to hide his fucking carcass either – we had to catch up with you." His eyes burned with a mad intensity, and he wrapped one arm around my neck, pulling me closer. "We'll deal with him, babe, on our own terms. I promise. He won't walk away free for what he's done to you. I'll make damned sure he never does this to somebody else."

I'd never heard such dark, bloodthirsty sincerity.

Skin wouldn't disappoint me. I could tell by the tone in his voice. So firm, so decisive, so eager to kill.

I trusted him, and that scared me. He waited by his bike while I ran inside and used the bathroom, wringing the last of the cool rain out of my skirt.

Ugh. I couldn't wait to get home and change into something clean and dry. For the first time in months, I thought about the reunion with my parents, wondered how many tears would add their wetness to my sopping wet clothes before the day was through.

The other guys didn't say much. They cast friendly, but distant glances my way, and climbed on their bikes with some sodas while Skin started his engine.

We shared a water the rest of the way, the only thing I could force down my throat. The last twenty-four hours' jitters sent an entire swarm of butterflies flapping through my belly. I wondered if I'd even be able to choke down my mom's home cooked food, assuming she hadn't given up on cooking at all since I disappeared.

Six months. Just kill me.

I couldn't believe half a year of my life had been spent in pure hell.

If I was lucky, I'd lose a few more to intensive therapy. I didn't want to think about all the traumas blackening my brain, all the pieces of my young, innocent self the pimp and his asshole clients had stolen away forever.

You're safe. Think about that instead, I told myself, latching onto it for support.

About halfway through the trip, I leaned close to Skin, relishing his body underneath my hands. "Hey, let me know when you want my home address…I can give it to you anytime. It's not too far off the highway."

He grunted, but didn't reply. Strange.

He had to have looked me up, I told myself, so maybe he already had it. That made sense. Just another half hour or so, and I'd be home.

If only it were so easy.

The knots in my belly deepened when we turned down a different exit, away from Knoxville proper, nowhere near the fancy estate where my parents lived. Another couple miles, and his bike rumbled down a short, unpaved service road, flanked by an overgrown forest crawling with kudzu vines.

"Um, Skin? I thought you were going to let me off at home? Where are we going?"

Again, silence. My fingers tightened on his stomach until I was clawing him.

No, no, no.

Please. Fuck. Please don't do this.

I trusted you.

I held my eyes shut as long as I could, praying I was wrong about my hero. I couldn't believe he'd lead me into yet another cavern of the hell I thought I'd left behind. But when the bike slowed down and I finally looked up, I couldn't ignore the stone cold truth.

If I had any tears left, they would've come spilling down my face when I saw the beat up looking clubhouse with a massive DEADLY PISTOLS MC logo painted across the wall. Two smoking pistols with a skull in the center, an emblem of death and destruction if there ever was one.

I couldn't cry anymore. I couldn't even breathe. I couldn't handle the truth ripping through me like daggers.

Skin wasn't what I thought.

My savior was just one more demon who was probably going to subject me to new tortures I couldn't imagine. The hero died that day. It didn't matter anymore that he'd been so kind, that he looked so handsome he'd thrown off all my instincts.

I hated him for betraying me, and his monstrous club too.

IV: Money, Money, Money (Skin)

This wasn't how it was supposed to go. *Fuck.*

Soon as I got her inside, Meg stopped talking. She wouldn't even look at me.

And who the hell could blame her? I'd stabbed her in the back and twisted it deep, the price of getting my boys on board to help save her life.

I couldn't have taken out all three motherfuckers alone in that dingy parking lot. Crawl and Sixty did it for me as much as the reward money I'd promised the club. Now, the only way I could keep myself from letting them down was by letting this gorgeous, damaged, blue eyed babe down so hard I feared she'd break.

I put her in my room and locked the door, walking away with the heaviest rock in the world sitting on my goddamned shoulders. Guilt was always an absolute bitch, the shit hanging over me now made me wanna drive off the nearest cliff.

Whatever, this wasn't the end. Not by far. I'd get her home sooner or later, just as soon as my brothers were satisfied.

There was no Option B.

Meg couldn't just jump off at her parents' house. They'd never pay up the quarter million to an outlaw MC. I had to make 'em, one way or another.

Hell, I had to convince *her,* get her to help me string her folks along 'til the cash was in my hands, heading for the Prez's office like tribute.

It was only a matter of time 'til the others found out. The Prez would fly into a rage when he learned we'd killed three Deads across the state line. Shit, we'd be lucky if it wasn't already hitting the news.

And if just one person at that piss stained motel saw us, remembered our patches, or maybe just enough to give a sketch to the cops…

Fuck, fuck, fuck. I wanted to put my fist through the nearest wall.

Instead, I headed for the bar, where my brothers who'd been along for the ride were already drinking. I looked at the clock.

It wasn't even eight in the morning. Christ.

Didn't stop me from ripping the cheap booze outta Sixty's hand and sloshing the rest of it in a tall glass. He grumbled, cursed, and protested while I poured the vile brew down my throat, hoping the napalm fire in my guts would temporarily wash away the crushing disappointment waiting for me in my room.

"Easy, jackass. It's been a long night," Crawl said, his eyes narrowed. "You running after the bottle because she's being a bitch, or what? Don't tell me she ain't even grateful?"

They both glared, demanding an answer. I shrugged and pounded my glass on the counter, turning around before I could say anything.

"I appreciate you boys having my back today, brothers. Really. I'll deal with her. I only need a day or two. Your job's done. Leave the rest to me."

"You can say that again, bro," Sixty said. "Remember the agreement – once the Prez or Veep find out about what went down, we're like ghosts. This shit was all you. We'll leave it to you, so long as you leave us the fuck out of it."

I nodded. Fair was fair, and I'd keep my word. I'd keep it with her, too, as soon as I managed to get her on board with getting her sweet ass home faster.

Too bad that was gonna be a helluva conundrum unless her loaded fucking parents decided to unload some money in our club coffers.

There had to be a middle way to do this. We had to get her home, get Dust the money we needed to hang on, and stop the full force of the FBI or the Deadhands from raining hell down on us.

There wasn't any sugar coating this shit. I'd thrown the club into chaos over a strange woman who'd twisted my dick in more knots than any woman should. Worse, I'd never even fuck her on top of it – not unless I wanted to land my sorry ass in a deeper pit.

The whiskey hit while I was out back, taking in all the fresh mountain air, the true drug I needed before I went inside to deal with her. I staggered inside, one hand on my guts, cursing myself for drinking so much of that cheap bootleg swill.

Fire tore through me, pleasurable and painful. I fumbled with my key in the lock for what seemed like five or ten minutes before I finally crashed inside, kicking it shut behind me.

She was huddled in the corner. The girl looked up like I'd just burst through the wall, her mouth hanging open.

The kindness in those blue eyes I'd always seen before evaporated. Now, those pearly blues shone nothing but hate, disgust, fear.

Fuck me. I'd given her enough shocks today, but what was one more?

Maybe the crude whiskey had more booze in it than I realized, or it was some sick combination of the long trip, the shootout, and taking this girl hostage. Whatever the fuck it was, I couldn't stand up.

She whimpered as I collapsed, crashing to the ground next to her.

A boot to the ribs woke me up. I jerked awake and rolled, my head pounding, using the adrenaline surge to slough off the hangover and reach for the switchblade I always kept on me.

Who the fuck was kicking me in my own damned room? If anybody wanted to come after me or Meg, I'd shred them wide open before they got in a second blow. I bolted up.

By the time I opened my eyes, I was crouched on one knee, my blade ready to disembowel the Prez.

"Shit!" I lowered it, ready to kick my own ass for my mistake.

He booted me again.

This time, I didn't fight. I fucking deserved it. Every swift, brutal, rib bruising crack.

"You stupid sonofabitch," Dust growled, motioning to Joker at his side. "Get him on the bed. Let's decide whether he deserves a chance to spill his guts about what the hell's going on before we gut him for real."

"Shit, come on! You've gotta listen to me, she's not what she looks like. I brought her here for a good reason, Prez, honest-to-God, I did!"

He wasn't listening. Not while the bulldog faced Veep raised me up and slammed me on my crappy bed. I heard Meg let out a scream behind them, cowering in the same corner where I'd left her.

I hated myself for putting her through *more* fucking violence after I'd tried to deliver her from it. Of course, my brothers would never hurt her.

None of us were black hearted bastards like the Deads. But they wouldn't hesitate to beat my ass to a bloody pulp in front of her if that's what they decided I deserved.

The Prez leered over me, his gray eyes searching, wrapping his hand around my throat. He squeezed so hard my windpipe pinched shut. I couldn't breathe. Rage creased his face, and the black stubble on his chin made him like a cactus sent to tear the life outta me.

"I practically had to rip this place apart to find out what the fuck happened. I promised the brothers I'd give you one chance, and one chance *only*, to talk. In my office. *Now.*" His hand pulled away and I jerked on the bed.

Sweet release. I inhaled so hard it started a coughing fit when he finally released me. Joker tore me up before I could get air back into my system. They weren't fucking around as they hauled me out of the room.

We marched past Firefly, who just looked at me and shook his big head. *You poor, miserable bastard.*

His expression said it all.

"Keep an eye on this whore," the Prez growled to him on the way out. "I don't know this chick from Eve, and there's no telling what she'll do. We don't need anymore goddamned problems, especially if she's a Deads' slut."

The Enforcer nodded. I looked past him, locking eyes with Meg for about two seconds. She was still staring at me as the Veep dragged me out, daggers and disappointment in her eyes.

Sixty, Crawl, and the prospects wisely kept their distance from the ruckus in the back. I was all alone when Dust kicked his door open. Joker dragged me in, hurling me into the chair across from Dust's beat up desk.

The Veep marched over to the door and stood guard while I sat up, coming face-to-face with my very pissed off Prez. I folded my arms, matching the intensity.

He wanted to skewer me, and I didn't blame him. But he didn't know shit. I'd tell him everything, explain why I put my ass on the line for this woman – or at least give him one good reason for involving the entire club.

"I never expected this from *you,*" Dust began, sinking down into his seat. "You're supposed to be our brains, at least when it comes to numbers. For fuck's sake – *three* motherfuckers you put in coffins today. Three! And I want to believe there's a damned good reason behind it."

"That's what I want to get to, Prez, if you'll just let me explain –"

"No." He held up a hand lined with thick, brutal looking rings on every finger "Not yet. How'd you manage it? You've never dropped that many bastards on your own. Something tells me Sixty and Crawl were in on this too."

Shit. I put all my energy into not letting my eyes wander from his iron stare. He was probing me, trying to decide if he ought to put the other two into the fire with me.

I couldn't let that happen. Not when I'd served them an IOU in blood.

"They're innocent. This is all on me, Prez. It wasn't as hard as you'd think. I shook down the pimp for intel, same fucking place where I met the girl. He's the one who sold her, passed her along to the Deads for transport to some fuck past Charlotte who bought the rights to her pussy. I went after them, and hit 'em just in time. Found them at a shitty motel. They were drunk, blazed outta their minds, not in any condition to fight. I'm surprised they didn't wreck their bikes on the drive down there. I'm not gonna pretend to be the meanest fighter in this club, but it was like shooting fish in a barrel. No lie."

Joker snorted over in the corner. "You really expect us to believe you're a cowboy, Skin? My little sister couldn't have piled up a bigger load of bullshit."

He actually sounded pissed. Surprising for the man who never let his guard down, hardly ever cracked his tight-wound, rock solid exterior, whether he was in the thick of battle, or dragging some whore to bed for the night in better times.

"He's right," Dust said sharply. "I don't buy it, and that means you're in deep shit. So are your friends."

"Go ahead and put them against the wall too!" I snarled. "Take out the three guys you need to call this MC a proper club. Shit, strip our patches and bury us in a ditch if you think we're all turning rat or defying orders. Prez, if you think I put this club in danger for nothing more than wanting to get my dick wet, you're dead wrong!"

"That's exactly what I think." Dust leaned back in his chair, cracking his knuckles. "You've always been soft, Skinny boy. That's why I kept you off the big runs, so you could be in the office, managing business. You're not a front-line fighter unless we're in deep shit. You're our support, our rock, too damned smart to wind up like your old man."

I clenched my jaw when he mentioned Dad. Fucking shit, that cut deep.

Bad enough to hear him acting like I was a goddamned secretary, let alone pretend he was doing me some big fucking favor.

"I've been in a dozen firefights and I've spilled my share of blood for this pistol, Prez. Don't tell me you've forgotten? I was thinking about every single brother here when I decided to haul her home, put my ass on the line. I was doing my job, thinking about the numbers, the lifeblood of this club." I paused, leaned forward, and spread my hands on his desk. "You think it's pussy that keeps me up all night? You're wrong. I know what keeps you up, though. You're wondering if we'll have enough in the vault next week to pay the boys their cut so they can keep themselves fed and fuel their bikes."

"Bullshit. I've never made it a secret how much this club's lifeblood matters to me. Without cold, hard cash, we're fucked. You know it just as much as me, handling the reports." He looked up, flashing a vicious smile. "Tell me something I don't already know, Skin, before I leave you alone in here with Joker."

Fuck. I didn't need to turn my head and look at the Veep to know he was looking at me with sadistic anticipation.

Something wasn't right in that boy's head. He'd gone screwy when my old man was still breathing. Never knew from what.

"She's not just another whore. I wouldn't have pulled her outta Ricky's hole if that's all she was. I ain't completely stupid, or reckless, or fucking this club with my dick." No, I wasn't. But the Prez didn't need to know I actually had a heart. "The pimp caught the girl and decided to sell her off months ago. She's got rich parents who are ready to pay up pretty damned handsomely for any info leading to her return. Ever heard of the Wilders in Knoxville?"

The Prez sat up like a dog catching wind of a juicy steak, but he kept his cool. "No. Can't say I have. How much money are we talking?"

"Quarter million. Pretty sure you could squeeze out more if you even give them a whiff you know something about their baby girl."

"Fuck. That's a lot of scratch." Dust leaned back in his chair, the wheels turning in his head so loud I could practically hear them grinding. "Tell me you've got a plan. We could drop her off at their doorstep tomorrow, but they're not gonna give that money to the Pistols MC, especially if the Feds are involved. Hell, Uncle Sam's glad we're almost out of commission. We're so far off their radar they barely even send goons to sniff around us anymore."

I had to think fast. For a second, the Prez and Veep eyed me so hard I thought they'd set my cut on fire. Sweat beaded on my brow, but I didn't earn my name by getting stumped.

They called me Skin because I'd saved this club by the skin of its teeth more times than anybody could count, especially from the IRS. Those bastards combed everything, looking for any little misstep to shut us down. As long as I wore the Treasurer patch, they'd never find a goddamned shred of evidence.

"I'll convince her to play along. The girl only needs

one hero – if I come forward and she's got my blessing, they won't be any wiser. It's probably her rich daddy who'll be handing off the money anyway. I'll smile for a press photo when they give me the check. I'll look nice and I'll be there as Parker – not Skin."

I stopped. Perfect timing because the Prez was shaking his head, trying to hold in laughter or else keep his fist from flying into my face. I couldn't tell which.

"That's weak, brother. Even by your standards. I expected better."

I shrugged. "Take it or leave it, Prez. We can talk about it in church, but I doubt the club's gonna come up with anything better. Me and this whore, we've built ourselves an understanding of sorts."

That was a total lie. Sure, I'd given her my ring, and she'd looked at me at first like the only man who hadn't treated her like a total piece of meat. Then I'd ripped her out of the fire, only to throw her into mine.

I'd betrayed her. This whole idea was insane, if the Prez decided to give it a chance. I had no fucking clue if I could really convince her, ever repair the damage I'd done.

But there wasn't another choice. Joker grunted in the corner, holding in his dead tone sarcasm. The Prez just stared, ready to open up on me, but I knew he didn't want to do it when I had him by the balls.

He knew this was our only choice too, the best shot we'd had in forever to inject some lifeblood back into this club.

"Yeah? What kind of understanding is that? One where she doesn't pay you back for holding her ransom with a blowjob and hands over a couple hundred grand?"

"Go ahead and be cynical. I'll prove how wrong you are. No different than that time you decided to go all in with the chop shops, and I told you that much expansion would bring the whole house down." I looked him dead in the eye. "I was right then, and it's no different now."

His lips twitched as his hand moved, scraping his heavy metal rings across the table. He looked at Joker.

"Step aside so he can get to work. He's got three days to convince me this isn't just bullshit." Slowly, Dust turned back to me, a mischievous gleam in his eye. "If I'm not convinced, I'm handling this myself. I don't give a shit who she is, or what we're putting on the line. The club needs cash, and we just landed ourselves a golden goose. Her parents *will* pay up one way or another, mark my fucking words. I'll use all the vinegar I've got if honey won't do the trick."

Joker grinned, cold and artificial as ever. Creepy motherfucker.

I stood up, nodded, and put my hand out to the Prez. He could be a total bastard and a stubborn SOB at times, but he knew how to motivate a man.

I promised myself I wouldn't let anybody down while we shook hands. I wasn't in the business of making promises I couldn't keep, and this one wouldn't be the first I'd failed to honor. Didn't matter that this happened to be the biggest conundrum since I'd put on the patch.

My word was gold. Always. The broken dove holed up in my room wasn't gonna be the first to turn it into mud.

I rode into town and picked up a fresh change of clothes for her. The jeans and shirts I picked out were probably a size too big, but fuck if I knew anything about women's clothing.

She'd wear it. She'd be happy. And I'd put a choke chain around my cock the whole time, whatever it took to kill the urge to fuck her senseless.

No lie, it was gonna take a miracle. Every second I wasn't balls deep in her was torture. My skin bristled thinking about her pressed up against me on the long ride home, how soft and sweet she felt, how hot she'd be to haul into my bed and fuck, fuck, fuck 'til we lit the bed on fire.

The last stop was at a local burger stand for some grub. I'd seen the old pictures of her, back when she had some wicked curves. A selfish part of me wanted to help pad her again, get her healthy.

No surprise, the girl had lost some serious weight in the pimp's clutches. She was beautiful now, but there was a total knockout underneath the surface, a girl who'd make every man who passed her ache to get her under him.

'Course, I didn't wanna wait. I wanted her *now*.

Having to forget about all the nasty things I wanted to do to her while we slept in the same room tonight promised to be a special hell. I'd have to tie my hands behind my back if we shared a bed, otherwise they'd end up stripping off her clothes, spreading her legs, holding her open for my fingers, my tongue, every swollen inch of me.

I'd heard her whimper several times before. Whenever I imagined her doing it louder in bed, pressed up against me, my thunder stirred my blood. My cock raged in my pants, a nuclear fucking warhead threatening to blow my whole world apart if I didn't slam her into the nearest horizontal surface and fill her up.

Fuck. I should've been thinking that kinda shit when I'd already screwed her over. Damn if I could help it. Meg's tongue, her tits, her sweet little ass clouded my head the entire ride home.

I focused on the guilt by the time my bike pulled into the garage, the only thing that would kill the dynamite hard-on throbbing in my pants.

I headed into the clubhouse, straight to my room. Found her curdled up on my bed, dead asleep, stripped out of the sopping wet clothes I half-worried had given her pneumonia.

My hand brushed her cheek, checking for warmth, fever. It was a small relief when she was cool to the touch, and pure hell as my eyes wandered her body, taking in everything that wasn't hidden by the lacy black bra and panties hanging on her.

Her eyelids fluttered open. She rolled sharply, almost fell off the bed and pounded the floor when she saw me.

"Didn't mean to scare you. I'm back with some food and clothes."

She looked at me like a scorned cat. I reluctantly

lowered my eyes, reaching for the bag from the clothing shop, pushing it into her arms.

"Go ahead and change in the bathroom. I'll give you some privacy."

Fuck, if I didn't want to eat those words. Privacy? Who the hell was telling her this?

It sure wasn't Skin. No matter how bad I felt about keeping her here for cash, I couldn't stop thinking about how hard I wanted to fuck her.

The bathroom door gently closed as she retreated inside, reappearing a couple minutes later, dressed like she was ready to ride out with me to the bar. I couldn't unsee what the jeans and shirt were hiding, and she scrunched up her face when she caught me looking at her too long, too intently.

"Jesus, you're a pig. I can't believe I thought you were different."

"Sure, go ahead and ignore the fact that I sent three miserable fucking Deads to their graves to get you here alive. I meant everything I said – I wouldn't have given you my ring as collateral if I didn't." I bolted up and stared at her, every kinda frustration known to man churning in my veins. "You're going home, Meg. No bullshit. The faster you work with me, the sooner it'll happen."

Ignoring me, she walked past, and looked into the bag I sat on my beat-up table.

"Eat, woman. You've gotta be hungry."

She wrinkled her nose and gave me a disinterested

look. "I'm not."

"Don't make me force something down your throat, babe. I've carried you this far, and I'm sure as shit not standing here while you starve to death."

"So do it," she said coldly, heading for the lone chair in the corner. "You're not my hero. I don't care how many excuses you make, Skin. You're just another man who's decided to use me. You're going to take whatever you want, make me do it your way, and I don't have any say. Don't pretend I'm wrong."

My skin sizzled, anger and disappointment building at my brain stem. I didn't like the defeat in her eyes, or the way she slouched her shoulders, shrugging off living another day when she was so fucking close to home.

"You can't give up now. Look, I'm not doing this because it's my choice. I couldn't have bailed you out in the first place if I didn't promise the other guys something." I stepped toward her, closing the space between us, waiting for her to look at me. "I'm still the same man you met in that whorehouse, the man who gave you the most important thing he's got for collateral. I'm gonna help you out of this for good, but I've got to help my club too, and they need the reward your folks promised."

"You're a criminal, Skin. No different than the rest of them – just a little less stoned and maybe less cruel."

What the shit? Was she trying to make me explode?

"Maybe," she repeated, still looking at the floor. "You want your money? Fine. I'll do what I can to convince my dad to give it up, whenever you're ready to let me talk to him. You know, if you aren't going to chain me up in here like Ricky and use me a few times before you decide to let me go. Looks like I wound up with a buyer after all, right?"

No more. I reached for her chin and grabbed it hard. She gasped, but the spitfire met my eyes, and I held her gaze.

I let it all come out in my stare. The anger, the frustration, the sheer need I had to save her while I prevented my club from getting completely shredded by Deads, without any funds to buy enough ammo to fight back...

Fuck, I knew she saw the desire too. I couldn't hide shit from this girl. If she didn't know how bad I wanted to rip her clothes off and stuff my cock in her mouth to shut her up, then she had to be blind.

"I don't need you to understand, babe. I need you to listen. This isn't a goddamned sex trade, and you know it. I'm not your new pimp."

"Do I?" The hateful confusion in her eyes almost made me question it too.

"If you don't know, you'll find out fast. Right now, you're looking at me like I'm one more twisted fuck who's here to pour gasoline on your life and watch it burn down. I'm no hero. I never said I was. But I'm your only ticket to true freedom. Just like you're my only way to save my ass, and maybe everybody wearing this patch. Go ahead and hate me like I'm nothing but another pimp, or a

Deadhand limpdick piece of shit sent to drag you away. Doesn't change the fact that we're up the same creek, and we can either sink our hands into the water together or drown."

She broke my gaze first. I watched her little jaw clench. At first, I thought she was going to fire back again.

No, she was fighting back tears instead, begging every instinct I had to pull her up, yank her into my arms, and brush away each poison tear sliding down her cheek.

My hand went to her shoulder and I squeezed. That did it, caused her to surrender.

Fuck it. She didn't fight as I drew her into my embrace, squeezed her so tight I threatened to crush the air outta her lungs.

I didn't understand what this strange, beautiful chick was doing to me. I wanted to protect her, break her, and scream in her face all at once. I wanted to fuck her as bad as I wanted to wipe away her tears.

Worst of all, I barely even knew her, and she had my ass invested like a gambler chasing penny stocks.

The outcome wouldn't be any better either. Christ, no.

I'd grown up a heartbreaker, and this girl sure as shit didn't need that. I resisted the urge to put my lips on her skin, tracing those fiery tears racing down her. She gushed sorrow and shame for the next couple minutes while I held her, stroked her hair.

I wished to high heaven I really was her hero, instead of her fucking warden.

I'd made peace with being the bad guy, the outlaw, a

long time ago. So, why the fuck did I actually feel bad with her?

"Work with me, babe," I whispered. "This can all be over faster than you think. You can rebuild your life."

"Okay!" she hissed at last, jerking away from me. "I'm sorry. It's been such a long day. I don't want your sympathy or your help. I'll work with you, Skin, but that's it…just enough to get your money."

The distance between us was suddenly like a gulf. Still, I stared at her, smiled, and nodded.

"That's all I'm asking. You get yourself square with the club, and you're free. This time, for real. You'll never have to hear shit from a man on a motorcycle or sleep in a dirty room again." I saw her look at the food on the table, probably getting ice cold. "You want me to warm that shit up for you, or what? You're not going back to bed 'til you put something in your stomach."

"I'll eat. Just not…that. It's the last meal I had before I was kidnapped. Ricky put something in my food at this diner. Doubt I'll ever enjoy a hamburger again. His trick worked to get me in his truck, and…"

She stopped, catching a lump of pure sadness in her throat.

Fucking shit. My heart sank. I held up a hand, silencing her, then walked over to the table and ripped it up. I crushed the whole bag into a tight ball and opened the door, hurling it into the garbage outside.

"If I take you out for something different, will you promise not to fuck me and try to run away?"

She shrugged. "Whatever. You know I won't. Even if your club isn't like the Deads, I know I'll have to look over my shoulder for the rest of my life if I squeal or turn you guys in. That's not what I call freedom."

My jaw clenched. She gave me the answer I needed to grab her by the hand and lead her to my bike. Didn't make me stop wishing the entire time that she saw me as something other than a cruel, calculating motherfucker.

Someday, I'd make her. One more promise piled onto my long list of impossible obligations.

We hit the local taco shack for a couple hours. I sucked on Mexican beers while I watched her pick at her food like a bird, but by the time we left, she'd finally eaten enough to make me happy.

I paid the tab and watched her slump across from me in her seat, her eyes half-closed, digesting more than just her food. Shit, the girl probably needed a solid year to process all the crap she'd been dragged through the last forty-eight hours.

I stared into my half-empty beer, watching the pale gold swirl, all I could do to keep my eyes off her curves.

My dick turned me into a monster. I couldn't stop imagining fucking her, even after all she'd been through.

And if we actually fucked, I'd be sure to fuck her over too. She needed something soft after the hell she'd suffered.

Too bad tender, gentle, soft wasn't in my damned vocabulary. The only thing swirling through my skull was rough, hard, and rougher. I wanted to take her so hard I left marks, stamped her skin from head to toe, let the entire world know she was mine.

I'd start by shredding her clothes and wrapping her hair around my fist. Meg's hot, virgin skin would burn beneath my lips. My entire cock throbbed each time I thought about dragging my mouth down her body, pushing my face between her legs, jerking her into my lips, tongue, and teeth by the ass.

Had she ever ridden a man's face before with her sweet cunt? Whether she had or not, there wasn't a fucking chance she'd ever had her pussy tamed with a mouth like mine.

I made women scream. I stole every molecule of air from their lungs. I caused them to pant 'til I let them attack my cock, and they fucked me ferociously, begged for my come, lost their minds before I finally gave it up.

This chick made me imagine the nastiest shit I had in years.

Her freak virginity made me want to claim her even more. If I got a chance, I'd shake every inch of her, fuck her over and over and over again, 'til every last trace of the dirty bastards she'd been forced to suck were gone forever.

"Skin? Did you hear me, or were you too busy playing with your drink?"

I looked up. The glass swirling lightly in my hand stopped.

Was she serious? Hell no, I wasn't listening.

Not when the pouty angel across from me turned my

blood molten every time I looked at her.

"Sorry. I've been busy thinking about how we're gonna work this to get you back to your ma and pa sooner."

Yeah, right. All I was really thinking about was hearing her call me daddy while she took every seething inch of me.

She smiled softly and shook her head. I'd put on a good front. "I said he never cared if I finished my food. Ricky, I mean. Look, I'm never going to kiss your feet for doing what you need to do. But maybe you're a little nicer than the last man who chained me up. Maybe."

"Yeah, whatever, babe." I'd rather have her kissing something else, but I kept that part to myself.

Reminding me of what the club had done – what I was doing to her right now – fucking gutted me. I hid that shit too. I couldn't go soft and let her assume anything. I also couldn't handle her getting under my skin, tempting me to do something stupid to get her home sooner, something that'd screw my brothers over.

Whatever morals I had died years ago, the first time I shot a rival man in the guts and watched him flop to death on the floor. Sure, the asshole deserved it, but you never come back whole from putting down a human being.

That's what I'd thought, kill after kill, growing a little colder every year, just like Dad. I hadn't known what the hell wrong was 'til I plucked her outta that whorehouse. I forced myself to look at her, even though my heart was filling up with black, toxic muck.

The woman across from me didn't deserve any of this

shit, however I justified it. Two wrongs never made a right, but between me and the club demanding money from her folks, we'd kept her alive.

"I won't try to run," she said, reaching for my hand. "There's nowhere to go without you. I don't know the rest of your biker friends from the pimp or the Deadhands. I shouldn't trust anything you say, but I want to believe, Skin, that you're not like them – I know you don't want to do this. I can see it in your eyes. That means something. Just a little bit."

Fuck. I didn't like anybody seeing past the barbed wire I put up in my cold face, least of all this wounded dove.

"Don't try to get all emotional on me, lady," I growled. "If you think I'm soft, you'd better get your head checked. I've done plenty of shit I'll pay big for one fine day in hell. I don't worry a lot about morals, beyond what's best for keeping my own ass safe and what benefits the MC. I'm gonna help you get out of the quicksand, Meg, but that's where this ends. You don't wanna get attached. I'm not your friend. Just your ticket outta here."

Her pale face softened. She nodded like she actually understood, fixing those glacial blue eyes on mine. I stared her down 'til she broke and blushed, then I slid out of my seat and grabbed her hand, leading her out to my bike.

We didn't say much as I drove her back to the clubhouse. She was probably getting tired now that her belly was full. I hoped it'd save me from having to deal with her anxiety tonight.

It was gonna be hell sleeping in the same room with

this chick, feeling her pressed up against me. Damn if I'd let her make me feel anything else.

I had to stop thinking sex.

This pussy shortage wouldn't last forever. I'd find others – lots of other sluts – and by the time I did, this stolen princess would be outta my life. I'd let the Prez put her reward cash to good use while I fucked myself completely free of her.

Women were fuck toys, and a special few turned into old ladies. Not for me. The only pillow talk that ever interested me was the filthy kind.

The chick with her little hands pressed around my waist while we roared through the mountains needed more than that. She was too screwed up for drama-free pounding after what Ricky the shithead did to her.

I'd save her from my dick, and I'd save myself from the love and tears that I knew would come raining down.

This was just another job, another mission for the club. One more chance to get things right after we'd been staggering around drunk on too much danger and not enough cold, hard cash.

Nothing more. So help me God.

I showered like I always did with the door wide open to my little bathroom. Having a woman in the room never changed my habits, not even this broken hearted beauty.

Still caught her looking.

For some fucked up reason, that made me grin through the suds and hot water hissing over my face. Her soft blue eyes took little snatches of my body whenever she thought I wasn't looking, too blinded by the water to notice.

Whenever I looked back through the cheap shower door, she jerked her eyes away, hiding her beet red face behind this mystery story magazine I'd picked up for her at a gas station.

Little minx, I thought with a growl, feeling my cock blazing to life. *Take a good, long look. It's only natural.*

Don't care if you're too screwed up to fuck. It doesn't change the fact that I want it anyway. Want it, need it, feel it so bad I've got hot coals burning in my balls.

Before I finished, I reached down and grabbed my swollen cock, giving it at least a dozen hard, quick strokes with my slick hand. Didn't feel a tenth as good as her pussy would wrapped around me, and I knew she was looking.

Hell, her eyes stayed fixed in dumb amazement on my dick up 'til I ripped open the door and stepped out, wrapping the towel around every raging inch of me and tucking it around my waist.

"Glad you enjoyed the show," I said with a smirk, stepping back into the room and grabbing my clothes.

She shrugged and shook her head furiously, too embarrassed for words. I walked back into the bathroom to change, wondering what kinda fireworks were going off in her head.

I wasn't stupid – I knew I shouldn't be teasing her like this after she'd just walked outta hell. But fuck, the girl needed a distraction.

If watching my dick took her mind off all the nasty things she'd suffered under Ricky, then I'd give her a peep show every fucking hour she was holed up in my room. Some strange, merciful part of me wanted to wine her, dine her, and fuck her 'til she couldn't remember her own name, much less what the last six months had been like.

My face turned psycho killer whenever I thought about it. I remembered Ricky, that sniveling, greedy piece of shit.

I would've killed him the night I went tearing down to save her if I wasn't in too deep a time crunch. I rolled on my jeans and looked at my gun, hanging on its holster. I pulled it out and felt the raw power in my hands, brought it over in my safe to lock up for the night, the same way I always did when I had a chick in the room.

Meg watched me walk out and put the gun away, slamming the safe shut with a loud clap.

I hadn't forgotten all the business I had with this girl, or the promise I'd made to her. She'd pay up and go home. We'd find a way to deal with the Deads and keep our club safe. But damn if I'd let that sick motherfucker slink away into the night, only to set up shop and do this to some other girl who never asked to be pulled into violence and slavery.

I'd end him one day. I'd do it with pleasure. I'd let Meg know when I did too, if only to give her closure so she could live the rest of her days without worrying about seeing his evil ass ever again.

"Take the bed tonight," I told her. "I'll crash on the

floor."

She sat up and watched me flop down with a pillow and a thin sheet. Shit was hard as concrete, really, but I didn't give a shit.

There wasn't much to my bed. Still better than the crappy cot she'd slept on forever in that whorehouse.

I closed my eyes for about a full minute before I heard her voice. I looked up, and she was staring over the bed at me, straight down with her gem blue eyes.

"There's enough room for both of us, Skin, if you'll behave yourself. I'm okay with us sharing. It's a cold night."

I grunted, mulling it over for a second. The raw need roaring through my cock threatened to strangle the gentleman inside me. Fine, whatever. I popped up and rolled into bed next to her, promising myself I'd keep my hands to myself.

She switched out the lamp a second later and pulled the sheets tight. I laid awake for a long time, thinking about how this whole twisted situation would blow over. We'd get the reward for the club, the day all this shit would finally be wrapped up by dropping her off at her parents' door.

I thought about the hundred ways I'd like to slaughter Ricky the pimp again. I thought about how I'd fight to keep this club intact and protect every last brother wearing my patch, how we'd butcher the Deads or anybody else who fucked with us.

I thought about anything and everything that didn't

involve me throwing the covers off Meg, tearing her panties off, and sinking my cock deep inside the hot, warm hole I wanted to fill with every fiber of my being.

All the dirty, bloody thoughts in the dark ended when she rolled toward me. I felt her heat, her sweet young body, pressed into me as naturally as a kitten curling up to its mother. The soft whimper leaving her lips told me she was asleep, doing it unconsciously.

Fuck it. I couldn't lay there a second longer without feeling her.

I threw an arm around her waist and pulled her tight, silencing the lust in my blood. She craved comfort, and I'd give it to her, if only for tonight.

There was something strangely peaceful about having this chick huddled in my arms. Didn't change the fact it was confusing as shit. I hadn't even fucked her, and we were spooning like lovers – something I never did with the whores I bedded.

What the fuck?

I was still thinking about how ironic life could be when the sandman finally caught up to me and dropped the five ton hammer on my head.

The next day, everyone was frustrated. Both the prospects ran into trouble with their bikes in the morning, and half our crew spent the entire day fixing them up.

When I came in to clean up, streaked in grease and oil, I found her in my room, a notepad and pen in her hand. She'd barely opened her eyes and muttered a few words this morning. I'd left her the paper and told her to start working on a plan that would get her parents' attention, without getting our club busted by any boys with badges.

"Didn't know you were into mud running," she said with a smirk, as soon as our eyes locked.

I gave her a stare. "You've still got your sense of humor. That's good. What else have you got?"

I walked over and ripped the notepad outta her hands. She yelped protest, but I ignored her as I flipped the pages, staring at a few lines of neat cursive scrawled several pages in.

It looked like the start of an outline, a bunch of question marks – never a good sign.

"Skin, give it back! I promise I'll read you everything. I'm having a hard time..."

"Yeah, no shit," I said, my eyes scanning what she'd written. "Letter to the press...anonymous call from a truck stop...dropping you at the Knoxville police in nothing but a sheet and a note stuck to your back."

I looked up as she grinned uncertainly. "Come on, baby. You're a smart girl. I know you can do better than this. What else have you got?"

"That's it," she said, blushing.

Bullshit. The way she jumped up from the bed and started tearing at my hands when I flipped a few more pages said otherwise. I pushed her away easily and turned my back, only stopping when I flipped another page and saw my own face staring back in dark ink.

Shit. It was good for an amateur. She'd done me

realistic, capturing my intense eyes and all the little details on my mug in all its glory. She'd even gotten the scar going down my cheek, the long gray line I'd taken in a knife fight several years ago with another drunken punk one fine night.

"Fuck me. What the hell is this?" I spun around, confronting her.

She looked like she wanted to sink to the floor. "I got bored. I used to sketch sometimes. It was a good way to pass the time at Ricky's place, and during long, boring lectures when I was in college. There isn't much to draw around here…so I did you."

I snorted. She looked on in horror as I grabbed the page carefully and tore it out of her notebook, then a few more pages I threw at her as I folded up the drawing and stuffed it into my pocket.

"This is all you get. No more distractions. I need ideas, babe, and you're the one who knows your family better than we do. Let's get this thing done so you can go home." I watched her nod weakly. "Relax. I ain't gonna throw you over my knee and spank your ass red or anything. Let's keep this professional."

"Professional?" she repeated, a sharp edge entering her voice. "If that's what you want to call keeping me here against my will and asking for these stupid ideas on the fly – okay. Sure, I can do *professional.*"

Her sass pissed me the fuck off. Why couldn't she see I was actually trying to help her, trying to save both our asses from this quagmire I'd chosen to get us into by saving her from the Deads?

"Look, you're gonna do this for me, Megan. This isn't a negotiation." I gave her my coldest look, forgetting about her wounded state. "I've got shit to do for the club. I'll bring you a burrito, and leave you alone to think so you can get some ink on paper."

Her blue eyes flashed fire. Hate. I watched her bottom lip sink into her mouth, like drawing blood was the only thing keeping her from going at my face with her sharp little nails.

I turned around and walked the fuck out. Got a couple steps down the hallway before I heard her slam into the door.

Beating, punching, kicking, screaming.

She was so loud, so shrill, so desperate, my brothers heard it all the way in the bar. They looked at me like I'd just dropped some poor bastard in front of 'em. Sixty flashed an uneasy smile, before hiding it a second later behind a fresh shot of whiskey. Crawl pretended I didn't exist.

Firefly cocked his head as I sat down next to him. Our huge Enforcer looked at me, the dark, sandpaper stubble on his chin twitching.

Fuck his amusement. Fuck his laughter. This shit wasn't funny. Not for me, not for Meg, and not for the club.

"Brother, you've got one fuck of a problem on your hands," he growled, slapping me on the shoulder. "Let her beat herself stupid. She'll give up after a few more minutes. These chicks only make it worse if they get their claws in you. Trust me."

He talked knowingly. Just then, I didn't really give a shit. I grabbed the nearest bottle of cheap, off brand whiskey and popped the cap. There wasn't time for a shot glass. I filled my mouth with fire and pushed it down my throat.

Only a snort. I'd learned my lesson that first night with her in my room. Shit, she could've killed me while I was passed out cold on the floor from this cheap swill. She hadn't, though, and that said something too.

"Whatever. Getting my dick wet is gonna be the first thing on the agenda once she's handed me our cash. The Prez'll throw us a bone before we get down to business. We'll celebrate. We'll drink and have a hog roast, bring the old girls to the clubhouse."

I wasn't kidding. I fully meant to fuck every drop of frustration out of my balls once my bird was mended and out of her cage.

No, fuck *mended.* That wasn't my problem. Her folks were rich – they'd buy her the best shrinks money could buy to get her head working again.

The second she walked outta this clubhouse, she wasn't my problem anymore.

Too bad you can't stop thinking about it, a dark voice said in the back of my mind, telling me how fucked I was. *You care too damned much. That's dangerous.*

"Sure, brother, just as long as the Deads don't crash our party first," the Enforcer said, knocking back another drink.

I watched Firefly grab the bottle and polish off the kerosene before I could get a second shot. Fuck.

The guys laughed while I walked behind the bar and dug around, finding nothing but beers and half-depleted drink mix. Shit had officially gone from bad to worse.

I couldn't drink her away, couldn't fuck her out of my mind, not 'til she gave me what I needed. Worst of all, I couldn't stop thinking about her.

I swung my fist across our shell of a once proud bar. Several bottles crashed onto the floor and shattered. Firefly beamed death at me, shaking his head, his fist visibly flexing, a reminder that he wouldn't hesitate to keep shit in line, including me.

"Somebody tell Tinman or Lion to clean this mess up the next time you see 'em. I need to make a run."

I made a hasty exit before they could give me anymore shit. Maybe I deserved it, yeah.

Maybe I deserved *all* this horseshit for letting her get to me, trying to play hero, landing the MC in deep.

I headed into town to pick up food, wondering if I'd have to fight her to eat later if I stopped at one of the little watering holes there to finish getting drunk.

I'd find some way to forget her, and all the nasty shit she made me think about. I had to, if I wanted to get through this alive and keep my sanity.

Poor, desperate, stubborn Megan wouldn't bring me down. I'd dump her off as soon as I could, collect the reward, and get on with the life I'd dedicated myself to.

She wouldn't strap me down on any big karma wheel and spin it 'til it ripped my damned limbs off. I'd always been a Pistol, by blood and by patch. I'd be one 'til the day I died.

I'd be a fucking fool if I let myself go to pieces over this ungrateful whore.

V: Caged Dove (Megan)

I wasn't sure when I finally gave up trying to beat down the door. The first few times I hit it, the rotten thing creaked and bounced on its old hinges, feeding my fantasies that I might actually smash my way out of here.

Of course it was insane.

I was too enraged to think about how I'd get through all the raging bikers outside, or how I'd ever find my way home if I escaped by some crazy miracle.

I embraced the anger, lived it until my shoulder burned so hot I couldn't even feel it.

Rage was all I had. When I was screaming and slamming my full weight into the door, hopeless and desperate, I didn't have to think about my miserable situation.

I didn't have to remember Ricky's vicious abuse, or how my friends and family hadn't done enough to track me down after I disappeared. Didn't have to remember I'd ended up as nothing more than bait for this disgusting motorcycle club, or how badly my stomach growled. It hounded me to shut up and take the food Skin would inevitably bring.

Skin. Fucking Skin.

Officially the last man in the world I wanted to think about, including Ricky.

I hated him, right down to the pale scar on his stupid self-righteous face. I hated the way my body reacted to him, the way I craved his warmth. I hadn't meant to roll into his arms last night.

It wasn't supposed to happen. And I definitely wasn't supposed to like it so damned much.

I'd woken up with him this morning, relishing his heat, feeling far safer than any woman should with a man holding her captive.

Truth be told, I hated him because he wasn't another greedy, abusive asshole like Ricky. He saved my life, and now I owed him and the rest of his nasty looking friends.

Moral gray area? Oh, yeah.

I couldn't sort the rights from the wrongs anymore. All I wanted was to go home and forget this nightmare forever, and if the bastard was going to make me plan everything out in meticulous detail, well…I would.

I'd show him I could get the money from my family with ease, if that's all it would take to get him out of my life forever. Ignoring the ache in my bruised arm, I flopped into the chair and picked up the pen and paper, using a magazine behind it for writing support.

I was completely ready to write down the first thing that came to mind. If my brain wasn't fresh out of ideas, stuck in this impossible situation.

Seriously, how the *hell* did he expect me to just collect the reward money and shuttle it to him without people asking questions? The minute I stepped through the family gate, I'd be bombarded. I'd probably have to face more questions than hugs and kisses.

I was about to break the pen off in my hand when I heard the lock jingling, and a second later, he stepped through the door.

The bastard had returned.

We barely spoke over the next half hour. He didn't even ask me about the paper in my hands, just passed me a bag from the same Mexican place we'd eaten at last night, and walked into the bathroom.

I ate my taco salad in silence. My face burned every time I looked up through the open door, staring at him in the steamy shower.

I hated him. Jesus, I did.

But just then, I hated myself even more for being completely unable to keep my eyes off him.

What the fuck was wrong with me? I'd barely escaped Ricky and all the cruel men who'd used me, and there I was pining after one more.

Skin hadn't beaten me up. He hadn't taken advantage, even though we shared the same bed. But he was just like them, deep down inside, an outlaw and a devil who wouldn't hesitate to fuck me with his hand around my throat if I gave him half a chance – or pissed him off just enough.

I tried to look away, dampening the sexy thoughts. Naturally, I couldn't. I didn't have a prayer with this naked, gorgeous giant only feet away, cleaning himself behind a thin wall of glass.

I watched him. I took him in slowly, running my eyes across him, every magnificent inch.

His huge, powerful body flexed in the shower, dark inked muscles ebbing and flowing like shadows as he scrubbed himself clean.

It was a cruel repeat of last night, except worse, because the tension was off the charts. Once, he peeked up over the short glass shower door. We locked eyes and my heart nearly froze from the embarrassment.

God. If he walked out of there and said anything about me looking at him, admiring his stupid sexy body, I swore I'd go to pieces.

I couldn't deal with this. We couldn't go on, sharing this cramped little room and enough sexual tension to blow up half the state.

Maybe it was my fault for giving him so much crap about keeping this cold and professional. Now, I was the one having trouble with those boundaries.

His body drew me straight into the flames when he pulled the door open and stepped out dripping wet, reaching for his towel. His huge thighs bulged, dark flames rippling on their sides. His entire body coursed like a canvass for pointing straight toward the huge, unthinkable part between his legs, the pulsing hard-on I'd felt when I first woke up in bed cuddled next to him, tight against my ass, crying out to fuck me.

I pinched my eyes shut, desperately fighting to smolder the flames of sick fascination for this man. We were cruising for a head-on collision before he was finally out of my life. No denying it.

He'd either fuck me first, or completely destroy me.

I looked down at the last few scraps of my food and suppressed a shudder. He walked in front of me with nothing but the towel around his waist a second later, giving me the stink eye.

"What? I'm almost finished – see?" Pursing my lips, I lifted up the empty tray. "Please don't give me any shit about eating every little bite again tonight. I'm really not in the mood."

With a snort, he ripped it out of my hand and walked it out to the trash. When he returned a second later, his dark brown eyes glowed amusement, a surprising change from the stern, frustrated sparks twinkling there before.

"Yeah, I actually believe you," he said coolly, staring down at me like a hawk eyeing its prey. "You got any fucking clue how hard it is to keep this professional when you're looking at me with a hunger for something else?"

Crap! I tried to hold every nerve in my body still, tried to keep my cheeks from burning scarlet red.

If only it were so easy. I forced myself to look at him, forcing out the words.

"I don't know what you're talking about."

"Bullshit, you don't. I'd have a hard time admitting I'm obsessed too, babe. That's why I'm laying it out there

– we can admit it without making this shit awkward. Just because we both wanna hit the sheets and fuck each other stupid all night doesn't mean we have to. We can ignore the urge. We can keep it *professional.*" The extra stress he put on that word tempted me to leap up and slap him across the face. "Unless, you know, you think you're ready to have a man you want to fuck. A man who's gonna use you in all the right ways without treating you like a cheap fucking whore."

He took another step forward, closing the tiny space between us. My eyes darted to the bulge rising beneath his towel. I thought about the huge, throbbing, rock hard cock I'd seen behind the fogged glass, every savage inch he'd stroked, probably thinking about me.

Skin's hand shot out, grabbed my chin, and twisted my face until I couldn't look away. "Look at me, babe. I'm telling you, I am not the fucking enemy. Believe it or not, I'd rather have you work with me to get you home sooner than drop this towel and feel your hot little mouth pulling my cock across your tongue."

Instant tremors. His words melted me from the bottom up, and my thighs pinched together, trying to stem the torrid wet heat. The asshole knew my pussy ached for him – and he was getting off on it, teasing me like no tomorrow, acting like I was the one making this so damned difficult.

Bastard! I still hated him, but the truth was undeniable – I wanted him so much it brought me to my knees.

I twisted my head, jerking away from him. Then I

stood up and pushed past him, heading for the other side of the room, before he could give me more crap.

"What the fuck?" he smiled knowingly when our eyes met again. "What's the deal, baby? We're just having a little heart-to-heart. I'm trying to lay it all out there, be straight with you."

"You're a pig," I snapped, shooting my eyes away so they wouldn't betray me for the thousandth time. "I don't understand what kind of sick game you're playing, Skin, but I want none of it. I just want to go home. Seriously. Give me another day. I'll have something for you, and then I'll be out of your hair forever."

The thin smile on his lips faded. His huge arms shot up and he folded them across the skull with the smoking pistols tattooed on his superhuman chest, leaving me one last glimpse of those hills and valleys he called a torso, a rugged landscape carved by testosterone and violence.

"Yeah, you're damned right you will. You think I wanna put up with this shit for even another week, you're flat out wrong. I'll hit the floor tonight. Don't worry about me. I'm gonna give you all the space you need to think hard and get this shit done."

He flipped the light out in the room on his way back into the bathroom, slamming the door shut. I slid into bed, cold and tired and so frustrated I could barely think.

I'd never known sexual frustration until now. Before Ricky, I'd gotten practically any boy I'd wanted, my pick, anytime. With the pimp, I hadn't had a choice who he forced on me.

Thank God for the icy raindrops spattering down on the roof over us. They gave me something outside this shoebox room to focus on, a chance to cool the fire in my body, and I let their soothing tempo carry me to sleep.

I woke up in the blackness shaking and crying. Skin's huge body was already pressed against mine, his chin on my bare shoulder, whispering in my ear.

"What? What the fuck is it? You'd better start talking to me, babe."

He sounded so soft, so concerned. It took me a minute to realize he'd kept his word, and my body wasn't responding to the surprise of him crawling into bed.

The nightmare came rushing back. I'd been dreaming about Ricky, all the times the pimp stepped into my room, unbuckling his belt, cornering me with that hideous gleam in his eye.

I twisted in Skin's arms, loving his masculine heat, his scent, the strength he enveloped me in. His rough hands reached up and brushed away several tears staining the pillow underneath my head before I could speak.

"What is it? Don't say a stomach ache. If those motherfuckers gave you food poisoning, I swear to Christ I'll ride back there right now and knock their fucking teeth out." I wanted to laugh at the rough, determined edge in his voice.

Jesus, no. If only it were that simple, I thought, letting my mind see it all again in crystal clarity.

"It's just a nightmare," I said softly. "Who the hell

knows. I'm probably processing the trauma of all this. I can't forget about Ricky. It's not the way he slapped me around or the men he forced me to take…it's the times he used me."

For a second, Skin's eyes lit up in the darkness. First horror, then nothing but stone cold rage.

"Bullshit. I thought he was saving you for a buyer?" The biker's hold around me tightened.

"Oh, he saved the most important part of me, sure. But he still took privileges." I swallowed the painful lump in my throat, wondering if I could really tell him the rest without crying. "He'd come to me every week or two, usually at night. Whenever he wanted to, really. He'd hit me awake – sometimes with his hand, other times his belt. He'd force me to get on my knees, pull down his pants, and do everything I did to those truckers for money."

I suppressed another sob, licked my lips, trying to see him in the darkness. His eyes said it all, even though his face remained the same killer, unchanging mask. I opened my mouth to tell him the rest, wondering if I was really helping myself or just worsening the pain, but his finger pushed down the center of my lips.

He held it there, hard and silent, squeezing me as I trembled in the darkness.

"Don't say anymore, Meg. I'm not a damned fool. You're brave to tell me, but I also know talk is cheap. It won't do shit to help you feel better."

I blinked in surprise, feeling another tear streak down my cheek. That wasn't the response I expected – especially when he was so right it hurt.

"He's a dead man, babe. Leave it to me. I'll wipe that brutal little pissant off the face of this fucking earth. I promise."

"Skin, no!" I pushed my head away so I could talk, shaking my head, spilling more tears. "You've already risked so much. Whatever else you've done to keep me safe, I recognize that. Don't put yourself in danger for me again. *Please.*"

I looked into his mad eyes while I begged him. It hurt to do it, but his gaze pulled me in the same way it always did.

Commanding. Unbreakable. Safe.

"I have to do this, and you're not stopping me. Neither will the club. I'll do it by myself. I'll catch him alone, babe, I've done this sorta shit more times than I want to tell you. He's not like the Deads. He's a weak, cowardly little shit. He'll fold the second he sees me coming." He paused, baring his teeth in the shadows, more fearsome and perfect than any biker's feral grin should be. "And if he doesn't, well fuck, that's even more fun for me. I'll make him pay for every last thing he's done to you. You can't heal 'til you know he's been evicted from this goddamned planet."

"Skin…" I wanted to plead with him, beg him not to dig our hole even deeper, but I knew it would be futile.

He proved it a second later when he jerked my head into his chest. I cried and shook and breathed his wonderful scent for what felt like hours. He held me close, rocking me like a scared child against his chest.

Why did I find such comfort when I had my face right up against the barbaric tattoos on his skin?

If the question had an answer, I wasn't going to find out tonight. By the time I knew what happened, I slipped into a deep, dark sleep.

Mercifully quiet, because this time I wasn't alone. When I opened my eyes the next morning, Skin was still there, awake and staring out through the tiny blinds covering his little slit of a window.

"Jesus," I whispered, sitting up when I saw the fury in his eyes in the full morning light. "Don't tell me you've been awake all night thinking about everything I said. You don't need to do anything, Skin. I just cracked last night, said too much. Can't we forget it?"

"Come on, babe. You already know the answer." A smirk twisted his dangerously kissable lips. "Let me get you some breakfast. Then I'll let you shower and get to work on the ransom plan, while I handle business."

He slid out of bed and began to dress, throwing on a clean shirt and his cut. I watched him the entire time, feeling my heart slip into my stomach, pulsing black, guilty blood.

"Don't do this. Please don't. I know I've given you a hard time because I'm all screwed up, but Skin, if I lost you –"

A wave of his hand cut me off. "Unless the next words out of your mouth have to do with how you're gonna convince your folks to get us the money, I don't wanna hear it. Mind's made up, babe, and nobody changes it once I've decided."

"Skin!" I jumped up and called out to him one more time before he adjusted the leather vest on his shoulders, and then marched out, locking the door behind him in one brutal twist.

He was gone. And unfortunately, the beautiful bastard was right again.

I had to accept whatever he was up to, even though it meant suffering alone all day worrying about him.

By the time the sun set and I had to switch the lamp on, I couldn't take it. I'd done nothing since he dropped off coffee and a sandwich this morning, without so much as a goodbye.

The paper sat gloriously empty, except for several lines I'd scribbled about how to save him. How ironic that he'd gotten me to care more about pulling his stupid butt out of the fire than my own.

I couldn't shake the exhaustion. The last few days had absolutely fried my brain.

I'd been too open with Skin last night. I never should've let my guard down. Never should've tempted him to bring more trouble down by wiping out Ricky.

Once he had his target, he was like an angry pitbull. There wasn't any holding back. He'd left for his destiny, and there was nothing I could do.

Nothing besides cloister myself in the corner and wait, praying the pimp wouldn't get to him first.

Another hour slipped by. Then two more. Panic crept in.

What the hell is happening out there? I wondered, biting my lip.

I wanted to do something. My hands and feet burned. They begged me to run to the door, pound on it and scream until somebody opened up, and tell them everything about what Skin was about to do.

But if his brothers weren't in on the scheme, then I'd only be giving him more grief, possibly putting him in greater danger.

I still didn't know anything about this MC. From what I could see, they barely tolerated me. The brothers gave Skin just enough space to watch over me as their personal cash cow.

Whatever, at least they hadn't demanded *other* favors. I shook my head sadly, wondering if I'd ever be able to think normally about any strange man again after what I'd been through.

Ricky fucked me up. Ricky, the Johns, and his nasty friends in the Deadhands, brutes who wouldn't think twice about using my mouth, or choking me until I complied with the next set of tricks they wanted me to turn.

I remembered Big Vic's vile cock in my mouth and cringed. He liked choking me, making me worry that he'd squeeze his fingers around my throat just a little bit tighter while he fucked me deep, filled my entire mouth with every evil inch of him.

He always laughed when I tore his floppy dick out of my mouth too, after he'd finished. I'd be on the ground, gasping for air, trying desperately not to panic. He'd roll off his condom slowly, making me worry he'd dump his waste all over me before he left.

You're a lucky bitch, he always said. *Goddamned lucky we like working with this pimp. One of these days, we just might decide to haul you back to the Carolinas to work for us instead, baby girl. Then you can suck this shit down your throat 'til you fuckin' drown.*

"No." I covered my eyes, mumbling, pushing away the bitter memory.

They couldn't hurt me anymore, whatever happened to Skin. Oh, God, what if something really did happen to him out there!?

He was the only man who'd been remotely kind to me in ages. And I wasn't even sure that was accurate. My brain was too screwed up to think.

I wanted somebody to slap me across the face, shake me, sort the rights from the wrongs. My own judgment was shot, destroyed forever by the deranged madman who'd had me for six months, the bastard I still couldn't hide from in my dreams.

Clenching my fists, I tried to breathe deep, anything to slow my shaking heart. I was getting worked up to the verge of tears when I heard the lock jingle.

My heartbeat thudded ten times faster when Skin ripped the door open and slammed it shut behind him, another bag from the taco place in hand, and something else. His phone?

"Oh my God," I whispered softly to him, standing up. "Are you okay? What happened?"

He didn't say anything at first. The biker with the savage scar on his beautiful face approached me like a lion, reserving his pride, stopping only to set the food on the table and lift up his phone.

"Skin? Skin?" I said his name a couple more times, studying him for telltale signs of blood, dirt, injuries – anything that might give me a clue what happened while he was out all day. "Talk to me!"

"Just shut your mouth and watch," he growled, pushing the phone into my hands.

A video started to play. I saw Skin's unmistakably huge hand gripped around a handgun. A man was down on the ground in front of him, looking miserable and dejected. It only took me a second to recognize Ricky's long, greasy locks. The pimp crouched on his knees, shaking, dead silent except for some distant fluttering birds off in the forest surrounding them.

"Don't do this, don't do this, please don't fucking do this – for the love of God!" The pimp sounded terrified.

Adrenaline shot through my chest. I watched as Skin brought the hand with his gun violently across the back of his head, knocking him to the ground. The camera shook, lost its frame, and came back about ten seconds later.

"Stop begging and die like a man, asshole," the biker snarled. "I'll bet she begged for mercy too. Of course she did, her and how many others? You reap what you sow, motherfucker, and now it's your turn to pay in blood, in pain, in your worthless life."

The pimp's face was in front of the camera now. He had hot, angry tears in his eyes, bruises all over his face. I gasped, completely blown away by seeing my old tormentor so beaten.

"You're gonna regret this, Skin. The Deads know all about the guys you killed. They'll come looking for me too, and when they find out what you did, they'll fuck up every last cowardly little shit in your club. The Pistols won't even fucking exist in a month's time – just wait!" His lips trembled and he drew a long, agonizing breath. "Just wait, Skin. You know I'm talking sense. It's not too late to throttle back, save your own ass instead of putting it on the line for that mangy, stupid, miserable little cunt. Christ, I should've fucked her and buried her in the brush a long time ago."

"Nah." Skin's voice sounded cooler all of a sudden. My eyes burned as he shoved the barrel of his gun into the pimp's bloody mouth. "It was too fucking late for you the instant I saw her. She's got time on her side, time to sort her shit out and heal. I'd say it's too bad your clock's run out, pimp, but, you know – it isn't. Eat shit."

I jumped when I heard the gunshot. Blood flew everywhere.

A few droplets spattered the camera, but most of it ran to the ground in the steady red trickle. What was left of the pimp's head slumped over the log where he'd been propped up and pinned down.

"Useless sack of shit," Skin muttered, right before the camera went black.

The last thing I heard was the shuffling of his boots and a nearby shovel plunging into the cold Smoky Mountain dirt.

My hands were shaking when he reached from behind me, gingerly taking his phone back, taking away the video forever. He gave me a squeeze as I fought the tears, the insane flood of emotion over what I'd seen, and then he stepped out in front of me.

I watched the big man put the phone flat on the floor, lift one leg, and bring it down hard. It crunched like nothing more than decayed wood, but he stomped it a few more times just to be sure.

"Skin…" his name left my lips before I even knew what else to say.

His dark brown eyes bathed me in their energy, safe and determined as ever. "You only gotta see that once, babe, but I had to show you. I had to prove to you he's been dealt with, just like I promised."

I could manage several steps to the bed before I collapsed, sitting with my hands across my face.

"I can't believe you did this," I said finally, meeting his fiery eyes.

"Believe it, babe. The bastard's dead, buried where nobody'll ever find him. My only regret's not dragging it out and making the worthless piece of shit suffer more for what he did to you and those other girls."

"The other girls – shit!" I sat up, suddenly in a panic,

wondering what would become of them.

None of the other whores were slaves like me, at least not in the same way. The drugs the pimp offered up with their meager salaries were the only master they had to worry about. But addiction was a powerful one, and half of them would starve in their beds, waiting for Ricky to come back and get them their next hits.

"Already taken care of." Skin folded his arms. "I went through the place and handed them their pink slips personally before I went to the pimp's house. His ratty little book keeper will find 'em, or else the girls will sober up in the morning. I gave all of 'em a shelter in Knoxville, not too far away, where they can go to get clean."

No fucking way. Smiling, I shook my head, scared I'd break down and start crying all over again.

"What? Don't tell me you're having regrets."

"No, Skin, you just really thought of everything. I'm impressed." I leaned forward and grabbed his hand.

He didn't pull it away as I moved it to my face. I took my time just holding it there, savoring his warmth, his energy, the raw power in the fingers that had held the gun when he blew Ricky's evil brains out.

"Something like that," he whispered, his face darkening. "He wasn't bullshitting me when he talked about the Deads before I ended him. But those fuckers were gonna come after us anyway. Killing the pimp won't change that, it'll just give them something else to dig into, maybe buy us a little more time."

I looked at him for a second before I jerked my head

away. It was too hard to hide the worry. I didn't want to get caught in the middle of a raging war between outlaw motorcycle clubs. But I couldn't ask him to put me ahead of himself, or ahead of this group he'd sworn an oath to.

My eyes ran across his patches, and the dark inks on his arms. Tiger stripes and swords mingled, skulls and tiny cards stamped in black. The canvass hiding the complicated man underneath was just as complex, a mesh of death and courage, blended together to the point where the two were nearly indistinguishable.

"Get some sleep and don't worry about any of this shit, Meg. I'll keep you safe, and so will the rest of the club. You're going home soon, babe."

"I need to thank you," I purred, my eyes inevitably dropping to the ridge where his legs met.

He tensed up when I put my hand on his fly. Skin's dark, handsome eyes followed me as I got in front of him and sunk down to my knees, ready to take another man's cock deep into my mouth.

Except this time it was a man I *wanted.* And I wanted to please him like nothing else, to make him lose control and show me everything underneath the surface. I had to strip him down the same way he'd done to me, if only to share souls with a stranger for one beautiful night.

"Babe, what the hell do you think you're doing?" he rumbled, fisting my hair as I unzipped his fly, reaching in for his cock.

"What do you think?" I actually smiled after I said it, something I hadn't done with a man since I'd fooled around with the rich boy and popular jocks in college. It felt like a lifetime ago.

"Megan…wait. You shouldn't." He pulled my hair so tight my hand stopped on his boxers, one pull away from grasping the huge, hot, rock hard length underneath. "I don't need any goddamned favors for saving your life."

"It's not a *quid pro quo,* Skin. Don't worry about that. I'm not the screwed up little girl you think. I have desires…*needs.*"

Crap. That last word hissed out of my mouth so sharp it caused me to tremble. My fingers instinctively tightened on his cock, wondering what it would feel like to draw him deep inside my mouth, inside my body.

My pussy tingled, wet and alive in a way it hadn't been for at least a year. Not even Crawford for the other boy toys I'd had made me burn like this.

They hadn't killed for me. They hadn't warped life and death. They hadn't mastered hell and carried me through it. And they absolutely didn't have a single thing on this giant warrior in front of me, this man who'd carved his glorious body by fucking and fighting instead of lifting weights.

He was stronger than anyone I'd ever felt, and it wasn't just because he'd saved me. Some of the truckers Ricky brought in to use me were huge, but they weren't as dynamic, as strong, as masculine as this perfect beast I wanted for the night.

One night wasn't a sin. One night with him wouldn't ruin me – on the contrary, it might bring me back to life.

"It's too early for this shit. You shouldn't even think about it 'til you go home and talk to somebody. Get some help. Get your head screwed on straight."

I looked him right in the eye and ran my tongue across my lips. His words told a different story than the hunger in his eyes. He wanted me, and for the first time in months, I remembered how amazing it was to be wanted.

"Come on. Don't be shy. You're not going to stop me if I pull this out and give it a little kiss, are you? I swear I'm really good at it. I'm clean. I'll make you feel so fucking good, Skin, if you'll just make me feel human again tonight." I swallowed, fighting the lump of angst and regret in my throat. "It's been so long…I haven't wanted a man until you. This isn't about repaying you for anything. This is about what *I* want, and I know it's the same thing you do too. Can't we just enjoy each other for one short night?"

He grunted, as if considering my words. Hell with it.

I wasn't going to give him a chance to think about anything. I practically shredded his boxers with my nails, tearing open his fly, pulling out the magnificent cock I'd only caught a few brief glimpses of in the dark, foggy shower.

"Holy shit," I gasped, feeling him spring to life in my hand, angry and throbbing. The fist in my hair jerked tighter when I ran my fingers up and down his length, giving him several quick pumps, a prelude to my lips approaching the thick, swollen head, slick with his pre-come.

"You do this, babe, and there's no going back. I don't do teases. I've been waiting to feel you wrapped around my cock from the first time I saw you in that dirty little room." He paused, pulling my hair harder, his lust almost ripping it out by the roots. "The second you put your mouth on my dick, I own you all fucking night, understand? And once you're mine, I'll never, ever wanna let go."

His words made me burn. I smiled and nodded, all I could manage with the fire between my legs blazing deep up my body.

I'd never wanted any man so bad before this moment. My grip on his cock tightened as his relaxed on my head, and I leaned into him, inhaling his scent, opening wide for the tip of his pulsing erection.

He tasted just as good as he smelled. Earthy, raw, masculine. I slid my tongue all the way over him, orbiting his crown, drawing him deep into my mouth.

"Fuck!" Skin roared, repositioning his hand until it was on the back of my head, controlling me, pushing me to take him deeper.

I did. Without hesitation, without a second thought, without wondering if I was losing my mind. I sucked him deep, surrendering to the sweet primal wave sweeping over my senses.

I took every inch of him I could manage, and it still wasn't half his full length. I attacked his cock with an energy I'd never had with any man, much less the filthy Johns in the whorehouse.

I rolled my tongue across his cock and moved my lips up and down. Alternating tender teases and furious strokes was new to me. The last few months, I'd sucked men off as hard as I could, anything to make them finish and leave me the hell alone.

But with Skin, I took my time, relishing every hitch in his breath, every curse, every time I felt his full, muscular frame ripple underneath my hands. I grabbed his thighs for support, forcing my mouth down deeper as he snarled.

"Fuck, fuck, fuck." He growled the same rough word in staccato bursts, urging me to suck him deeper. "You keep that up, babe, and I'll give you a mouthful of come. That's what you want, isn't it, you sweet little slut?"

God. My legs tightened like vices and I flicked my tongue across him harder still.

Men had called me all kinds of terrible things in the trucker spa, until I grew numb to their words. But Skins' sweet and spice reminded me what it was like to feel dirty and enjoy it. It was only the start too, the very beginning of all the filthy, twisted things I wanted him to do to me.

"Don't you fucking answer me with anything but those lips," he said, his voice getting deeper with his pleasure. "I want to shoot off in you, wipe away every last trace of that miserable piece of shit I killed. I want you thinking about my dick morning, noon, and night, Meg. I want you to remember my hands, my tongue, all over your tight little body long after this clubhouse is just a distant memory."

I moaned, all I could do not to come completely unraveled.

"Suck. Harder. Show me how bad you want it, woman. I want you to rob every goddamned drop of seed out of these balls with your spitfire tongue."

Sweet Jesus. His words made my entire body throb, flogged me from the inside out to do everything he commanded.

It wasn't hard with my pussy burning me alive. Something about this man did terrible things to my body. I imagined fucking him, giving up the precious thing I'd kept through my hell.

I knew I'd lost my mind, but I didn't fucking care. Not with my lips wrapped around him, drawing out his pleasure, thinking about how wonderful his power would feel between my legs, slamming me into the mattress. I wanted to give him my virginity without asking anything for it, not his money, his life, or even his love.

I went into overdrive. I used every trick I'd ever learned with my mouth for pleasing a man, giving him a whirlwind of lips and teeth and tongue. All while I completely lost it, shoving my hand down my pants, moaning with my mouth full of his cock when I found my swollen clit and felt the wetness he'd summoned, turning my panties into a ruined mess.

"Oh, Meg. Shit. Don't you fucking stop for anything, baby. I'm gonna give you what you're craving. Fuck it out of me," he growled, jerking my face up and down his length, merging me into his powerful strokes. "Fuck it out of me with your tongue. Show me how much you love it. I wanna watch you swallow every damned drop while you frig your little clit to the moon."

I did, with pleasure.

The next few seconds he swelled in my mouth, so impossibly big I thought he'd hurt me. He roared and shook from head to toe as he tensed up and emptied himself into me, fucking my mouth in swift, desperate strokes, flooding my mouth with so much come I couldn't take it all.

He spilled out my lips. I swallowed everything I could manage, every jet he sent hurling down my throat. Not that it was easy to focus with my fingers working overdrive between my legs, pushing me to the brink – and then straight into free fall.

He swelled, erupted, filled me with hot, musky seed shooting across my tongue. His climax overflowed, grunt by grunt, and I moaned into the flood of come.

I came with a mouthful of his cock, his come. I felt his warmth and his energy radiating across me as my own body exploded, shaking and moaning and sweating in heavy, tense ripples. My climax opened up a hole in the world underneath me and swallowed us both.

For a couple of beautiful minutes, I found total release from everything I'd suffered, a completion in Skin, my feminine canvass glowing in his masculine stars.

He made me feel everything he'd offered before, but this time there were no barriers, no holding back.

We came together, long and hard.

I only started cleaning the sticky mess he'd left dripping down my neck when he finally pulled out, sliding one hand across my face, a softer touch than he'd ever used before.

"Look at me, babe," he ordered, when I'd finally wiped most of it up.

For a second, I hesitated. I worried how I'd feel when I finally met his eyes again, scared that we'd just made a huge fucking mistake.

But when our eyes connected, there was no regret, no terror. No ifs, ands, or buts.

"That was amazing," I sighed, smiling as I gave his softening cock one last rub.

"Was?" He cocked his head, looking at me like he really didn't understand. "Stand the fuck up."

I bounced up and he wrapped his arms around me. His face came in close and he inhaled my scent, breathing through my hair, entangled yet again with his strong, incredible fingers.

"Yeah, I mean, it's over now…we have to get on with all the other stuff. Right?" I'd never sounded so nervous with a man after having him naked.

But Skin was the first man in ages to make me come, and the only one who'd done it with such an intensity, without even touching me directly between my legs. He'd done it with his energy, his strength, whatever strange spell he had over my body.

"You're cute, babe, for real." He smiled, staring deep into my eyes. "I meant every word I said. If this is just a one night thing, then I'm gonna spend every minute fucking you. You know I searched your purse the first time we brought you in. Have you been good about taking those pills, or what?"

My heart came to a screeching stop and took a few seconds to reboot in my chest. Was he really asking to take my virginity – and was I going to give it to him?

I reached up for his face, running my fingernails across it. *Yes, yes, a thousand times yes.*

Everything about this man tripped my buttons. It was like he was made for me, and I'd found him in the most fucked up way possible.

Mostly, I adored him because he let me forget. He helped me imagine a different future, even if he was the very thing holding me here in this stupid clubhouse. It didn't matter – Skin told me I could take control, on my own terms, and maybe someday I could be more than a spoiled party girl or a broken ex-whore.

"Babe, I need an answer, and I'm not gonna wait all damned night." He grabbed my hand by the wrist and pressed it to his cock, making me feel him ballooning, hard and hungry as ever for me.

Very slowly, I nodded, blushing like a prom girl.

"Take me, Skin. I meant what I said too…I'm yours for the night. Just for tonight. I don't want to forget you when all this is over." It took everything I had to hold his gaze without looking away. "Give me something to remember."

My words unchained something wild inside him. Even *wilder* than what I'd seen so far, and it was ten times as insane when he threw me on the bed and started tearing off my clothes.

Off went my shirt, my jeans. He growled as he unhooked my bra, flipping me over while his hand went below the waistband to my panties, shedding them in one rough fist.

He didn't waste any time kicking off his clothes either. The same half-naked body I'd watched and admired before revealed itself, except this time I knew it was going to be all over me, taking me, claiming me.

His hot, aggressive lips touched mine. It was like he transferred his manic energy, kissing me so hard I couldn't even think about teasing him, needing his mouth on mine as much as I needed air. My lips parted, and his tongue sank into me, taking control.

Skin's tongue frolicked with mine for the next several minutes. He kissed me in ways I didn't know men could kiss, and I feasted on his passion, everything I sensed in his kiss and in his heart.

His hand slid between my thighs. Two stiff fingers pushed into my soaked pussy, catching me by surprise, so sudden and intense I nearly flew off the bed.

"Relax, babe," he whispered softly, a mischievous smile on his face. "You picked the best man in the world to fuck you for the very first time, and I'm not gonna let you down. I'll just leave you hoarse from all the screaming you'll be doing tonight, fucking my mouth, my hands, my cock, fucking me 'til you can't. You'll love it."

"Yes!" It wasn't even a question, but I added my voice anyway, staring at him with such heat in my eyes it was starting to scare me.

We kissed while he fingered me. Skin's marvelous thumb pressed on my clit, and I went wild, rocking into him, bucking my hips over and over and over.

I thought he was going to send me straight over the edge again, but he had other plans.

If his fingers were bliss, then his mouth was heaven. Nothing prepared me for his face sinking down, stopping to tease my nipples with his teeth and tongue, before he stamped a hot trail all the way down my body.

His lips stopped at my pussy for a small eternity, teasing me with his hot breath and stubble. Shallow licks caressed my inner thighs, then drove higher, straight over my clit. My fingernails dug into his head and I tried with all my might to push him into me.

The bastard resisted, enjoying his amusement, teasing me until I couldn't hold it anymore.

"Please lick me, Skin. Fuck me. I'm dying. *Please.*"

I begged him for all I was worth. And tonight, that was everything, as I learned when he finally gave in and let me have what I'd wanted.

He taught me real passion. The bad boy between my legs savaged me with his mouth, pulling my legs open, throwing them over his shoulders while I trembled and gasped.

His tongue fucked me, sucked me, and did everything in between. Raw heat pulsed out his mouth, covering my entire slit, before he began to focus his licks and forceful kisses around my clit.

I clawed at the sheets underneath us, losing control in the space of a heartbeat.

"Oh, hell, Skin, that feels so good…too fucking good. Shit! You're going to make me…"

It sounded like I wanted to say *come,* but really it was *yours* on my tongue.

I couldn't get out another word as climax crashed over me. Every muscle in my body tensed and the fireball building in my womb exploded, rippling outward, giving me the greatest pleasure of my life.

Incredible. Better than anything I'd had, except what I knew I'd feel with his cock slamming into me.

Skin's mouth fucked me into total submission through the whole thing. His pleasure dragged me so deep for so long the fiery stars filled my vision, engulfing me completely, scorching me from the inside out.

Somewhere inside me, the wounds Ricky inflicted broke open and drained.

I came back to life with his hand gently moving across my face, wiping away tears. He held my head, kept me from shaking, panicking, freaking out.

"Let it out, baby. Get it all the fuck outta your system before I shake you so hard you'll be crying over the pleasure instead."

I pushed my face up to his, and we twirled tongues once again. His taste completely addicted me. I worried I'd go to pieces by now, but my body craved more, begged him to go all the way, to fill me and fuck me like no man ever had.

Like no man ever would.

No, I couldn't let myself think like that. I had to just enjoy the moment. If we did the sane thing, this would all be over tomorrow, just like it should be.

Breathe in, breathe out. Experience everything Skin had to offer for one amazing night. Just one night.

This wasn't love. This wasn't worship. This was fucking, plain and simple, two people throwing themselves into one wild attraction to sate their urges.

His hands gripped my legs and pushed them apart. His rough stubble grazed my neck as he traced a line along my throat, dipping to my cleavage, and then back up again, where he caught the skin on my neck and sucked it hard enough to bruise.

His cock moved against me, teasing, wedged against my clit. I threw my arms around his neck and squeezed, all I could do to stop myself from panting and going to pieces.

"Feels like I've been waiting half my life to feel this pussy wrapped around my cock. You ready for me, babe?"

I stared up at him through narrowed eyes, wondering how he had the energy to speak when we were so fucking close.

"Yes! Please, Skin. I want you inside me." Blood brushed my veins like sandpaper, melting me from the inside out.

No exaggeration. I hadn't needed anything this bad in my entire life, except my own freedom.

He bared his teeth and kissed me again, rubbing his

cock harder through my folds, one thrust away from claiming me forever.

"You'll have to do better than that. I don't believe you. Is this what you want, babe?" He rocked his hips into mine, grunting as my wetness coated him. "This, yeah? If you wanna feel me fucking you straight through this mattress, then you'll beg for it, Meg. Beg for every damned inch."

"Please!" I panted, feeling like the floor was dropping out underneath us. "Please...please...you're *killing* me, Skin!"

He let out a small snort. The steady rhythm in his hips brushing mine grew harder, more urgent, as if I'd finally said the magic word.

"Bullshit. We haven't gotten started yet, babe. You'll die and come back to life a few more times before I'm through with you." His hips shifted, and I felt his cock's tip poised at my entrance, throbbing heat ready to own me. "You're mine now, woman. Hell, you were mine the second I laid eyes on you in that shithole. We're just making this formal with sweat and flesh since we've already spilled blood."

His words lit me on fire. But it was nothing compared to the hard, sudden thrust of his hips. His fullness sank into me, gliding through my depths, stretching me open and taking me hard.

"Skin!" His name hissed across my tongue like a mantra.

He reached behind my head, seized my hair, and jerked

my head straight. His strokes came, gradual and harder each time he pounded into me, staring deep into my eyes the whole time.

I saw fire. Smoke. Mountains coming down inside me, an avalanche of pleasure blanketing my soul.

The ruins of my old life suddenly set free, all the pain rocketing away from me, fueled by this ecstasy. Skin fulfilled his promise in every thrust, fucking me like I'd never imagined. There was nothing soft or tender about it, and I realized that wasn't even close to what I'd been looking for.

He took me like a man should, forcing me to feel every inch of him, every flex of his muscles. He reminded me I was a living, breathing woman, one who craved his sweet release a little more every time his cock slammed into me.

"Oh, God. Don't stop, don't stop, don't ever fucking stop," I murmured, losing myself in the rising tide of ecstasy.

"Come on my cock, woman. I'm gonna pull out and walk away if I don't feel you clenching all over me in the next minute."

Oh, shit! His threat only made me fuck him harder.

The tearing and mild discomfort I'd felt when he stretched me open faded in the frantic pleasure shooting through me. My hips rose, bucking against his, taking his cock deeper with every stroke.

I loved how we fused, one in the moment, working without worry toward our own sweet release. And he guided me there, dragged me along, a leader I wanted to follow with my everything.

Growling, he fucked me harder, so rough my ass slammed deep into the mattress each time he went deep. The bed shrieked beneath us, but it had nothing on the scream building up in my core, the explosion ready to wreck my body.

"Come, baby girl. Come like the beautiful woman you are. Come so fucking hard you see stars and nothing else. Come now!" His chant threw me over the edge.

I scratched his neck so hard I was afraid I'd drawn blood. Everything below my waist tightened, convulsed, gushed, and I lost all my senses. My vision blurred and I turned into a shaking, writhing mess.

The release I found beneath him devoured me completely, like riding an atomic wave. I came forever in that sweet, merciful place where there was no pain or regret or fear, just soft warmth and raging passion.

Skin was a drug. My brain crackled like he'd given me a hit of something I'd never leave behind without wanting more. That scared me, but not so much I'd dream of letting him go tonight.

Not like there was much choice either.

He barely let me come up for breath as my climax faded. His face looked more intense than ever, rivulets running off both of us. He power fucked me straight through it and kept going, working his cock deeper.

The fire his friction kindled seemed almost endless. A minute or two after I'd come once, the ache in my womb was building again, and this time I wanted to feel his release too.

I dug my nails into his neck and rode him harder, jerking my body up and down in mad waves, begging for his come before the words even left my mouth.

"Make me come again, Skin. I want to feel your cock explode inside me. Don't let me come alone this time. Come with me. Please. Please. *Please!*"

His face twitched when I begged the last time. He jerked my hair harder, growling as his hips picked up speed, taking me so fast and hard it probably would've hurt if we hadn't built up to the perfect tempo together.

"You think you know what you do to me, babe? You don't know shit," he growled, his voice darkening more with every word. "I'm gonna fuck you senseless. I'm gonna fuck my balls dry all damned night. I'm gonna give you something to remember when you're home in your mansion, one good memory to cherish, so fucking incredible you'll frig your clit to me even when you're married to some boring, white collar chucklefuck. You're *mine* tonight, dammit, and my come's about to be yours."

Please do! I thought, right before everything in my head turned to static.

Please, Skin. Please. For fuck's sake, please!

My body raged. My muscles turned to iron as I locked onto him and rode him for all I was worth, panting and moaning the whole time, becoming his vessel.

He fucked me like a madman for at least another minute. Neither of us could make a sound except for the ragged, savage grunts spilling out of us.

Then he plunged into me one last time, holding himself against my womb, swelling so big I felt the torrent for a split second before it began.

"Fuck!" Skin roared first.

"Oh. My. God." I was right behind him.

We came. Savagely, relentlessly, wildly.

Our pulses mingled and our bodies rippled with carnal delight. His fire tore through me, a blaze set by the molten seed he spilled inside me. His cock jerked inside me over and over, rooted so deep, filling me until I overflowed around him.

I'd lost it with him a couple times before, but this…this wasn't even on the same planet.

Climax swept me up in a tsunami of heat, skin, and his feral curses. I took one last glimpse at the dark, violent ink seething on his chest before my eyes pinched shut.

My orgasm throttled me, caused my pussy to tense around him, sucking greedily at his cock. The begging wasn't over, even though I couldn't speak. Every inch of me wanted more from him.

More, more, so much more.

I didn't know how I'd walk out of here with my sanity intact. Hell, Ricky and his Johns had shattered it long before I ever heard the name Skin. But the biker's name was all I could feel in my soul now, filling the holes torn wide open by the pimp and his bastards, as surely as he filled my flesh.

I opened my mouth and tried to scream his name one more time. It didn't work. Nothing more than a squeak came out while we were frozen in bliss. When the firestorm lifted and I could finally breathe, he buried me in another kiss, wiping away the new fears and obsessions he'd planted in my head.

Tonight was ours, and I was okay. Hell, I was *good,* something I hadn't been since the last year at university.

I ran my hands up and down his chest, owning the moment. I had to stay here, every precious second, one with Skin and the night.

It was all I could do to stay happy. I ignored the foolish part of me that wanted him to own me forever.

VI: Conscience (Skin)

I couldn't shake the whole night fucking her. My eyes were still sore as I sat there in church, waiting for the Prez to get his shit together, listening to the steady *thud-thud-thud* of Joker slamming the knife on the table next to me.

The Veep's place at the table had about a thousand little cuts from all the years where he'd put his hand down flat on the old wood, stabbing his switchblade between his fingers. For some reason, it seemed weirder than ever today, watching him lost in his own tortured world 'til the Prez put a hand to his mouth and let out a sharp whistle.

"Fuck!" Sixty snarled next to me, covering his ear. Loud noises got his fucked up ear, ever since he'd been too close to a grenade going off a couple years back.

Joker stopped trying to take his fingers off and looked up at the Prez. Dust gave him the same dirty look I'd seen a thousand times before.

Same old club. Same old shit.

What wasn't the same was the way I'd fucked that sweet, wounded woman sleeping off the sex in my bedroom right now. It was twisted, it was playing with the last fire on earth I should, but damn if I regretted a thing.

No. No way. Fuck no.

My cock throbbed, wishing I'd kept her up for another hour. But then I wouldn't have gotten a lick of sleep at all.

Shit. What the fuck are you gonna do?

The question kept tossing in my mind. If only the incredible sex was all I could remember. Too bad fucking her brought these other feelings, this need to treat her like more than a piece of meat and a hostage.

"Let's get on with it, shall we, boys?" The Prez said darkly, training his dirty look on me next. "Your turn to brief us first, brother. The whore's your business, like you promised. You've had plenty of time to cook up a plan to get what we're owed. Spill it."

Fuck. I wracked my brain through last night's haze. It took all I had not to freeze up as all the brothers looked at me, waiting for this grand scheme I was supposed to have hatched by now to get us the quarter million.

"We let her walk."

Boom. My words wouldn't have been any less surprising than a pipe bomb going off underneath our table.

Several jaws dropped. The Prez cocked his head like he hadn't heard me right.

"Skin…what the fuck? You'd better be kidding me, brother."

"Don't think he is," Firefly said, standing up and flexing his fists, his huge jaw twitching. "The girl's got him by the balls. I heard those two yesterday. Up all night, fucking their little hearts out."

Fuck, fuck, fuck. All the sirens blasted in my head, especially when I saw the stocky boy walking around the table toward me, angling to make this shit physical if I didn't think of something, and *think fast.*

"Come on, guys, it isn't like that."

"Bullshit!" Firefly spat at the floor, ripping me up by the shoulders.

The bastard had brute strength. I couldn't get a good grip on him to fight back and free myself before he slammed me against the wall, rattling every bone in my body.

"We're disappointed in you, Skin. Your weakness has always been pussy, just like your old man." He grabbed my throat and tightened his grip before I could say shit. "We've been more than goddamned generous with you. Now, you're the only boy getting pussy in this joint, and you wanna let this bird fly and leave the club empty-fucking-handed – after all we've been through!"

I saw his other fist coming up, ready to break my nose. Shit.

My knee came up and slammed into his gut. I knew the big Enforcer's weak point. It didn't fail me here, he stumbled back against the table and doubled over, struggling for air.

Everybody else was already up on their feet.

I tried to make a break, and ran right into Joker. I got in the first blow, but he had the edge, pulling at my cut and holding his cold blade against my throat.

"Try to run, brother, and I'll skin every fucking symbol of this club right off you."

I held my breath, knowing he meant business. Hell, I'd watched him do it a few times to assholes who deserved it. The Veep was crazy enough to do it to one of our own too, as soon as the Prez said jump.

Speaking of the Prez, he was heading toward me. Angry, sharp determination flickered in his pale blue eyes. His lips peeled back, and I saw the gold tooth set in his mouth shining like a beacon, illuminating the only words that could bring me mercy or pure hell.

"Prez, go easy, aren't we jumping the damned gun?" Sixty pipped up. "He's gotta have something for us. Skin's all brains. He's never let us down. Cut the man some fucking slack."

Crawl nodded at his side, sweeping his dark hair over his face, unable to hide his worried expression. Both my brothers backed me up, and they'd try to save my ass if it came to a vote.

Assuming you're worth saving. The nasty thought ran through my head.

I had to give them something. I had to prove I hadn't lost my mind from getting pussy whipped.

Shit, I had to prove it to myself. I'd just had the best fuck of my life, and I'd promised her the moon, but damn if I'd let her get to me.

I owed this club my life. I looked up as the Prez approached, steadying my gaze, refusing to give a shit when his eyes flashed murder.

"Firefly's right. You've got your head all fucked up by this stray pussy cat we've let you take in. You've got ten seconds to start talking, and tell me why I shouldn't have the club drag her out back and find out the best way to get that money from her rich folks ourselves..."

Shit. She wouldn't survive a club interrogation. The guys wouldn't hurt her – I didn't think – but they'd scare the shit out of her, undo everything I'd tried to give her last night, dig up all the shit the pimp had done to her.

Good thing I came ready. I had an Ace in my hand, a little extra card I'd picked up from the pimp before I shot his shit-for-brains out. It just might stall them from doing something reckless and stupid.

"Send one of the prospects out to the garage right now. There's a black bag out there, next to my bike. I was saving it to bring to your office privately, Prez, but since you want all this shit out in the open..."

Dust's eyes widened with dark amusement. *You'd better not be fucking with me,* they said.

He looked at Crawl. "Step outside and tell Lion to bring us whatever the fuck he's talking about. Hurry up!"

Everybody waited while our brother opened the door and said a few words to the prospects standing guard. Lion and Tinman both took off, returning a minute later. The Prez saw Lion's scruffy face holding my leather saddlebag, sagging with the shit I'd stuffed in it.

"Come on, up on the table," Dust ordered, waving him forward. As soon as the prospect dropped the bag, he gave him another wave, and Crawl shut the door behind him, locking them both out 'til they'd earned their bottom rockers.

"Go on. Open it. It's not a full quarter million, but it's a sign of good faith. This club's all I think about, Prez. Here's your proof that's true. I *won't* let us walk away with our pockets hanging out, and I'm not gonna stand here and listen to the shit that's being talked about me."

"Firefly."

Soon as the Prez said his name, the Enforcer moved, ripping open the zipper. His eyes bugged out when he saw the fat stacks of cash spilling out on the table, mostly smaller bills like fifties and twenties, mingled with hundreds.

It was a complete fucking mess. I wasn't sure how the hell the pimp counted it. Hell, maybe he'd been too drugged up when the Deads dropped off his down payment for Meg, or else too busy shitting his pants.

He'd done enough of that before I blew his worthless brains out. I took a quick estimate and pegged it around twenty-five thousand. There'd been twice as much to start, but I'd divided that and given it to the whores when I opened up their rooms to deliver their pink slips.

Sure, they might go out and blow the shit on street smack, but at least it'd get them outta that rat's nest and into the city. The closer I got them to the shelter listed on that paper, the better.

Dust pushed Firefly and the other boys aside, reaching into my bag, pulling out fistfuls of cash and spreading it across our table.

"I'll be fucking hog-tied." He was still fisting big stacks of bills when he spun around and looked at me. "Where the hell did you get this?"

"Settling accounts. The pimp had a payday twice as big as the shit we confiscated from him last week. That was his down payment for selling her off, and it's ours now."

"Aw, shit." Dust's fists dropped, holding the cash limply at his sides, shaking his head. "Don't tell me...you killed the stupid sonofabitch?"

"Yeah." No sense in hiding it.

None of the men in this room were stupid, even if they couldn't crunch numbers or cloak our operations from the Feds like I could.

"Fuck me alive."

"It was bound to happen sooner or later. You know it, Prez, and so do I." I swallowed, preparing for the biggest gamble yet. "The fucker was tight with the Deads. He was a cash cow, besides being a walking sewer. I don't regret a damned thing. I brought the club some red meat and buried his carcass in the usual place, where nobody'll find his bones for a hundred years. Sure, the fucks from Georgia will notice he's missing, but they're coming for us anyway sooner or later, after what happened to their guys..."

Sixty, Crawl, and I shared an uneasy look. I wasn't gonna say anything more about that and blow their cover, even though the Prez had probably figured it out.

"This is going in the club coffers," Dust said slowly, the anger in his eyes receding. "You've earned yourself another chance – one week. That's all I'm giving you. I swear on my father's patch, Skin, if you fuck us over, and don't get us the rest of what we're owed from this gal, I'll send the guys to pick her up and drag her ass back here, kicking and screaming."

He stared right through me to the wall, where we had old photos and trophies framed for the club. His old man's cut hung there, patch facing out, one more relic among many in all the glories the Deadly Pistols had lived and lost.

"We've got about enough here to start another girlie bar, this time in Knoxville city limits. I'm going with the business plan I should've let you talk me into the first time. Whatever else happens, we'll do this shit right. This is our second chance. I'm not pissing it away." The Prez stepped up, looking me dead in the eye. "If you fuck us over, Skin, if your *toy* fucks us over, I swear to Christ I'll make her work off every single red cent she owes. Don't think I haven't noticed what you're fucking. She's got the tits and ass to be a slut. She'll be the first chick we put to work shaking what she's made of, seven days a week, even if we have to put a kinky mask over her face to keep any nosy assholes from noticing who she is. If she doesn't pay up, mark my words, she's *ours.* Club property."

Asshole. I didn't say it to his face, despite the anger howling through me. I was too busy thinking about how bad I wanted to make her my property. Mine, mine, and mine alone.

Joker's knife pulled away from my neck. I instinctively reached up and rubbed the impression he'd left, smearing a tiny blotch of rusty blood between my fingers.

"One week, Skin. That's all you get." The Veep's dead eyes were more lively than usual. Creepy as a hungry fucking snake. "I'm game for bringing her back here and putting her to work myself. Nobody fucks this club. Not even the men who've given it their blood."

Firefly still looked like a bull ready to charge, but his rage was deflating too. With a heavy sigh, he turned his back and walked to his spot, ripping his chair out to sit.

"Prez, with your approval, let's sit down and call a vote like gentlemen. I'll let this fucking guy live another week and set his girl free. He's bound by the club rules – they both are. Skin here's done some stupid shit, but he ain't a rat." He looked over the ranks of brothers, ending with me. "Trust is all we've got when we're outnumbered three to one by the Deads. He's right about one thing – they're coming. And they damned sure will rip our heads off in a heartbeat if we're fighting each other."

The Prez nodded. Everybody followed his lead as we headed for our seats.

The vote went fast, the yeas rolling in one by one, unanimous.

When it was my turn, I only had Meg on my mind, hoping to high hell I wasn't making the biggest mistake of my life.

"Start packing," I growled, kicking the door shut behind me.

Meg flashed me a smile. I'd caught her walking outta

the shower, a towel wrapped tight around her, tempting me to tear it off.

She shifted her weight, forcing me to see the contour of her hips. "You mean you're taking me out to dinner tonight? What, are we dating now, or something?"

The girl winked, and my blood turned into fire.

Fuck. My dick remembered everything we'd done last night, everything she had waiting beneath that flimsy little towel. I'd fucked her for hours after I spilled my seed inside her the first time, and it still wasn't enough.

I wanted more. I wanted it so damned bad I had to fight with everything I had to shut down the instinct to march over, strip her bare, and fuck us both seven ways stupid.

But I didn't do goodbye fucks. Especially when I'd finally gotten the clearance to get her home without any huge hangups. I had to do it *now,* before the Prez changed his mind, or Joker helped him in all his ruthlessness.

"You heard me, woman," I said, turning away from the beautiful sight in front of me and ripping open the closet. I pulled out all her new clothes and began throwing them on the bed, wondering if she'd want any of this shit once she was with her rich family again.

"Jesus, Skin! Slow down." Next thing I knew, she stood next to me, tugging on my arm. "Why can't we talk like normal people? Tell me what's going on?"

There wasn't any time for that. As soon as I had her outfits laid out, I grabbed an old bag from cleaning my cut, and started to throw her shit in there, leaving her a pair of jeans and a tank top to change into.

"I said, you heard me. You're going home. Nothing else to say."

Her jaw dropped. Her big blue eyes became wide moons in front of me, moons I'd stared into last night while we fucked, her chestnut hair tangled between my fingers.

My dick begged me to slow down, and so did her expression. But I wasn't listening to either of them. This mission couldn't wait, dammit, and nothing was getting in my way when I had a chance to get her to total safety.

"I don't understand, Skin. It can't be that easy."

"Things change, babe." I shrugged, tying the bag shut, ignoring her. "Quit acting like you're all upset. This is everything we've been waiting for since I dragged you to the clubhouse. I'd be a damned fool to give it up, and so would you."

"Home..." she repeated the word like she needed to just to grasp the meaning again. "Holy shit. What will I tell my parents? I still haven't figured anything out. I mean, I had some ideas, but I woke up so late after last night, and none of them are very good."

"You'll have a week tops to sort that shit out in the comfort of your own home," I said, grabbing her by the wrist. I led her into the bathroom and set her change of clothes on the toilet next to her, stepping outside with my back turned while she changed.

Fuck, my eyes burned knowing she was naked behind me. I heard her clothes rustling slowly, as if it took her massive energy just to move.

I couldn't turn around, no matter how much my body begged me. If I gave in and saw her in the nude again, I'd want to keep her here forever. I sure as shit wouldn't let her leave without one more fuck, one more fiery, passionate fling on the bed next to me, grabbing her sweet ass and shaking her 'til she almost broke while I slammed myself in so deep my balls bruised her.

My fists tensed at my sides. Lucky for her, she didn't have a thing to worry about.

I wasn't gonna fuck her and send her home with an even more screwed up head. Just like I wasn't gonna look her in the eye right now and let her see what she'd done to me, turning me into a lustful, possessive mess.

Me, Skin, the rock hard motherfucker who never got attached to any pussy. I'd always been the man to fuck and forget. Hell, I *still* was that guy, it was just harder this time, because I'd spent more time having her in my bed than most girls.

"You have to tell me what's changed. What's the catch?" Her voice darkened.

I turned around and faced the only woman I'd slept with as opposed to just fucking. The only woman I'd dreamed about wearing my brand, and maybe the only chick this side of Nashville who never fucking would.

"Prez had a change of heart. I convinced him. It isn't right to hold you here like our personal cash cow. Lord knows you've had enough of that shit." She folded her arms, shooting me a skeptical look through all her shock.

The girl wasn't stupid. Shit, that made me want to fuck her more, hard enough to rattle the brains in her pretty head.

"You're expected to deliver the money, babe. That shit hasn't changed. Quarter million, solid, straight from your folks." I gave her my coldest look, trying to make her realize how serious it was without scaring her. "Consider it a finder's fee, the price of rescue, operating costs, whatever the fuck you want. Truth is, everybody knows what's on the line here. The club's interest in the reward money is the same it always was. Big difference is, now you've got a chance to get it over to us while you start to put your life back together. Come on, I know your family's rich. Two hundred and fifty big's a drop in the damned bucket, isn't it?"

She cocked her head. "Okay, fair enough. And what happens if my parents say no, Skin? What if the police ask too many questions? What if I can't convince them?"

I had a crystal clear vision of everything Dust told me. I saw myself being held down by all the brothers and punched in the face, over and over 'til Joker broke my nose, plus a few ribs. They'd have to beat me stupid to make me stand down while they pulled her outta her house and forced her back into slavery, this time shaking that killer ass for grubby motherfuckers in our nudie bar.

No, no, fuck no. I won't let that happen.

"You'll pay your debt one way or another," I growled, looking around the room for anything else she'd left behind. I saw her mystery magazine and threw it in the bag too, plus a bottle of water for the road.

"What's that supposed to mean? Should I be worried? Looking over my shoulder?" Her questions ended in a hiss of resignation. "Just tell me one thing…are you actually setting me free, or not? I can't tell."

Shit. I didn't say anything for several seconds, not 'til I turned and handed her the heavy bag.

"Make sure everything's in there. Next stop is my bike so I can take you home." Her face wilted, and she nodded glumly as she realized I wasn't gonna tell her shit. Not before we got outside, anyway.

When her bag was stuffed into my Harley's trunk and I handed her the helmet, I let it spill. None of the brothers were around to hear shit, but I still would've said it, even if they were.

"Babe, I'm dead serious about you figuring out the reward. I threw the club a bone to get them off your ass, but they're gonna be right back on it soon if you delay too long. Here's a burner." I reached into my pocket, and passed her a cheap pre-paid flip phone, the kind we always used for jobs that had to stay anonymous. "You call me anytime. Any trouble, any update, or when you've got the cash, ready to go. And yeah, it's gotta be cash, stacked up neatly in a briefcase or thrown into a damned barrel. I don't give a shit. Just get it to me, and you'll never hear from me again."

"Understood." She took the phone and pinched her eyes shut. I couldn't tell if she was sick from the renewed worries I'd just given her, or if it seriously hurt her to think about a life without me.

I inwardly snorted. *Dream on, you poor, lovestruck bastard.*

"Hope you don't need to give them much notice. I'll drop you off wherever, right outside the gate or in your own driveway, just say the word. Hold on tight." I made sure she had her hands around my waist before my bike's engine roared.

We headed out into the mountains, the autumn breeze nipping at my cheeks. At least it wasn't raining like the night I'd rescued her, soaking us all down to the bone.

I tried to think about anything except the beautiful, broken woman riding on my bike. She'd come through for us in a few days. I didn't doubt it one bit. I'd meet her one more time, then drop the money for the Prez, and he'd throw one fuck of a party.

We'd have girls, booze, more hogs and steaks on the fire than we could even eat. We'd gorge ourselves on good times and brotherly love. We'd drink the evening away, and fuck ourselves raw at night, cuddling up with two or three girls at a time, just like the good old days.

I'd have some hot brunette with ice blue eyes riding my dick while another one bucked her pussy on my mouth. It should've been enough to make my dick throb while we bounced up and down the mountain roads.

It always was before. Hell, it was all I'd ever known before Megan, before killing Ricky, before I fell on my ass into this big goddamned mess.

So, why the fuck didn't it cut it anymore? Why did

thinking beyond this bullshit just fill me with numb, gray dread?

I clenched my jaw, gritting my teeth, throttling the bike harder on the next bend. She held me tighter, pulling herself instinctively closer to stay steady and safe. I slowed as soon as I realized she didn't need to ride this hard.

But damn if her hands didn't stay tight when we were coming off the highest slopes. If anything, she was digging her fingers into me, just like she'd done last night.

Last night, our only night together. All I'd have to remember her by, and all I'd ever give her to remember me.

I'd fucked her so damned hard, but I wanted to do more. I wanted to fuck her a dozen times more, each time harder than the last, the only thing that might stand a tiny chance at driving her outta my system.

I knew then I was really and truly fucked.

Thinking about the woman riding bitch behind me was what really set my balls on fire. Not an orgy with three whores wearing too much lip gloss and silicon in their tits.

Meg was all natural, all woman, and I wanted her to be *mine.*

She turned me on like no woman ever had. When we fucked, I was fucking to leave marks, a makeshift brand on her that would tell the whole damned world I owned her. I fucked to make her convulse and scream herself hoarse. Mostly, I fucked to make her shout my name, the only name I ever wanted hanging on her lips while she pinched her arms and legs around me tight and lost control.

Yeah, it was insane, stupid, and a thousand shades of wrong. Just then, I didn't give a single shit.

I squeezed my bike's bars so damned hard the vibrations of the road shook my heart, and it still wasn't enough to wipe her outta my system.

I didn't give a fuck about senseless. I only cared about keeping her safe, keeping her in my world, never letting go. My eyes followed the faded lines on the road 'til I was almost in a trance, all I could do to keep myself from pulling into the nearest lookout, dragging her into the woods, and making her realize I hadn't said shit about *my* payment.

The money was for the club. She'd handle that one way or another. Me?

I wanted her naked and fused to my cock, legs spread wide while I rammed my dick into her and emptied every last drop of come from my balls in her pussy, her mouth, all over her perfect fucking skin.

I'd saved her several times. Something about that made it even more fucked up that I wanted to ruin her, wanted to drag her away from her prissy little world forever, into the darkness with me. I wanted her in my bed forever, the bed she belonged in, where she'd wear my brand and call me her old man. And she'd fucking love it every time.

Fuck. I shook off the twisted fantasies long enough to see the signs growing more frequent.

We were approaching Knoxville when I spied the little filling station. I made a hard turn into it. Filled up my half-depleted tank, everything I'd need for the ride home, when I had a lot less precious cargo on my bike and a whole lot more hell on my brain.

Meg never even got off to stretch. She was staring down at the pavement when I paid and got back on the bike, ready for the home stretch.

"Babe, you should be the happiest woman in the world when you get home and that gate slams shut behind you. Why the fuck don't you look it?"

"I can't forget last night," she said, looking up and locking eyes with me. "I'll never forget you, Skin. What we did…"

She gnawed at her bottom lip. My whole cock ached, remembering what those sweet lips felt like gliding along my flesh.

Fuck me. Of all the excuses I'd expected her to give, it wasn't that.

I reached up and palmed her face, feeling her sweet cheek on my fingers. If only for the last time.

"No regrets, yeah? I wouldn't have done shit if I knew it was gonna make you hurt more. You need to get over everything that happened and live your life, baby. It won't be easy. But you'll do it. You're one helluva woman – a survivor. Anything you do after all the shit you've suffered is gonna feel like a stroll instead of a frantic fucking sprint to the bitter end."

"I know," she said softly, rubbing her face into my skin. "It's the end I'm worried about. The end of us…before we've even started. I mean, if there was an us. You know what I mean, yeah?"

My eyes narrowed. She had me by the balls, but I played dumb. Showing her any of the flames pouring through my blood right now wouldn't do a damned lick of good.

It would only make it harder to close the book on this, harder for her to heal, to forget, to move the fuck on like she needed to.

"I know two healthy people shared a bed for a few nights and did what people do. That's it. It ain't nothing to worry about, woman, and it sure as shit ain't anything to cry over."

Fuck if my words did any good when I felt the warm, salty wetness rolling down my finger, a single teardrop slipping out the corner of her eye.

I wiped it away and squeezed her cheek one more time, drawing my face into hers. "Give me one more kiss. One for the road."

She did. We kissed long and hard, absorbed in this wild thing we had, oblivious to the impatient prick in the pickup behind us, waiting for my pump. I pulled her into me and really fucking kissed her.

Hotter and harder than the night before. More intense than I'd ever kiss a woman for as long as I lived, tracing her tongue with mine for a few sweet seconds, then leading it around and around in a dance we'd both dream about 'til we jerked awake in a cold sweat.

"I'm not going to forget this," she said, her voice a harsh whisper.

"No, you won't, but you're not gonna let it fuck up the

rest of your life. I won't let you, babe." I grabbed her face, traced her jawline, pressed my fingers in 'til I stopped and felt her tremble. "This is the kiss that sets you free. Nothing more. Now, strap on your helmet and hold me tight. You're going home."

I could hear the strain on her voice when we roared through Knoxville and hit the streets leading to the prime acreage tucked just outside the city's good side. She gave me directions, and I took them like a man, hating every fucking word coming outta her mouth because they were leading us closer to the end.

The real end. Everything she feared, and everything I'd fought too damned hard not to acknowledge.

The street lights were on by the time we hit the country and rode by the big houses. She leaned into me, resting her soft face on my shoulder, whispering the last few digits to look for in my ear.

I saw them coming up on a big stone wall, glittering in gold, markers to my private hell. My bike jerked to a stop, later than I wanted because it was so fucking hard to let her go.

"You got a way to tell them to open up, or what?"

She gave me one last squeeze and hopped off my bike, shooting me a look like I'd just talked nonsense. I knew I had a second later, when I saw the intercom built into the wall, next to those high iron bars. The gate was too tall, too sleek, too pointy for any man to climb over – not unless he was really determined.

My mind started working, figuring out how the fuck to

get through. Just in case I needed to, of course. I wasn't planning anything.

Yeah, right, I heard inwardly, the passionate side of my brain about to snap the leash held by cold logic.

"Helmet, babe!" I called after her, just as she grabbed her stuff and trotted quickly toward the gate.

She spun around and flushed. The redness on her cheeks did terrible things to the spike between my legs. Fucking great. It was all I needed to see when I was doing my damnedest not to think about how much I'd miss her sweet cunt clenched every inch of me when she lost control.

"Sorry," she said softly, passing me the spare black helmet. "Seriously, Skin, I know this is hard, but I appreciate everything you've done for me. You'll get your money. I'll call you the second I've got it ready to go."

"You do that." I reached for her hand, squeezing it tight, one last time I couldn't resist. "Get your shit together, Meg, whatever it takes. You've got a second chance, and I wanna see you in the papers in a few years, knocking the absolute piss outta anything you choose to take on. Ricky's rotting where he can never hurt you, and I'll make sure my boys deal with the Deads. You're free. This last little payment's just an afterthought."

She forced a smile. We both knew damned well the money was *very* important, but I wasn't gonna ruin the moment, even if I had to tell her a few white lies.

She knew the truth. And I had a feeling she saw it in my eyes, everything I tried to bury, wishing it would go into the deep, dark earth as easily as the pimp's broken bones.

"I wouldn't be here without you, Skin. Thank you, so much, from the bottom of my heart."

I let her throw her little arms around my neck and give me one last hug. When I was done enjoying her tits pressed close to my face one more time, I gave her a gentle push, putting on my angry rebel mask again.

Wetness spattered my ear. At first, I thought she was turning on the waterworks again, but the thunder and darkness rolling in overhead said different. Thank God for small miracles, giving me the perfect excuse to wind this up clean.

"Go on and get the hell inside. Last thing I need is you catching cold."

The last smile she flashed me was all real. I watched her run to the intercom and hold the button down, muttering a few words, soft and uneasy.

I had my bike primed by the time the gate slid open, and two dark figures showed up on the distant doorstep to the big house, between the Greek columns. The taller silhouette took off, running toward her as she went through the opening, as fast as his legs would carry him.

That was my signal to take off into the night, and I did.

I rode the storm hard, moisture coalescing along the stubble on my face. Taking the mountain curves like a demon outside Knoxville, I smiled when the wind picked up. I opened my mouth and howled like a fucking demon, just as lightning cut the sky.

I'd find a way to survive this chick, even if it killed me. I had to. No woman changed me or twisted me up in knots, much less this dove from a world I'd never understand, the world where she belonged.

When I took this patch, I swore nobody would ever fuck me over, much less myself.

If blackening my heart was the price of giving Meg a second chance, then I'd do it. I'd make myself so hard and cold that even Joker would look at me like I'd gut his ass over a dirty look.

VII: Home Sweet Home (Megan)

"Megan?! It's really you, isn't it? Oh, God!"

Daddy's arms couldn't stop shaking as he threw them around me and threatened to squeeze the life out of me. He held me tight, a familiar, happy hold I hadn't experienced since I graduated High School, back when I was his perfect princess.

Too bad the only embrace I could feel was Skin's. His were the only lips I thought about when I watched my dad's moving, praising God for my return, blasting me with a thousand and one questions.

I already missed him, and he'd barely been gone for five minutes. How fucked up was that?

I didn't have time to think long about the past. Somewhere in Dad's embrace, Mom's kisses began to hit me, the last straw I needed before I officially broke down.

We stood in the rain for a long time, a family reunion bittersweet to the core. By the time they finally let up long enough to let me walk toward the house with them, I wondered where I truly belonged.

The huge family estate loomed over me like something

from a dream. It didn't feel like home anymore, and it didn't feel safe either.

The only place I'd ever found that was in his arms, and now he was gone from my life forever.

"Start over, Miss Wilder. Tell us everything again, this time from the top." Investigator Harlow shot me an easy look and put his finger on the camera's red on button.

It was the third fucking time that day I'd been asked to give a statement. So much for rest, much less easing back into my old life.

They'd been waiting for me when Mom brought me back from the clinic that morning. The doctors were thorough – what else when they were the best money could buy?

I'd gotten a clean bill of health. No STDs, no broken bones, no bleeding ulcers.

No surprise, my parents were already pushing me to take a therapy retreat to clear my mind. Really, I think they just wanted to stamp out the bruises left by my trauma as soon as possible so they could have their bratty, carefree daughter back.

"It's okay, honey. Just do what the nice man says, and you'll be off to Georgia before you know it." Dad reached over and squeezed my hand.

His smile seemed so brittle. Mom left the room after the first statement, unable to hide her horror when she heard about everything that happened to me.

They didn't know what to do except send me away to a

spa in Georgia with orchards a plenty and world class psychologists. Hearing about the savage abuse I'd suffered brought tears and anger at first, but then it brought total paralysis, weak little looks from my mom and dad like I'd been tarnished forever.

They didn't know how to bring me back to life. Hell, neither did I, but this endless interrogation wasn't helping.

"You heard it all the first two times," I snapped. "What else is there to say? Here, let me break it down for you – I was kidnapped, pimped out for six months of my life, and sold to a man on the black market one state over. I never found out his name. I don't know anything except what Ricky said, and it wasn't much. He couldn't even bother driving me down there himself."

"Yes, yes, you told us all about the trucker spa. We're well aware it's been a seedy prostitution racket for years."

Really? Then why the fuck didn't you raid it and close it down? I thought, chewing my bottom lip.

I swore I could still taste traces of Skin there, the only thing that comforted me. He'd want me to be strong right now. No, he was *counting* on it so I didn't spill the truth about his club and land them all in a world of hurt.

I had to take a few more of this asshole's questions without standing up and running off to my room.

Harlow looked down at his notepad and frowned. "What doesn't add up, Miss Wilder, is why the place is totally closed down. Abandoned. Patrol says it's always been a twenty-four hour operation until now, but when my men showed up last night, there was nobody home.

Not a single girl to corroborate your story. And no sign of Richard Proby to boot. It's like he's dropped off the face of the earth."

"Oh." I swallowed, putting on my best face to hide the fact that I'd watched the pimp die. "Well, somebody obviously tipped him off. He must've found out about my escape, and knew I'd talk. I don't know where he is, honestly. I've been on the run for weeks, hiding out in the woods."

"Honey…" Dad's hand tightened on mine, begging me to keep composure.

I ripped my arm away from his and looked at the detective. I didn't need his damned sympathy. I didn't need anything right now except to be left the hell alone to recuperate.

"And that's the part of the story I'd like you to repeat. It seems a lot of details are being glossed over, darling. You told me all about how the pimp beat you, sold you to other men, tried to break you. I believe that part, and I'm very sympathetic." What bullshit. The look on his face was nothing but a frustrated man doing his job. "What doesn't add up is how you got away from his underlings…"

"I already told you," I said, looking right into the camera. "It was raining bullets. They stopped for gas, just before we hit the state line. The man in the front seat was fiddling with his gun. I saw my chance and I took it while the other two were using the bathroom. They didn't have the guts to chase me with bystanders around."

"Yes, the state line, you mentioned that before. So,

you're saying you never entered North Carolina at all? And the men charged with transporting you had no affiliation with the Deadhands Motorcycle Club?"

"Absolutely not," I said.

Damn. Sweat beaded on my brow. It took all my energy not to shake. Lying like this in front of my father, the law, and God tied my intestines in knots.

If anybody found out, I had a feeling I'd be up for all kinds of perjury, but I didn't care. Anything for Skin. I owed him big time after he'd pulled strings to get me home.

I wasn't saying anything. I wasn't even going to mention the phrase 'motorcycle gang.' I couldn't screw over Skin. That meant leaving the Deadly Pistols and the Deadhands completely out of the equation in my lame ass story.

"I don't know where Ricky hired his men. Maybe they were thugs just like him, or inbred cousins. Who knows. I never saw them much before they picked me up for the trip, and I never saw them again after that night. Lord willing, I never will."

The detective cocked his head, folded his hands, and leaned forward. "Look, Miss Wilder, we're aware the pimp had connections with the biggest outlaw motorcycle gang several states over. I'm asking you to please take a moment and think. Are you *positive* you never saw anyone like that while you were a prisoner? No patches, no bikes, no dirty business going down with outlaws?"

"I don't know what I saw, to be frank. Most of the men he brought to my room, I was only focused on one part of them, trying not to gag."

My father winced next to me, and the color drained from his face. My heart sank. I felt bad about that.

My parents were good people, but they weren't emotionally equipped to handle my abuse. There was no worse torture than thinking about his precious baby being reduced to a common whore.

Of course, he was only hearing about it second hand. I'd lived it.

The nightmare was still alive in my head, coming to me in little flashes. I latched onto them and let my face crack, twisting in agony, looking up as I sniffed back tears.

I had to play the wounded dove card if I wanted to walk out of here sometime today.

"Are we done yet? Haven't you heard enough? I don't get what you want me to say – I barely got away from him with my life. Whatever you're asking me about bikers and bad guys, I don't know about any of that. I was too focused on survival, okay? If these Deadhands were ever there, I never saw a thing."

Harlow stroked his short, gray beard and leaned back in his chair, studying me. His lips started to move, but before he could say anything, Dad jumped up, making the chair screech across our kitchen floor.

"That's enough, detective. I thought this was going to be short and sweet?" He reached up and flicked his spectacles back into place on his nose. "My daughter hasn't even been home for a full day. She needs to rest. Why don't you come back later this week? I'm confident you'll get more out of her when she's settled in."

"Sir, I told you from the beginning it's imperative we get all the facts straight while they're fresh," Harlow snapped.

"And they'll be plenty fresh a few days from now. She might remember more once she's cleared her head. Let me get my girl some help, and you'll be welcome back anytime. Please."

I watched the men exchange an icy look. Finally, the detective caved, sighing as he reached for his briefcase under the table, and began to gather up his things.

"This flies in the face of procedure, Mister Wilder, but seeing how you're so well respected around these parts, I'll let it slide. Let's set something up for Thursday."

"Of course," Dad said simply, resting one hand on my shoulder.

I looked down. For now, I'd dodged another bullet, but the shots were going to keep coming, weren't they? So would the stress.

I didn't have a clue how I'd ever convince my parents to get me the money for Skin and his club. But I had to, if I ever wanted this to end.

If I couldn't keep up my end of the bargain that brought me home, then a few more tense discussions with the FBI and a perjury charge were going to be the least of my worries.

The next few days were a blur. Both my parents fell all over themselves offering me food, tea, and water every afternoon I stumbled downstairs after a fitful sleep. They babbled at me like I was a baby, barely able to feed myself, asking me in hushed whispers if I wanted to see a shrink today.

No. I needed my space. I had to figure out the money question before I did anything else.

Plus, the minute I told them I was fine, they vanished. Mom dove into her exercise in the gym downstairs and soap operas for more hours of the day than I'd ever seen her watching them. Dad's long nights at the office grew longer. Sometimes he didn't show up until almost midnight, creeping in and practically jumping out of his skin when he saw me at the kitchen table, picking at leftovers.

I wondered why I'd come back at all. Sure, they were happy I'd shown up alive and safe, but that was it.

The cracks in the family were deeper than ever, a thousand times more unbridgeable than they'd been when I was just a party girl with a cushy job in the family business. I'd disappointed them then.

But now, taking up space in their home as a former whore in need of serious therapy?

They couldn't handle it, and neither could I. The tense atmosphere roiled my brain, prevented me from thinking about the money my entire future hinged on.

One morning, Mom woke me up early, telling me I had a visitor. I was sure it was that stinking detective again, come to finish what he'd started earlier in the week.

When I saw Becky standing on the doorstep, looking

like she hadn't changed a day since our fateful evening skinny dipping in the Smoky Mountains, I had a new shock to deal with.

She flew forward, tackling me before I could make it down the last step to the entryway.

"Oh, girl, I'm so, so sorry!" She smothered me in desperate kisses, the third person in just as many days. "Can I take you out to lunch? Just like old times?"

I managed a weak smile. "Sure. Give me a couple minutes to get my things."

We didn't talk much in her car. She'd traded in her old Lexus for a hot pink Camaro, something appropriately showy and vibrant for my best friend.

A year ago, I'd have been completely green with jealousy. Hell, I'd have hit up Dad right after the drive, demanding my trust fund, whatever it took to land me a car even better than hers.

But all the flash didn't phase me. I stretched in the comfortable passenger seat, watching the Tennessee valleys roll by us, remembering how marvelous they'd looked on the back of Skin's bike.

He'd taken me to a world that was rough, mysterious, and often dark. But he'd also shown me a strange kind of beauty, just like he'd shown me that I was still beautiful, even when I'd believed Ricky had stolen it from me forever.

I missed him, goddamn it. Horribly.

Half an hour later, we sat in our favorite cafe in Knoxville, waiting on some big wedge salads with a side of fried okra to share. Just like old times.

Except it wasn't.

The food, the décor, and Becky's sweet little smile were all the same. It was myself I couldn't recognize.

Not when I sipped my iced tea and tasted the sweetness that was almost nauseating, the same stuff I'd drank by the gallon before the pimp. My reflection in the glass looked so plain too. The last time we'd come here, I'd been dolled up in makeup and a fresh perm.

Now? My eyes robbed all the attention from my high cheekbones and pale face, blue whirlpools that stayed dark and endless no matter how hard I tried to put it all behind me.

"I need to come clean about something," she said suddenly, dropping her fork. "Meg, please don't hate me for this, but I'd be a bad friend if I didn't get it off my chest right away. Remember Craw-daddy?"

Shit, did I? It took me a minute to remember the plain little weasel before I nodded, the last man I'd ever kissed before the train of faceless, filthy animals who used me. Before Skin revived me, stamping his hot lips on mine, the only thing in the last six months that made me feel alive.

"We're kinda an item now." Becky flashed me an uneasy smile. "Just wanted to get that off my chest right away! I can't keep anything from you. Best friends forever, right?"

I shrugged. "Congratulations. I'm happy for you, Becks. Really."

I tried my best to be sincere. It must've worked because

a second later she grabbed her glass and held it up, offering her cheers.

We clinked and I actually smiled. Hers didn't last long, though. A few seconds later, she was staring at me with her brow furrowed, giving me that look I'd seen from everybody this week, like I'd fall to pieces from the slightest breeze.

"I read all about what happened online. There weren't a lot of details, but God! I can only imagine what you've been through." She lifted a bite of salad on her fork and chewed it unevenly. "It must've been awful if you really don't give a crap about Crawford and me."

"It's all in the past," I told her, taking a long pull from my iced tea, wishing it had Long Island in front of it. "Seriously, don't worry about it. I'm busy getting my life back together. Don't have time for any business with men."

"Yeah? You're really giving up on the whole hubby hunt?" She eyed me sadly. "I mean, it makes sense. Pretty ironic I ended up where you want to be, right?"

"Whatever, Becks. I've got some serious thinking to do before I ever let a man into my bed, much less my life. Kinda comes with the territory when you've been trashed and abused."

At first, she nodded eagerly, hanging on every word. I dug into my food, watching the cool, emphatic expression on her face become a curious smirk.

"Wait, who is he?"

The fried okra I was chewing almost fell out of my

mouth. I dabbed at it with a napkin, taking my time, before I finally faced my best friend's wicked psychic powers.

"What? Who?"

"The boy who's got you all twisted up! You almost had me fooled for a second." Smiling, she wagged a finger. "Thank God, Meg. Thank God. I was worried they'd left you traumatized."

She saw through me like nobody else, not even my own family. I thought about trying to hide it, but there wasn't any burying the heat on my face, the blush that gave everything away beyond all doubt.

"Look at you!" Becky gushed. "Wow, you're really into him, aren't you? Don't tell me, let me guess…it's the man who saved you from – well, you know."

She couldn't bring herself to talk about the brutal pimp who'd kept me captive. Was it really so obvious?

"It's nothing like that. Honest." I hesitated, but only for a second. "Okay, fuck it."

Her mouth dropped when she heard me curse, about to confess to everything. I couldn't hold anything in when the idea hit me. It struck me like a bolt of lightning, so strange and unexpected I wondered if Skin's savage way of thinking had infected me when we kissed.

It wasn't just my best friend sitting across me anymore, looking on with concern. She could help me help *him*, bring me closer to the man who'd given me a second chance, all I wanted when I looked into the gray void of my future.

"Can you keep a secret?" I said, leaning closer to her.

"Swear on my life." She held up a hand, and for the first time I saw the giant stone on her finger, probably an engagement ring from Crawford.

"You aren't wrong. A wonderful man saved me, but he's into some bad stuff. I couldn't tell the media or the police to keep him safe. I owe him my life. I owe him everything for getting me away from the bastard who sold me. He's the only reason this is all over."

Over. I couldn't believe it really was, but I said the word with finality and impact. Becky stared wide-eyed, probably imagining a small glimpse of the way they'd used me.

"You've always been there for me, and I know you'll keep it hush." I reached across the table, snatched her hand, and waited until I saw her nod. "I also need you to do me a favor. A big one. It's a secret, Becks."

"Okay."

For a second, she straightened her back, looking around to make sure nobody else would hear. Then I watched her slide off her seat and sit down next to me, her ear close to my mouth.

"That pretty pink Camaro wasn't a gift from Crawdaddy like the ring, right?"

"No." She shook her head.

Good. Then she won't actually miss it when I smash the lovely thing to bits.

I left her at the nearby gas station before I drove toward the park. Knoxville's sunsphere flashed by, tucked beneath the high rises along the skyline. I drove recklessly, ready for what I had to do, praying it wouldn't leave me seriously hurt and twisted.

But I'd risk anything to get out of this. Anything to get back to him.

I couldn't believe she'd actually agreed. I'd laid my heart on the line. I promised her it wouldn't hurt.

Opening up hurt, but I did it to be convincing. I told her about Ricky and all the Johns who'd fucked my mouth. I told her about the night the Deads came for me, how they'd nearly forced me in the hotel, and how Skin and his crew had killed them all at the last second.

I told her about the way he'd grown on me, the passion when we fucked, the insane love I suddenly had for this bestial, irresistible man. I'd actually used the L-word too. Once when I told her about the feelings Skin gave me, and again when I told her how worried I was about him, how he had obligations in the underworld that had to be met at any cost.

He needed a quarter million, for his own good, and for mine. And I needed to count on my best friend to trust I wasn't crazy and loan me her car, promising I'd get her something better as a wedding present.

Somehow, some way, we'd make this work. We had to. This crazy fucking plan was all I had, and it was a miracle she'd agreed.

She had tears in her eyes when she handed me the keys, asking me if I was sure about it for the dozenth time. Each time, I nodded coldly, refusing to entertain any second guesses as I climbed into the driver's seat.

The amazing car must've cost at least a hundred grand with all its custom features. A little less than half of what I needed from my trust fund. But if I could get Dad to open it once, then it wouldn't take much to squeeze a little more out.

I knew my grandparents left me at least a couple million. Paying for tuition out of it had barely depleted anything when I'd snuck peeks at the statements. Everything I'd need to live a sheltered, pampered life for the rest of my days – the life I didn't want with Skin.

He'd shown me something different, and he was worth the risk. I was ready to throw it all away, anything to help him, whatever it took to get me face to face with the only man on the planet who'd made me feel whole.

And I did.

When I saw the big oak tree near the pond, I lined up the car. My foot pounded the accelerator and refused to let up. I'd barely had ten minutes to get used to it on the streets, and now the speed floored me.

I never saw what happened to the front of the car. The airbags deployed a split second before I blacked out and the entire world started spinning.

In my fragmented daze, I saw Skin, beautiful Skin. I pressed my lips to the scar lining his cheek and dug my nails into his back. I kissed him long and hard, waiting to be reunited, aching for him through the flashes of sirens and voices and then the soft murmur of a doctor standing over me.

His lips moved across mine, reminding me of everything I'd missed, and why. These lips made me ache. These lips teased and commanded. These lips were the only ones I wanted to think about kissing for the rest of my life, even if they turned my whole world upside down one more time.

Even if they made me crazy. Even if they killed me.

I love you, Skin. I really do. Call me insane, delirious, or damaged, but it's true.

I imagined saying those words and looking into his deep, dark eyes. A smile tugged at his rogue lips, but before he could say anything, the black wave behind him crashed over us, pulling me into nothing.

I woke up the next day with a terrible headache, but no worse for wear. Daddy stood over my bed with a mortified look on his face. An elderly doctor came in and said a few words, told me I ought to thank my lucky stars that I hadn't broken anything.

The accident only left a small bruise on my collarbone and some sore muscles, besides the pounding headache.

Dad's concern overpowered everything at first. He sat with me quietly for the next couple hours, through one more scan, until they decided I was good to go.

He waited until we were in his car to open up on me.

"Start packing your bags when we get home, dear. Your mother and I have decided you're beyond our help. We've been patient – too patient, I fear. No more." I opened my mouth to speak, but he shushed me with a finger to his lips. "Don't, baby. You're messed up and it's not your fault, I get that. I'd be a devil for expecting you to be any other way after you suffered with those demons. But I can't sit by while the police are knocking on my office door every other damned day and my only daughter's trying to kill herself! Becky told us what happened."

For the first time, fear stabbed at my heart.

"She did?" I swallowed, balling my fists so tight it hurt, praying my best friend hadn't betrayed me.

"Yes, and I hope you're very thankful for wonderful friends like her. She said she forgives you for hijacking her car. The poor thing barely drove it off the dealer's lot a month ago, you know. I'm not going to drag you on a guilt trip, Megan, but we're all lucky she's decided to turn the other cheek without pressing charges."

I let out a long sigh of relief. Jesus. She'd saved me, sticking to the alibi we carefully concocted in the cafe, before I dropped her at the gas station and took the hot pink Camaro on its last fateful ride.

"Okay, whatever you say, Dad. Let's set something up. I'll spend a week at the spa talking to whatever shrinks you want me to. I'll tell them everything. I won't come back until I'm fixed."

He looked at me, his eyes softening. "I'm glad to hear you say that."

We shared a soft, understanding look. The last one I allowed before I let the pain rip me in two. My face contorted so hard it hurt. I barely had my palms over my eyes before the hot, poison tears streamed out in waves.

"Oh, honey. No, no, no, it's going to be okay," Daddy said, bringing a hand to my shoulder. "What is it? You're scared?"

I shook my head, voice cracking through the tears. The hurt was all authentic, a little slice of everything I'd suffered over the last year, but I was using it strategically for the next step in my plan.

There'd be time to feel guilty about that later. Right now, I needed the money, and I absolutely *had* to see Skin.

"No, Daddy. It's not that. I just can't believe I wrecked her car!" I looked up and grabbed his arm. "Stop with the sympathy. I'm tired of everyone treating me like a wounded pet since I came home. You saw what I did – I went crazy. I lashed out. I completely fucking ruined my best friend's car, and she's going to hate me forever!"

Cue more shrill blubbering. The f-bomb caught him by surprise too. I watched Dad struggle for composure for the next few miles up to our house.

"God, what I disaster I am. I just wish there were some way to make it up to her, some way to repay all the kindness she's shown me…"

As we pulled through the gate, I really lost it, crying my eyes out. I wanted a response, damn it, preferably one that was open to the idea of undoing all this damage.

"Meg, stop," he said sharply, pulling into our big ten car garage. "I can't believe you're worried about money. Have you forgotten we always take care of our debts? This family never lets anybody down who's done us a kindness.

We're Wilders, after all. Here, let's go into my office."

Nodding glumly, I followed him. We went inside and headed straight for his study with the fireplace and the tall walnut shelves, the same place he used to read me stories as a kid. Maybe I had a pang of guilt that second, standing there while he rummaged around in his desk drawer, but it wouldn't stop me.

I'm sorry, Dad. You'll understand one day. We both will, if everything goes the way I'm expecting.

I watched him pull out his check book and some paperwork with our attorney's logo. "Now, how much do you think it'll take to put things right with Becky? That was a custom model, wasn't it? Let's say, a hundred and fifty thousand, drawn straight from your trust?"

More than I expected, I thought with a sigh. *But not enough.*

"Actually," I sniffed, blotting at my eyes as he handed me a tissue. "Becky told me she paid over two hundred grand. And she said something about tax troubles with her mom, I don't really know, something about taking all of her money in cash."

"Cash?" Dad's eyes went wide. "My, I didn't realize Harold and Penelope were in that kind of trouble. Are you really asking me to pull money out of your account and hand it over to her in a briefcase or something like a mafia don?"

I flashed an uneasy smile. *Close enough.*

"I'm sorry, I just think it'll be easier this way. I don't want any more screw ups. She's sticking by me, and I'll be *devastated* if I lose my only friend right now. Please don't spend a dime of your own money. Take it all from my account. Let's make it an even quarter million."

He cocked his head. "That's a lot for a low-end luxury ride with all the bells and whistles. Are you sure, Megan?"

"Cross my heart. I want her to have more than she needs, anything to show her I'm serious about her friendship. She needs to see how *sorry* I am." I sat down in the chair, satisfaction and guilt mingling in my blood as Dad sighed, ran a hand over his face, and slowly folded.

"All right. We'll grab it tomorrow and I'll drop you off for lunch – you're sure not driving yourself. But after the interview with the detective this week, you're on your way to therapy for the rest of the month. That's the deal. Got it?"

"Of course." I smiled. "Say, maybe when I'm better again, I can handle my own affairs? I know you've been giving me access to the funds when I really need them, but it makes me feel like a kid. Granpda said –"

"I know what your grandfather said, Megan. It's your money." He clenched his teeth. "And yes, it's abundantly clear to me now that you're not the same girl you were when that man took you away from us. But as for who or what you've become…well, I think we're both figuring that out. Fair?"

"Fair," I repeated, looking at the ground.

He'd come around sooner or later. I'd have the money I needed for Skin tomorrow, and then I'd work on flying right so I could get the rest to actually repay Becky. Of course, the stuff about her family having tax trouble was a little white lie – it was quite the opposite.

I half-expected her to pull up to the cafe in a flashy new car. The money I threw at her in another month or two to replace the car would just go toward her elaborate wedding, and hopefully show Crawford he was with the right woman for life.

The day went fast. I went to the bank with Dad in the morning and got my cash. The tellers took nearly an hour to make sure it was all there, processing the jumbo cash order and filing it neatly in a cheap leather duffel bag we'd picked out.

Then it was off to lunch with Becky. She squealed when she saw me and ordered us desserts, skipping the healthier fare completely.

This time, talking to her was a lot more like old times, two young women scheming over men and mischief. I danced around who exactly Skin was, and what he did for a living.

Hell, I didn't actually know. I knew the club was tight on cash, which was why getting this to him was so serious, but he had to earn money some way, didn't he? They all did, and it couldn't be legal.

We parted on good terms. I promised her I'd have the money as soon as possible, and she told me to drop it off when I could make a day of it. I owed her a date to look at wedding dresses.

After lunch, my father picked me up and brought me

home, with just a brief warning Detective Numbnuts was waiting for me. I pretended the bag stuffed with cash underneath my feet was empty. Thankfully, Daddy was totally oblivious, too caught up in having this agent at his house once again to check.

We sat down at the kitchen table with Harlow. He brought out his camera for the third time, and I repeated my story verbatim.

Kidnapped. Forced. Abused. Escaped.

No bikers. No handsome, dangerous men named Skin. No accomplices for the dead pimp from the Deadhands MC. No devils who'd murder the man I'd fallen for if I didn't get him his cold, hard cash.

For a detective, he didn't hide his frustration well. "I'm going to review the files again, Miss Wilder. If I find any discrepancies, rest assured our next chat will be taking place down at the station, rather than in the comfort of your own home."

Daddy shot up like a bolt of lightning. "Are you really threatening my daughter with a prison interrogation in my own house? Sir, I'll remind you who was the top contributor to the Senior Senator from the great state of Tennessee last year – you're looking at him. Don't make me get some calls flying back and forth between Washington and FBI headquarters. We wouldn't want to soil the nice, professional relationship here. But I'll do what I need to, if you leave me no choice."

Harlow looked genuinely disturbed. I tried not to laugh, loving how my father brought the hammer down when it really mattered.

Of course, I felt even worse about the lies I'd just told.

Had Skin already dragged me too deep into his world, away from the normal, law abiding life I'd known before? Or had Ricky damaged me forever before the biker even got his hands on me?

I didn't know, but one thing was clear – I'd never settle for a quiet, normal life again. I'd plunge into the darkness and navigate the lesser evils if it brought me closer to him.

Therapy in a Georgia spa wouldn't do anything for me. Nothing would, except feeling Skin's powerful, tattooed arms around me, pressing my face into his rock hard chest, inhaling his earthy, masculine scent.

"We'll talk again when she's back from her retreat. Good day." Harlow packed up his things and scuttled like a scorned cat.

"The nerve of that man…" Dad walked to the small liquor cabinet in our kitchen and poured himself a drink, ripping off his spectacles.

I felt bad. But I felt worse about my plans to sneak out later with the cash in hand, right after I used the burner phone hidden in my dresser to call Skin to the gate.

"Daddy, don't worry about him. Seriously. I'm going to be okay, no matter what happens. He has to give up sometime. I don't know why he's so adamant about tying what happened to me to these dead bikers in North Carolina."

"He says it's important, something about drug and terrorism laws. I really don't care, Megan." I watched him knock straight bourbon down his throat and slam the glass on the counter. "You're home, you're going to get some help, and that's all that matters. If there was more to your escape like the good detective thinks, I don't care. You're here. You're safe. And one day, you'll open up and tell me, won't you?"

My heart skipped a beat. Shit.

He knew. Somehow, Dad knew I wasn't being completely honest. My stomach turned to lead, and I wanted to crawl into the kudzu tangled forest out back and die.

"We'll just see about that," I told him. "I promise I'm going to be okay. Don't worry about me, whatever happens. I'm going to get well again, and you're right, whatever happens from here is going to be between *family.* Not this nosy detective who won't let me get on with my life."

He stared at me for about a minute, piercing me with his bright blue eyes, the same ones I saw staring back at me in the mirror every day. He hoped I'd give him more, but I couldn't.

If I told him about Skin, about the club, all about how I wouldn't be standing here alive if it wasn't for the hardened biker and his Pistols…I'd never get away tonight.

Dad broke and looked out the window while I grabbed a drink of water and slipped away upstairs. Someday, I'd tell him the truth. He deserved it.

I needed to face it all, open and honest, the truth about

myself and the last six brutal months of my life.

I was ready. I had to be if Skin decided to make me his. And that was one thing I was ready to discover, no matter the price.

VIII: Made Whole (Skin)

Four days. Almost an entire fucking week since I'd dropped her off at her parents' door, never to be seen again.

I didn't give a shit about the money. I missed her, and I couldn't stop, not even among all the brotherly backslapping and celebrations for our coming windfall.

Dust put my down payment to good use, working on plans for the new strip joint and holding nightly bashes to raise moral.

Girls threw themselves at me, just like they always had. I shoved them the fuck away.

I didn't want to do anything but drink. We finally had Jack and Jim flowing by the gallon again. I took bottles to my room and sauced myself to sleep, usually after long rides into the mountains. I always stopped when I came near the half-covered path leading down to the hollow where I'd dismembered the pimp.

His rotting flesh and bones were stuffed into a hole where nobody but the black bears would ever find him. They'd gnaw his bones 'til it was like the fuck never existed. Ashes to ashes and dust to dust.

Good fucking riddance. I'd saved her several times over. I'd killed for that chick. And I just had one regret.

What I regretted was letting go. I never should've taken her home without one more kiss, asking her to be my old lady.

I didn't think she'd actually accept. Shit, the girl was from another world, a rich family who'd probably sweat a little bit and pull over if they saw us coming down the highway next to them. She'd been beaten, used, and abused by the bastard I'd killed and the scum who gave him money.

She'd need a good shrink and a lot of fucking money to get her life on track. Fortunately, thanks to her rich folks, she had both of those.

I was the worst kinda medicine she could swallow, bitter and wrong. I wasn't blind, but it didn't make me wanna lay off her any less. Damn if I didn't want to pour every drop of myself down her system. I wanted to overload her with desire, make her crave me, flatten her against the cracked wall out back, rip her panties off, and fuck her 'til she screamed my name.

I was completely, irreversibly screwed, and the rest of the guys knew it too.

They kept their distance during the wild nights when the girls came flooding in. Sixty and Crawl gave me nothing more than a wink and a brotherly nod when I threw my unwanted women their way.

A lot of the familiar faces who'd sucked me off before

wanted another crack at my dick. The other boys were plenty easy on women's eyes too, but they liked the silent, brooding type, I guess. I'd always fit the bill, second only to the Prez himself and Joker.

Unfortunately for the girls, the Prez was too damned busy to spend time fucking them. And Joker – if he still had any marbles at all, they were all below the belt. He fucked like no tomorrow, and sometimes the bitches in his room screamed like he was taking 'em apart.

The crazy bastard had lost his mind a long time ago, turned into a dead-eyed killer. Fuck if he'd lost his wild oats, and everybody was surprised he didn't have a few dozen bastards running around town by now at the rate he pounded pussy.

I walked through the clubhouse after sunset, having the bar almost to myself. Firefly was over in the corner, a hot little blonde on his lap, playing games with her lips and the dark wings tattooed around his neck. He always did the same shit with his girls, and they were all over him as soon as they had their legs around his waist.

I fished out a fresh bottle of whiskey and popped the cap, ready to head for my room after a few swigs. Loud country blasted on the old jukebox, the kinda shit my old man used to listen to, back when the club's biggest worry was throwing bonfires. It was ancient history now, before any brother realized the danger settling in, before they figured out how big and aggressive the bastards outside Tennessee had grown, how they were dead set on making a run for our territory.

"Hey, what the fuck, Skin?" Firefly called to me, tugging at Goldie's locks as she giggled on his lap. "Lighten up and have a little fun. You look like you're gonna pass the fuck out if you don't whip that bottle at the wall first. Don't get any bright ideas. Just because I'm partying doesn't mean I'm not on the job."

I rolled my eyes. He took the Enforcer role deadly serious, playing hall monitor when he wasn't breaking up fights between brothers or drilling us to see how fast we could get our guns.

"Here, your majesty, have another drink so you can relax," I growled, sloshing whiskey sloppily into his glass, and then hers. "One for the lady, too. It's the least I can do to take the edge off this blowhard, yeah?"

She looked at me and giggled, slapping Firefly's shoulders. "Oh my God, fireball! Why didn't you tell me your friends were so hilarious?"

"It's *Firefly,* baby, and don't you fucking forget it." He shot her a stern look. "Here, looks like you need something to remember me by."

I snorted as he jerked her hair tight and gave her a long, hard kiss.

Fuck if I didn't think about Meg, though, having her beautiful chestnut locks tangled around my fingers again, the other hand on the small of her back, pumping her hips up and down on my cock.

So many ways I hadn't taken her yet. So many ways I wanted to the second I got her sweet ass back here.

"Shit, Skinny Boy, don't you have some numbers to

punch on a computer or something?" He looked away from me at his ditzy date for the night. "I've never been shy about having an audience 'round these parts, but it's kinda creepy if it's just you."

Christ. That meant he was going to fuck her behind the bar, if he didn't just shove his cock into her right here. He wasn't wrong – I didn't need to see that shit.

Watching Firefly fuck a girl barely old enough to drink wasn't my kinda porn. I had plenty of that shit waiting in my room, but even the perfect Dixie girls on the screen with their ruby red lips and fake tits didn't hold a goddamned kindle to the woman turning my crank.

"I'm not gonna cramp you, brother," I told him, deciding to leave the whiskey with them. "You're right. I've got more important biz to settle. Somebody's gotta keep this club from going up in flames, after all."

Firefly gave me a sharp look, but he decided to let it go, too obsessed with Blondie wiggling on his lap. I was halfway to my room when I heard her hit the counter and cry out as he sank into her.

Irony was an absolute bitch tonight. Before Meg, getting my dick wet was the only motivation I had to bring the club more cash. Now, there was pussy galore, and it still felt like being stranded in the desert because none of those hot, pink holes were the ones I really wanted.

They only belonged to one woman. Not even the buxom young redhead I found stretched out in my bed, naked from the waist down.

The used condom on my floor told the full story, as did the bright red hand prints left all over her ass. Snarling, I grabbed her by both hands and whirled her around, shaking her outta her stupor.

"Okay, who the fuck was in here and left their trash in *my* fucking room?" She yelped and looked at me like I'd just jumped out of her nightmares.

What the shit? I noticed the handcuffs hanging off her plump wrist for the first time, dangling between her legs as she blushed and fought to cover up her pussy.

"Um, I'm really sorry, Skin. I'm not supposed to say. Joker told me we'd be okay in here, and he'd just gone out for a smoke or something…"

"Joker?"

Fuck me with a cactus. I'd heard enough. The Veep was outta control, dragging his shit through my gutter. With a growl, I grabbed her wrists and led her to the corner, where I found her half shredded panties. She got the message when I pointed, picking them up and struggling into what was left of them while I watched.

The chick's ass wasn't half bad, but she had nothing on Meg. That woman was perfect, raised to perfection because she was a damned aristocrat, rather than a blue collar baby or a farm bumpkin like most of our casual fucks.

"Get that condom off my floor on your way out, too, woman. And if you see him, tell the Veep my room's not his personal landfill. Don't care if he's an officer or not."

She nodded and flashed me a nervous smile one more

time before she backed out, Joker's bloated condom in her hand, and closed the door behind me.

If there was ever a sign I needed to move the hell outta here and get my own place, now that we had a big paycheck coming in…

I rolled into bed and dozed. It wasn't easy after I'd ridden in the cold all day, scoping out the places in Knoxville for the Prez, all the sites where he wanted our girls to shake tail and bring the club more money.

Of course, it'd be a drop in the bucket, and not even good for laundering much money if we ever got the *real* cash pipeline going. But that wasn't gonna happen overnight. Dust's grand schemes meant clearing our way to the sea first, the path the Deads and other thugs were blocking through the Carolinas and Georgia.

The yanks in the Prairie Devils or the Grizzlies wouldn't even sit down with us 'til we had something to offer 'em. I dreamed like a goddamned geek, numbers and logistics, the only distraction my brain knew when I wasn't thinking about Meg's perfect little lips wrapped around every inch of me.

The heat of her mouth was still burning up my brain when my burner phone screamed to life. I jumped up and grabbed it, doing a double take when I saw her number.

Thank fuck. It's gotta be about the cash.

"Yeah? Where should I meet you?" I growled into the receiver, the instant I heard her soft little breathing on the line.

"Wow, so much for hello." She paused, and my dick

swelled as I imagined her smiling. "You can pick me up right outside my house. Just after eleven, maybe? Will that work?"

"See you then, babe."

I snapped the phone shut and checked the clock. I had about an hour, maybe a little more, just enough time to shower off the stink of motor oil and sweat from my pussy withdrawal.

I grinned, thankful I was sober. Just when I'd started missing the booze too. Good thing I'd decided to dump the whiskey off with Firefly and his whore for the night after all…

I had something better coming. And I was gonna fuck her so hard she'd never go anywhere else again.

"It's all there," she whispered quietly, stuffing the big duffel bag in my trunk. "Every last dollar. You can count it when we get to the clubhouse and –"

"Enough. The first thing I'm doing once we're back there's the last thing we did before I took you home. Fuck, I've missed these lips."

Somehow, I kept it polite. I managed not to rip her clothes off right there, or tell her how bad I wanted to shove my tongue up her pussy 'til she cried.

But there was nothing nice about the way I threw my arms around her, pulled her into me, smashed my lips down on hers. My tongue sucked at hers hungrily, a prelude to where my hands were going. They went down, stopped on her ass cheeks, and squeezed.

The moan she hissed into my mouth told me we were on the same page. Shit, she knew my hunger too. Her nipples poked through her bra and the thin autumn sweater she was wearing, an outfit so conservative I couldn't wait to shred it to tatters.

"Let's get the hell home, babe. Plenty of drinks waiting if you're in the mood. The boys are celebrating."

"No," she whispered softly, staring up at me while I sat her on the bike and fixed her helmet. "All I need is right here."

Her arms hooked around me. The embrace blew my mind, and threatened to do the same to the nuke hammering in my pants.

Christ. How the fuck could a woman feel so perfect riding with me?

It was like she'd been made for the back of my bike, made for my bed. I'd never bought into that soul mate horseshit before, but every second with this chick was making me wonder if I'd been wrong about it for nearly thirty years.

I loved how she rode pressed up against me while we roared down the highway, taking the mountain bends beneath the moonlight, dipping up and down the valleys filled with Smoky Mountain mist.

Dew prickled at our skin. Even the land itself was wet and teasing. If this wasn't a night to lay a woman down and fuck, then I didn't know one.

Hell, this was a night for more than that. I'd claim her, damn it, and do it good and proper. We'd have a proper reunion at this little mountain bungalow I had about twenty miles from the clubhouse, right on the edge of the big national park.

I'd never brought a girl out there before. It was the place my old man used to go to think, and sometimes he brought Mama and me along for the ride. I'd inherited it after she passed, but I kept it locked up tight, except for the times I wanted to reflect, all alone, away from the brothers and the violence.

I'd never been ready to share that shit with anybody 'til her. Not 'til tonight.

We got to the clubhouse in record time. I parked my bike and grabbed her hand, leading her inside. Loud classic rock bounced through the air, the latest tempo the brothers inside were drinking and fucking to.

A loud moan greeted us behind the bar. My eyes darted to the spot where Firefly had his bitch for the night bent over, slamming his cock into her and growling every time he went deep. The Enforcer never stopped being a hothead even when he fucked, taking his girls out in the open, and hanging 'em out wet to dry the next day.

The bastard looked up, his eyes dark with sex. I gave him a knowing stare. He snorted, never skipping a beat with the slut under him.

"Wow, you weren't kidding about the party!" Meg smiled, so excited and seductive I wanted to drag her out back right there, behind the trees, and put my mouth on hers 'til she couldn't show any teeth the rest of the night.

I didn't like the way Firefly was looking at her. The

fuck had a taste for threesomes sometimes – who among us didn't? – but there was no way in hell I'd let him ask my girl.

"Something like that," I growled, leading her toward the hall hand-in-hand. "We're just here for business. I've got a better place for us to go after this. Let's get this over with."

The cash stuffed bag sagged in my hand. I carried it in and headed for the Prez's office, hoping he hadn't gone home yet. I sure as hell didn't want to deal with Joker after he'd borrowed my bed for his nasty fun.

Firefly sat at the bar and fixed his eyes on Meg as we stepped inside. We exchanged a look and he nodded. He wore that tired, satisfied glaze in his eyes that he always had after he'd fucked his testosterone calm for awhile. I noticed Blondie snoozing in his lap as we walked by, heading for Dust's office.

"Leave the talkin' to me," I said between taps on the door. "This is club business, baby, even though it involves you too."

"Yeah, about that…I was hoping we could get some reassurance from your boss about what's going to happen to me."

"What?" I shot her a sharp look, just as the door opened.

The Prez had a beer in his hand. He squinted at us like two trick-or-treaters who'd just shown up on his doorstep on the Fourth of July.

"What's she doing back here?" His eyes instantly fell to

the big black bag in my hand. "Holy Moses. Is that what I think it is?"

I nodded. All it took for the Prez to reach for Meg and pull her into his office without another word, while I followed them in.

He walked behind his desk, sucking down his beer and hurling the can in the garbage. The bag hit his desk with a plop. His thick, scarred hands landed on it and I watched his fingers give it a squeeze, shaking almost imperceptibly while he went for the zipper, looking like a man about to pull down a lady's dress.

Fat stacks of twenties and hundreds wrapped in bands spilled out the opening. He pursed his lips and whistled, so sharp and unexpected Meg barely suppressed a laugh.

"It's all there, Prez. You can count it down to the dollar. She says it is, and I trust her." Smiling, our eyes met, and I tried to lay off thinking about how bad I wanted to be inside her just then.

Come on. Hurry the fuck up. You've got your business here, man, and we've got ours.

The excitement in Dust's cool gray eyes raged louder. Then he said the words I dreaded.

"Skin, have a seat. Help me count this loot and get it inventoried for the vault."

Megan took one look at the sparks in my eyes turning to smoke. This time, she couldn't hold it. She laughed, high and sweet and beautiful, and kept on doing it when the Prez looked at her like she'd lost her mind.

About an hour later, I couldn't get the stink of fresh money off my hands. "It's all there, Prez, see? Just like I told you. Right down to the final dollar."

"Yeah, yeah. You weren't bullshitting. We've got our second chance for this club right here, and it's all thanks to turning your mistake into a miracle."

"Mistake?" Meg spoke for the first time in forever, sitting in the corner, next to the club's old filing cabinet.

"My words, not his, beautiful." Dust thumped his chest. "Our boy's got too big a hard-on for him to realize you're trouble, sweets. You oughta be thankful."

"Yeah, trouble...about that." She stood up and walked over.

I grabbed her hand, trying to stall her out. She wanted her assurances, but there was a right way to approach the Prez and a wrong one. I didn't want him chewing into her, no matter how good his mood was from our newly fat cash supply.

"Now that you've got your money, I need to know that you're never going to come after me again, Dust." She walked past me and stared at him like a wildcat. "I want assurances that we're good on both sides. I need to know I've paid my debt, and whatever trouble Skin caused is done."

"Assurances?" The Prez glared at her, considering her request.

The girl had courage, I had to give her that. 'Course, she didn't realize what he'd done. She hadn't seen him throttle bastards to death with his bare hands, or take rival prospects out back when his old man led the club, making them scream louder than anybody else could, 'til they sang and gave us whatever we wanted.

Dust didn't get to be Prez thanks to his daddy. He'd gotten the patch because he was as hard, uncompromising, and relentless as he was reasonable.

"Yeah, sure, I'll give you my word. Here, girl, reach out your hand and shake."

I watched him take her by the wrist. I couldn't breathe 'til I saw the familiar handshake I'd seen him use before when deals went down. Dust grabbed her wrist and pressed his fingers deep, like a Roman soldier feeling for a dagger.

I'd read about that when I was growing up, going through a spell where history's badasses intrigued me. Didn't have a clue where the Prez picked it up – it had to be intuitive, because I'd have bet every dime I had against him ever paying attention in any history class.

"There, babe," I said softly, running my free hand through Meg's dark brown hair as they broke hands. "Satisfied?"

"No, actually."

Fuck. My eyes jumped to the Prez. I could see the cold, frustrated, predatory edge creeping into his eyes.

"I don't have time for games, little missy. You'd better name whatever the fuck you're after or drop it. I've given you my word, and any brother around here will vouch that it's pretty damned valuable. You think I'm a liar?"

Instinct took over. I stepped up, got between them,

and looked the Prez dead in the eye.

"You know she isn't, brother. The girl wants to know she's safe, and I don't blame her, but you can't give her the assurance she's looking for. That's my job." Meg's bright blue eyes flashed wonder and confusion.

I grabbed her by the wrist and jerked her into my chest, wrapping my arms snug around her sweet body, everything I wanted to own for the rest of my days.

"What's going on here, Skin?" Dust growled.

"I'm claiming her as my old lady. Right here, right now. Nobody's gonna stop me. This club won't ever make demands from a woman wearing a brother's brand."

For a second, the whole world stopped. Meg tensed in my arms, scared and uncertain, but her eyes were wide. Filled with the desire, the need, the admiration I'd come to love.

The Prez just gawked, taking a few seconds to collect his senses. "Bullshit. You don't really mean it...do you?"

"You know me by now, Prez. I don't do idle talk. I don't say shit I don't mean, and I'd never even pretend with something like this. She's mine, dammit, I swear it." I looked at Meg, ignoring his wild-eyed stare. "She was mine from the minute I saw her in that bastard's whorehouse. Mine from the instant I pulled her here and decided to get her home. Mine when she came back tonight. This is just making things official, putting a pretty formality on what we both knew. Now, I'm gonna make sure everybody in the whole damned world knows it – or at least every man in this club."

"Jesus, Skin." She whispered my name softly, her lips trembling.

Fuck it. I wasn't gonna let her break down or spit the confusion written on her face. I grabbed the back of her neck and pushed her to my lips. We kissed pure hellfire there in Dust's office, all while he watched in total amazement.

"I'd say you've lost your damned mind, Skin, but it's clear you've actually put some brains into this. Fuck me." I forced myself off Meg's lips and looked at the Prez as he circled back behind his desk, shaking his head. "Listen, you two, before you make a big damned mistake…if she wants to get out of all this shit, this ain't the way to go about it. Does this girl even know what becoming an old lady means?"

I looked into Meg's deep blue eyes. No, she didn't, but I'd show her everything she had to know.

I'd lead her by the hand as sure as I'd master her in my bed every night. I already owned her, inside and out, and this was just making things official.

I claimed right here, right now, because I'd decided I couldn't let her slip away again. Not when she got scared of the club, or scared of me.

Not when she feared for her life, or wondered if she really fit in here. Not when she had any damned doubts about what I had for her beating straight through my ribs, the manic beat she put into my heart.

"I'll lead her every step of the way, Prez. That's between her and me. Give us twenty-four hours, and she'll be back here wearing my brand, PROPERTY OF SKIN."

"Let your old lady answer for a change, if that's what she really wants to be," Dust snapped. He sat up in his scrappy leather chair and pointed a finger at her.

"You've got my assurances, whether you think I'll honor that handshake or not. You don't need to do anything rash with this poor, desperate bastard if you don't want to. Say no, and I'll make sure he doesn't ride your ass. This is *my* club, and I've got the final say when it comes to who gets to be part of it. You really want to get yourself in deeper? Because there's no going back once you've got his name inked on your pretty flesh. You're his property then, and one more extension of the club."

Fuck, the Prez made it sound like lock and key with no rewards. He didn't tell her that becoming mine meant I'd kill for her, keep my loyalty to this woman in blood, surrender the wild I'd known my whole life for her embrace.

I waited for her reaction. The next five seconds were the most tense of my entire fucking life.

I'd done everything here on a whim, going by nothing more than the love in her eyes. Now, I was about to find out if that pure, sweet energy would be enough, or if the beautiful baby girl in my arms would panic, break, and go running back to the comfort and privilege she'd always known.

Don't do it, I thought, clenching my jaw. *You know where you belong, babe.*

Here. Now. Forever.

"Honestly, I don't know what I'm getting into here," Meg said slowly, pausing just long enough to make my damned heart stop. She spun around, flattening her hands on my chest, smiling at me. "But if it brings us closer together, Skin, I'm ready for it. I'm ready to take on anything. You saved my life and taught me I didn't die back in Ricky's place. You showed me I could have another life. You're all I could think about at my parents' place. I dated plenty before the pimp took me, and I never found any man with a scrap of what you're offering."

"Babe, fuck, just say the word," I whispered, tightening my hold on her back, fighting to keep my hands off her perfect ass.

"I love you, Skin. And, well, I'm game for whatever this old lady thing means. No regrets. No going back." She turned and looked at Dust, pushing her cheek onto my chest. "Just keep my man safe, Dust. That's all I'm going to ask from your club. If what he's telling me is true, then I'll be out of your hair for good, right?"

"Shit, you're sweet. Innocent and a little dumb. Nah, it's worse than that, girl. You haven't bought yourself a ticket outta anything." Dust's smiled, and his shoulders straightened. "Becoming an old lady means you're part of this family. If anybody owes anyone else here a damned thing, it's the club promising you protection, the same as any brother."

We both broke into a smile. I couldn't keep my lips off her. I didn't give a shit about the bulldog with the PRESIDENT patch watching us neither.

We plunged into a new flurry of kisses in the Prez's office, hungry as all hell, feeding the fire we shared, flames that wouldn't be dashed 'til we finally consummated this thing.

Hard, deep, and long. I wanted to fuck her so damned hard she'd forget the first time. This was a night to remember, the most important one of our lives, and I'd spend the next few hours shaking every curve so hard she'd weep from the pleasure.

"All right, kids, that's enough!" Dust snarled, standing up. "You've both got twenty-four hours to change your minds before I announce this to the rest of the boys. Skin, you'd better bring her home with your brand inked in her skin, or I'll tear your damned ears off for leading everybody on. You, girl, make up your mind for good after tonight. Now, kindly get yourselves a room, and get the fuck out of my sight."

We stepped out and I closed the door, a split second before I grabbed her and threw her against the wall. We picked up right where we left off, out in the hallway, our lips dancing a desperate tango.

Tango? Fuck that. I'd never been much for dancing.

I shoved my tongue in her mouth, found hers, and dominated it. I pulled at my baby's bottom lip 'til I heard her whimper. Her breasts pushed into me, her nipples hard underneath all the fabric, and I stole the breath from her lungs.

My hips hooked to hers and I pushed. Hard. I wanted her to feel how hard and ready I was for her, how bad I wanted – no, *needed* – to fuck her.

Getting her branded was just the first step. Taking control and owning her, well, that was deadly simple, and also a helluva lot more fun.

"Come on. We've got one more stop to make before we can get the fuck outta here."

"Huh?" She stopped and smiled, her eyes questioning mine. "You mean there's somewhere else we can go besides your room?"

"Yeah, there's a place not far from here, a family place I've had forever. It's a nice night, and not too cold." I inwardly snorted, deciding not to bother dancing around this shit anymore. I leaned in close and hissed fire in her ear. "Obviously, I don't give a shit about the southern wind. This place doesn't have much for heat, but I'll make you burn between the sheets. You're mine, Meg, and that means I'm gonna spend every spare second fucking you senseless. I'm not stopping 'til you're soaked like a sauna, not 'til your sweet cunt's massaged my dick dry half a dozen times or more."

"Oh, God." Her eyes fluttered shut as my hand grabbed her thigh and squeezed.

Fuck if I could take a second more. Grabbing her again, I led her to the bar, praying Firefly would still be there, maybe a little more sober now that he'd gotten in his fun for the night.

I found him with Blondie's head on his lap, a beer in his hand, staring lazily at an old Western playing on the flat screen without any sound.

"Aw, shit." He took one look at Meg and stubbed out his smoke in the ashtray. "Your little toy's back? Did she bring the Prez the cash, or what?"

"You'll find out tomorrow, brother. All the club's business has been taken care of. Every man wearing this patch is gonna be pretty fucking happy, let me tell you." I walked closer, tugging Meg with me, who'd suddenly gone shy in my grip. "Keep the bullshit on your tongue. If I hear you call her a toy, a whore, or a stray again, I'll put my fist in your face, and I don't give a single fuck if you know it's coming. I need ink, Firefly, if you're not too fucked up to draw. She's mine, brother, and I want my brand on her tonight."

His jaw dropped. "No fucking way. Skin, the human calculator with a porno fix, settling down?"

He shook his head once, twice, three times. I nodded, coldly, staring him down. Why the fuck did everything take so long around here?

Finally, it must've sunk in. Firefly leaped up from the bar and caused his girl to jerk up awkwardly, losing her headrest.

"Congratulations, brother. I'm done giving you shit." His big arms held us both, crushed us to his massive chest. "Let's get this woman inked up. It's about time this club had some good news."

Amen to that.

Meg watched me nervously from the padded chair. She'd chosen to take my brand on her shoulder, a perfect place for me to see it whenever I told her to wear something loose in the warmer weather. Better still when we were naked and I mounted her from behind.

I'd watch my brand appearing on her skin like a damned target, all the encouragement I needed to fuck her harder, mark her from the inside out. My balls churned, aching to unload inside her, watching as Firefly kept her arm pinned down with one hand, and used the other to scrawl the design we'd picked out with the ink gun.

"You're doing so good, baby. This is the last pain you're ever gonna feel for me. I promise." I grabbed her free hand and laced my fingers through hers.

I couldn't tell if she wanted to laugh or cry. Her whole face twitched, on the verge of going to pieces.

Her smile said everything I needed to know.

We'd only talked about the design minutes before Firefly went to work. I watched him etch a heart on her shoulder made from iron bars, just like the gate in front of her home. The center was all open, and the Enforcer stenciled PROPERTY OF SKIN, DEADLY PISTOLS MC TENNESSEE onto her flesh one glorious letter at a time.

By the time he was working on the finishing touches, I couldn't hold it. I leaned in and crushed my lips on hers, tasting what belonged to me. Fuck if she didn't taste even better already – something I'd have thought was impossible.

"She's all good to go, brother." Firefly turned off the ink gun and grinned, admiring his work. "Lucky man.

The girl was hot before, but now? Shit, ya'll are lucky I've got somebody to keep me company tonight."

I shot him a withering look. Joking or not, I didn't take kindly to other men sniffing around her, even my own brothers. Jerking her up by the wrist, I pulled her into me, holding onto her extra tight, grazing my stubble across her bare neck.

She shuddered. Fuck if it didn't make me imagine her rippling underneath me.

Christ, she'd get fucked tonight. Harder than a boulder dropping. I'd slam my cock in and out of her 'til sunup, marking her as mine, making her understand beyond any shred of doubt what her tight little body did to me.

"We're done here, Firefly. Thanks for playing artist for the night."

"There's nobody better in this MC. You taking off for the night, or crashing here?"

"Yeah, we'll be back when the Prez says it's time for church. Or whenever this little lady wants to go home. Try to keep Dust from spending every damned cent of what we just inventoried. I know morale's been low, but fuck, we've finally got ourselves a second chance. We deserve it."

I was talking about the club, but I held Meg's eyes the entire time. My new old lady never wavered, catching the hidden meaning in everything I said.

"Yeah, we do," she whispered, just as we headed out. "A second chance, and a whole lot more."

They'd be the last words I'd let her say tonight before I fucked her incoherent.

We left the clubhouse and rode underneath the moonlight. It was going on two o'clock in the morning, a bewitching hour, but I wouldn't trade this ride for anything.

She pressed close to me in the cold, purring in my ear during the ride to my cabin. My cock pulsed in my denim each time I felt her breath, imagined feeling her tongue wrapped around me again.

I wanted her to suck me off, almost as bad as I wanted to take her pussy over and over with my mouth, my cock, my hands, whatever would make her go to pieces. I hadn't fucked her enough yet – not nearly enough to wipe away all the traces of Ricky and the bastards he'd sold her to for pennies.

"Hold on tight here," I told her, a quick warning before we entered the final stretch.

My bike growled up the last bend, an unpaved dirt road through the forest. She yelped surprise, ducking underneath the low hanging branches, bringing her so close to me my entire body ached.

She stirred me up like a goddamned fire.

I needed to fuck. Not just in the pure, crazy, animal sense, though that was there too. I needed this woman like I needed to cleanse my own soul, meld bodies and heartbeats 'til I emptied everything I had inside her.

No chick was ever worth truly draining myself for 'til Megan. And now that I was about to give her a proper honeymoon as my woman for the very first time, no other girl ever would.

We rolled up next to the lake and I parked the bike. My hands burned to touch her. I pulled her up and ripped her helmet off, sneaking in another kiss, bending her over my bike and holding her while we kissed, one last taste before we headed inside.

"If I'm going to be your woman for the night, yours forever, there's something I want to know…"

Why did she sound so shy all of a sudden? My lips pulled up in a smirk and I leaned in close, teasing my lips across hers without closing in another full kiss.

"Anything, babe, as long as it ain't club biz."

"Your real name can't be Skin. What was it before?"

My eyes widened. I'd never had a woman ask for my given name since I'd put on the patch. That shit belonged to another world, and it was never supposed to have a voice once my folks were gone.

They'd been the last to call me by my name, and that was the way I'd intended to keep it.

But hell, I'd never dreamed of claiming an old lady 'til now. I'd never brought a woman to this place, into my private world, beyond the bike, the bar, and my cramped little room in the clubhouse.

"Walk with me. Let me show you the lake."

"But!"

I cut her off. Taking her by the hand, I led her down the steps going down to the old dock, the same place me and my old man launched our boat for fishing. Those were the best times I had with Dad, when he was away from the club.

"You wanna know my name? Fine, babe, I'll give it to you, but you're gonna know the rest of me too."

"What is this place?" she whispered, smiling as we gazed up at the stars, pristine and reflecting on the calm waters.

"Family cabin, like I said. It was my grandpa's, and then my dad's after him. It's mine now, seeing how they're gone. It's been my second home since I was a kid, back when everybody called me Parker."

"Parker?" She beamed. "That's a beautiful name. So much nicer sounding than Skin."

"Don't be fooled. Skin's who I am now. Parker's just an afterthought, Meg, a memory and a secret that doesn't mesh with the rest of my life anymore. I never meshed anywhere 'til I put on the patch and took my road name." I clasped her chin and held her face for another kiss.

Goddamn, her lips tasted good. All of her teased my tongue like whiskey and honey. I thought about all the places I'd let my mouth roam tonight, at least 'til it decided to find that hot, wet place between her legs and smother her clit.

She moaned as I broke the kiss. "Can't I use it a little bit? Parker, I mean? It can be our secret, just like the new tattoo."

"Whatever, babe, go ahead and say it when we're alone, if it makes you feel better." My arms tightened, pulling her close. She didn't realize what a gift I'd just given her. "That ink on your shoulder's like a contract or a vow, yeah, but it's not a secret. Hell, I *want* every brother to know you belong to me. You're a marked woman, mine 'til the death. You got it?"

She didn't answer me with words. I barely had time to tuck a stray lock of her chestnut hair behind her ear before she leaned into me, tempting me with those lips.

My hands swung lower as we kissed. They found her ass, clasped it hard, and squeezed, pulling her into me, a prelude to everything we'd do inside my place. Cozy, naked and truly alone.

I'd fuck her 'til the Smoky Mountains echoed with our cries. My cock twitched, hounding me to rip her jeans and panties clean off. I pushed my hips into hers and broke the kiss, slowly spinning her around, walking her up to the place before the horny motherfucker in my pants caused me to take her outside.

There'd be plenty of time for that over the next few days. Tonight, I wanted to fuck her behind the walls, ease her into being mine completely behind closed doors, and then mine forever out in the open with the night sky watching us.

"Why Skin?" She whispered on the way up, wiggling her fingers in mine.

"You never heard? Every road name has a story behind it."

"Don't tell me." Her smiled faded. "You skinned somebody alive, didn't you?"

I chuckled. Shit, the girl could make me laugh, but I couldn't let that distract us from what was about to happen tonight.

"Nah, I like tanning asses a lot more than I enjoy skinning them. Only women's. They named me Skin because I started saving the club's ass. First with Uncle Sam, and then in more important ways. Seems like this MC's always been living by the skin of its teeth, and that's the way I roll too. Living anywhere but the edge ain't worth living at all."

We got to the door and I wiggled the lock. No sooner than we got inside, she pounced on me, moving me to slam her against the wall and bury my lips on hers.

"I love it!" Meg cooed. "Your name fits what's happened with us, too. You know this isn't just because you saved me, right? I really do love you, Skin. I want the man behind the hero…all of him."

Fuck. Her hand settled on my cock and she pressed her fingers against me, gave it a firm pinch.

I put my hand over hers and moved her fingers up and down, forcing her to feel my heat, how hard and hot and ready I was for her. She whimpered when she felt me pulse behind my jeans, ready to bust through them and take her on the damned floor right here.

No, I couldn't do that shit. I had to shut the animal screaming inside me up, if only for a second.

She deserved better tonight. We deserved more.

I wanted her in a nice, cool bed. I had to fuck her good and proper, slam her into the mattress when I emptied myself inside her. I wanted to hear her screams bouncing off the walls like gunfire, and fuck yes, I wanted 'em reverberating in my ears forever.

With a growl, I spun her around, swept her into my arms. "Come on, baby girl, let's get our asses to bed. Just one rule in this house."

She quirked an eyebrow and laughed. "Yeah, what's that?"

I walked her several more steps through the small cabin before I answered, passing the little kitchen. When we were at the threshold to the bedroom, I set her on the floor, smoothed her ass with one hand, and then worked my way up, ripping off her shirt before she could draw another breath.

"No clothes. Not 'til I tell you to get dressed again. You're here to be wet, bare, and ready for me every waking minute in my house. Follow the rules, and you'll get fucked constantly."

I smiled as she moaned, my fingers grabbing at her jeans and jerking them down. I never fucked around with the rules. Soon as I laid 'em out, they started *now.*

"And if I don't?" Meg purred, teasing me with words, almost as good as her naked skin.

"Then you'll get punished. Spanked, tied up, and fucked so hard you won't be able to dress yourself anyway."

I had to show her I meant business. Grabbing the waistband to her black lace panties, I tore them down her legs, and popped back up with my palm ready. I slapped her ass so hard she jerked forward, sputtering surprise and delight.

Fuck. Finding out she had a pain slut streak almost caused my cock to blow on the spot.

"Oh, God. You're a bastard sometimes, Skin." She turned toward me, one hand on her little ass, rubbing it seductively. "But I love you anyway."

"Yeah, I love you too. Now, undress me so I can show you how a man fucks his old lady."

We stepped into the bedroom and stopped near the bed. I watched as she went to work on me with trembling hands. Moonlight spilled through the flimsy old curtains, just enough to see her pupils blow up when I dropped my cut and helped her roll off my shirt.

Chicks always melted when they saw my chest. I flexed, feeling the power in all my ink, feeding the feral need to fuck her pussy, already dripping between her sweet legs.

"Hurry it up, woman, before my dick punches a hole through my pants. You wanna feel every inch of me inside you tonight, or what?"

She smiled nervously, dropped to her knees, and worked on my jeans. I unfastened my belt and shoved them down, fishing out my cock. Goddamn it felt like heaven just to give it some fresh air.

Better, maybe, because her hot little mouth was poised over it. I looked into her moonlit eyes with one command on my lips.

"Suck, baby. Suck me as hard as you want me to fuck you tonight."

The girl didn't need to be asked twice. I watched Meg's beautiful glossy lips take my tip in her mouth and flick her tongue against it.

Little tease. I fisted her hair and pushed against her head, bringing her down, drawing me deeper into her perfect mouth.

"Fuck!" I growled. Her warmth surrounding me, taking me to another universe, one where there was nothing but my testosterone and her hot, ready holes.

Her tongue glided over me, circled the ridge underneath my cock, sucking up all my pre-come like a good girl. And I leaked it like a ruptured fucking line, my cock swelling a little more each time she pulled with her lips, doing things with her mouth no girl should've been able to do.

I hated the motherfuckers for what they'd done to her in that whorehouse. Had she sucked any of those sick bastards half as hard as she used her mouth on me?

Couldn't imagine it. Didn't want to. The only cock she'd ever obsess over again was already in her mouth, and damn if I wasn't hell-bent on keeping it that way.

"Look at me, baby," I whispered, pulling gently on her hair 'til I saw her eyes. "Just keep sucking. Don't stop for anything."

Her eyelids fluttered and she sank down on my dick, as far as she could go. The surprise heat and the moan rippling in her mouth around my cock almost caused me to come on the spot like a fucking school kid.

Shit! I regained control and brushed her face more gently, encouraging her, giving her the absolute safety she needed, all I'd ever give her for the rest of her life.

"I love you, Meg, you know that? Love you when you've got your lips all over me. Love you when you're laughing, or spitting venom with that hot little tongue. I loved you from the first night I held you in my arms back at the clubhouse, feeling your heat, your pulse against me. You're my whore in this bedroom, babe, but you're gold in my heart. You're my old lady. I don't give a shit how fucked up it seems. It is, and that's all that matters."

I expected her to stop, to freeze up, maybe to spill a few tears. But I knew I'd done well when I felt her lips tighten. Hot breath brushed over my cock as she inhaled my scent, drew me deeper, sucked me like her entire life depended on it.

"Ah, ah, fuck me alive!" My balls tightened after another minute of her furious sucking. I was ready to spill my passion straight into hers, but that shit wouldn't do when I needed to claim her tonight.

"Enough." I pulled on her hair and drew her mouth off me.

"You don't want to come in my mouth, Skin? You taste *so good.*" She wiped her lips like a good girl, flashing me a pretty smile.

Tempting. Too bad I wanted to fuck her breathless just a little bit more.

"Hell yeah, I know I do. Don't play dumb with me, babe. You already know exactly what I want. I'm gonna see if you're wet enough to take every inch of me, and then I'm fucking that pussy 'til dawn."

I watched her rosy nipples harden. Taking her hands, I

jerked her up, walked her over to the wall between the bed and the window, and pushed her head down. I threw her hands against the wall and held them there, pressing my power on her.

"You don't move an inch unless I tell you to. I'll hold you up. You're not falling to the ground on my watch."

I kissed down her back and sank to the floor. My lips went to work automatically, stamping hot kisses upward, starting at her knees. My tongue flicked her skin when I got to her thighs, feeling the heat growing every inch I climbed, stopping just short of the sopping wet sweetness in the middle.

"Hey, I don't know about this. I've never come standing up before. Not sure I can…"

I wanted to laugh in her face. The girl had a lot to learn about her own body. Couldn't wait to show her things she'd never dreamed of.

Her scent drove me wild. I brought my mouth up and pulsed hot breath across her pussy, forcing her to rock her hips.

"Please, Skin." Meg begged me with words and with her body, and I growled my satisfaction. But I wasn't done with her yet. Not by half.

"No talk," I warned her. "You can make noise, girl, but it'd better be the sexiest fucking nonsense I've ever heard, especially if you want this."

I pushed my face in and dragged my tongue across her slit. She threw her head back, shaking and murmuring. Her thighs quaked in my hands, and I put my hands on them, shoving her closer to the wall and pinching her skin tight.

Her clit throbbed behind it all, but she'd be howling like a banshee before I got there. My lips circled back to her thighs, faster this time, before I returned to her pussy and brushed her with more quick, delicate strokes.

Piece by piece, she came apart. Her legs shook harder. She breathed fire.

Panting, moaning, pleading for me.

Exactly where I wanted her.

I didn't truly give her the tongue-work she wanted 'til she rubbed against the wall. The girl was looking for support, relief, anything to save her from the firestorm I'd started in her body, the staggering *need* to have me take total control of her pussy.

Every precious inch of her was mine now. Mine to protect, mine to own, mine to tease, rule, and use as I saw fit.

Luckily for her, I finally saw fit to give her the tongue she was dying for just then.

"There!" she screamed, as soon as I fucked my licks into her, her whole body tensing.

She was really on edge, but not for long. I laid into her with everything I had, pulling her 'til she sat on my face, holding her in mid-air like a gymnast I'd trained to fuck under any circumstances.

Her whole body hitched when I finally moved forward and found her clit. My tongue lashed over it again and again, cutting short, mean circles, digging into her with just the right pressure to send her crashing into O land.

She screamed through her teeth when her pussy tightened. Hot, luscious cream gushed all over me, and I lifted two fingers up, plunging them into her as she convulsed.

She fucked my fingers and my mouth like a goddamned animal. It was so hot my cock throbbed hellfire, aching like a magnet in front of metal.

I'd never known need like this. My blood turned to needles, digging at my veins, telling me to fuck her like a junkie needs his latest hit.

Something primal from deep down inside me dragged itself up and caught me by the throat. I wanted to bury myself balls deep and spill everything I had, whatever it took to meld with this woman, anything to put out the wildfire searing my bones.

I licked and finger fucked her 'til she collapsed against me. Then I stood up, wrapped my arms around her waist, and squeezed her tight while we kissed.

She moaned when she tasted her own sweetness on my lips. She cried out louder when I rubbed my swollen cock against her ass, showing her how bad I needed to fuck her into submission.

"You feel that, babe? There's no hiding anything with you. No secrets. No games." I brought my mouth close to her hot, red ear, grazing my teeth against it. "I'm gonna turn you around in another second. Get on the bed, all fours, and put your ass up. Your pussy's mine for the night, and it ain't resting 'til you're overflowing."

"Oh, God." She spun and kissed me harder.

I could've sucked her tongue all night if I didn't need to fuck so bad. I gave her another gentle slap on the ass and watched as she did what I said, admiring her legs shifting apart for me, her perfect ass going up in the moonlight, presenting and prone for me.

Too bad I couldn't stand to admire the sweet scenery for more than a second.

I crashed into bed behind her and put one hand on her ass, fisting my cock with the other, guiding myself into her. She stiffened and moaned when I sank in.

Fucking hot. But nothing compared to the sounds she made when we started to fuck.

And fuck, we did.

I slammed my hips into her long and hard. Short strokes, shallow strokes, long thrusts, and everything in between. I took her hair in my hand like reigns and slapped her ass while she bucked into me, pounding her deeper, feeling her creaming all over my hungry fucking cock.

Didn't have a damned clue how I held it together for more than a couple minutes, but I did. She was the first to lose it when I really started to power fuck her.

She tensed up, clawed at the sheets, and screamed my name over and over.

Skin, Skin, Skin!

Just like a mantra. I sank my teeth into her neck, hard enough to leave marks, and fucked her harder, straight through her first climax, mounted on every inch of me.

"I don't think you wanna feel my come inside you yet, woman."

"No, no, I do," she whimpered, almost in a trance from my thrusts. "Please, Skin. *Please.*"

Fuck, I was starting to love that word. But when I finally let go and pumped my seed into her, I wanted her pussy to clench me so hard I passed out.

"You can do better than that. Come on, sweet girl." My palm went down on her ass hard, making her jerk. "No bullshit. Make me believe you want it."

When she recovered from the love slap, she began to buck me back. Hard.

The chick became a total demon beneath me. Her pussy met my thrusts with a passion I could feel all the way down to my bones. Her perfect ass bounced backward and snapped against me, calling me to fuck her harder.

So I did.

I fucked her like a whore, a lover, and the woman I was meant to be with 'til the end of my days all in one. I fucked her that way because that was exactly what she'd become, and I aimed to keep her.

Mine, goddamn it, I thought with a snarl, feeling the fire building in my balls.

Mine when she's naked or dolled up for the town. Mine when she's young and vibrant, or old and wrinkled. Mine when she's looking at me with tears in her eyes, holding our first kid at her breast.

Too much. Imagining my baby in her shot me into outer-fucking-space.

My hips went wild, smashing into her, pinning her to the bed as I fucked her in long, manic, mattress pounding strokes.

"Fuck, Meg, you're so damned tight. Come the fuck with me! Now!"

Her pussy clenched around my cock before I'd even finished saying it. My cock tingled, and I drove into her deep one more time, rooting myself against her womb, feeling the explosion come.

I came so hard I forgot to breathe.

Every muscle in my body tensed, primed for squeezing every drop I could into her, spilling it in her sweet pussy in hot, molten jets. My cock spat fire for what felt like an hour, and I still couldn't get enough, growling as I forced out a few more thrusts to grind it deeper.

I wanted to own her every way possible, dammit. And someday, when she went off those stupid pills, I'd be working on the son or daughter I'd take on fishing trips on the lake outside.

I'd loved my family a long time ago. Never dreamed of building a new one 'til now, when I pulled her face to the side by the hair, and put my lips on hers.

"You're driving me insane because I love you, babe. Don't give a shit if I wind up in a straitjacket, as long as it's with you."

No bullshit. I wasn't letting this woman go for anything. And if any man ever caused her a single tear again, I'd die first, murdering the sonofabitch with my mad hands.

IX: Too Close to Paradise (Megan)

Everything here was beautiful.

I woke up blissfully sore the next day, and found the bed empty next to me. The last thing I remembered was drifting off to sleep with my face on Skin near dawn, breathing in his scent, loving the afterglow when we'd finished fucking more times than I could count.

A breeze hissed through the open window. I gasped when I sat up and stretched.

The trees outside looked incredible. They wore their autumn hues all the way down to the lake, jack-o-lantern orange mixed with reds, yellows, and just a dash of lively green.

I smiled, searching for my clothes. It took my nose a little longer to wake up. Then I noticed the heavenly smell in the air as I slid on my panties.

Breakfast.

I fought not to tear up, wondering if I'd actually died before he saved me, and maybe this was heaven. I was about to head out to the kitchen to meet him when my phone pinged.

Daddy's text made me groan. I couldn't believe I'd forgotten to check in with my parents when I'd taken off last night.

I typed something quick back, told him I'd be home in another day or two, after spending time with Becky. I said a small prayer he wouldn't actually check in with her. I left it short and sweet, adding a brief note about how excited I was for therapy, and turned the phone off.

I hated lying to him, when he'd done so much for me. But Dad wouldn't understand this – not yet – just like he wouldn't understand that the only therapy retreat I needed was already right here in front of me.

"Shit, babe, you're awake." Skin walked in, wearing nothing but his jeans low on his lips and a smile. "Just in time for eggs and pancakes. Get out here."

I smiled as he took my hand and dragged me to the breakfast table. The first couple bites told me the boy knew how to cook, and that made me grin even more.

"What's up? Not enough salt?" He shot me a sharp look when he saw me staring out the window, chewing my food.

"Sometimes I can't believe I'm really here. With you. Doing this."

Skin smiled, folding the long scar on his cheek. "Believe it, woman. If you want, we can spend every summer doing this. Can't imagine any other way worth spending the time when I'm not with my brothers. I'm gonna hit the town looking for places outside the woods next week, before winter creeps in."

"Oh, we're moving in together already?" I couldn't hide the hope in my eyes.

"Damned straight. I'm not gonna let my old lady live with her folks forever. What kinda man would I be? Shit, come shopping for places with me. It'll give you something to think about."

I reached across the table for his hand. "I'd like that. This is all happening so fast..."

"Yeah, it is. When I spot something I want, I move like lightning, babe. You'll figure that out fast, if you haven't by now."

"No, I kinda had a clue." I took another bite of my food, chewing slowly, enjoying the warmth and strength of my fingers in his. "What makes a man like you so decisive? There's got to be more to it than...well, that."

I motioned at his beautiful chest with my fork, staring at the Deadly Pistols MC tattoo blended into his huge muscles. The smoking gun and skulls across his torso seemed more like a birthmark than something he'd gotten later in life, intricately and forever part of him.

"There's more, yeah. But it all begins and ends with this club, the only family I ever had, especially once my folks died."

I frowned. He'd mentioned it before, but it really hit me for the first time. Guilt filled my heart, reminding me how I'd lied to my two perfectly sane, loving parents.

"My old man bit the dust when I was just shy of fifteen. The club had a run in with the wrong gang hauling meth on a run through Kentucky. They chased our guys right off the damned road with their trucks, and Dad caught the worst of it, a bullet through his back and a cracked skull in a ditch." He held up his hand, studying the big Pistols ring there, the same one he'd given me as collateral in Ricky's spa.

"This is all I've got left of him. It's a good reminder how quickly things can go to shit. I live my life moment by moment, babe. Sure, I'm a planner when it comes to numbers, but fuck if I hesitate when I'm onto something good, or taking out any threats to the things I love. It's all I know how to be, and it hasn't let me down yet."

"You're a good man, Skin." I smiled softly, squeezing his hand. "I had my doubts after the rescue…but not for long. I get why you did what you had to. You risked your life for me when I was just a stranger, you and the other guys in your club. I wish I'd gotten a chance to thank them."

"You will. Bring 'em beer or BLTs, and they're good." His eyes flashed with a jealous, possessive energy. "The only man you gotta be concerned about pleasing from now on is right here in front of you. You're mine, babe, and I'm never letting go. Not for *anything.*"

His tone made me shudder. He was really, truly serious. He spoke with an anger ten times deeper than my dad's when he'd thrown the detective out.

This man had killed for me once, and he'd do it again in a heartbeat.

I finished my breakfast and sat back in my chair, safe and satisfied. It was the first time I'd felt this way in months since he'd saved me from the pimp.

"It's a beautiful day," I said, loving how the light came through the window and caught his hazel eyes. "Can't we take a hike?"

"Sure, but there's something I've gotta take care of first." He stood up and walked over to me, pulling me up with both hands.

His lips crashed on mine. The addiction in my body reawakened, tingling for him already, no matter how many times we'd enjoyed each other last night.

"What's that?" I purred.

"Turn around." The edge in his voice told me he wasn't asking.

As soon as I did, his hands were around my waist, tearing down my jeans and panties in one stern tug. I gasped at how quickly he unraveled me, how fast he made me go from wet to completely soaked.

Completely his.

Skin took me right there. He bent me over the kitchen table and mounted me like a bull. He held me by the hair and fucked me hard, so damned hard I whimpered, loving his masculine force colliding into me.

Halfway through, he grabbed my shirt and pulled the loose corner down, just enough to expose my shoulder. "Fuck, babe, I can't get enough of how good my brand looks on you. I wanna see that every time I've got my dick buried in you to the hilt. You hear me?"

I did. I tried to moan a reply, but nothing except hot breath came out as he moved his hips faster, slamming into me, taking me to the edge.

"Every. Fucking. Time," he growled, quickening his thrusts.

I couldn't hold it. I never could with this man, and it thrilled me to surrender to him again.

"Come with me, Parker. Please!" It was all I could force out before everything below my waist convulsed.

We rocked and came together, just like that, grunting in total heat. His cock slammed into me, deeper than before, and he held it there while he swelled.

Hot, potent come pumped into me, scorching me from the inside out, and wiping away what was left of my sanity. I let go and became a mess of pure pleasure, rocking on his erupting length, coming together in one sweet, frantic rhythm.

He kissed me again and slowly pulled away. I felt his seed running down my leg. Something about that made me smile, just being a vessel for this wild man.

"Shower?" I asked, stepping out of my fallen clothes.

"Sure, babe, and I'm coming with you. We'll clean up together. Then I'm keeping you full of me the whole damned day, overflowing, whether you like it or not."

I smiled and took his hand. "Lucky for you, I think I love it."

By mid-day, I thought I'd gone to paradise. We walked deep into the forest, bright and magical in all its hues.

I scrounged up what I could find in his fridge for a picnic, mostly sandwiches and beer. We talked and laughed, hiking into the wild, one with nature and each other.

I know how sappy that sounds. But I was love-struck, opening my heart for the first time as a brand new woman. I never thought I'd meet such a deliciously handsome, warrior like him, a man who made me feel completely secure, whether I was on his bike or in his bed.

We stopped next to a small creek and sat on giant boulders to eat our lunch. Skin sucked down his beer and passed me a canteen of water, pulling me into his lap as he did.

His dark brown eyes captured me and drew me in. I couldn't resist his face. My fingers reached up and traced the scar going up his perfectly square jaw.

"How'd you get this?" I asked, wondering if I should bite my tongue as soon as the words were out.

"Knife fight in Sturgis, not long after I'd earned my bottom rocker." He smiled. "Trust me, the motherfuckers had it coming. I scarred their asses ten times as bad as what they did to me. I got off lucky – a couple inches higher and they'd have taken out my eye."

Frowning, I shook my head. "Don't you ever get tired of it? The constant danger and fighting, I mean?"

He laughed. Deep, rich baritone that seemed to shake the whole forest. His feral edge should've disturbed me, but truly, it didn't do anything but make my nipples tighten and my pussy tingle.

"Babe, this club's what I live for. It's the only life I've ever known, the only one that makes sense to me."

"But you're a smart man," I mused, running my fingers along his stubble. "You're like the club's accountant, aren't you? You could do so much more with your life."

I tapped the small TREASURER tag underneath his name patch. Skin nodded.

"Yeah, the boys would be lost without me. Lucky for them, I know how to handle the IRS just like the shitheads who disrespect our colors. There's nowhere I'd rather be than behind my bike or drinking with my brothers."

He paused, deep in thought, and then snorted. "Well, fuck, maybe I can add one more place to the list..."

"Yeah? Where's that?"

His hand ran through my hair, took my locks in a fist, and pulled them tight. "In you, babe. And I'm not just talking about that sweet pussy I'm about to fuck right here. I'm talking about having you with me on the open road, having you in my room, my cabin, my bed. Fuck. I gotta get you out of your parents' place the second we get back. I can't stand having you anywhere else. You *belong* with me, babe. Here's the proof."

His hand flowed down my neck and stopped near my new tattoo. It was still a little sore, but I didn't care. I smiled, overwhelmed with new passion, and put my lips on his.

Skin never did anything half way. He kept his word, flipping me around on his lap. His hands worked my jeans and panties down, and he took me right there, sitting on the rocks, squeezing my breasts through my shirt while he fucked up into me.

The closest I'd ever come to something like this was my last night as the old Megan Wilder, skinny dipping with the girls and the dopey rich guys.

Now, I was being pinned down and fucked in front of the universe.

Skin grunted, his pleasure rising, pushing his lips against my throat. I moaned, trying to keep it quiet, and failing a few seconds later.

His free hand reached for my clit, found it, and applied his expert pressure as his thrusts quickened. Blood rushed to my head before it arced lower. The distant foaming creek became a roar in my ears, mixed with his curses, his growls, his commands.

"You better fucking squirt for me, woman. If I pull outta you and my balls aren't soaked, we're not going anywhere 'til you do. Come on, baby girl. I know you can do it. Scream with the birds and the bees out here when you come on my cock."

Oh, God. Like I could resist.

I wasn't sure what the hell he was talking about, I'd never done anything like that in my life.

My pussy burned like never before. My hips bobbed up and down on his. I started grunting too, so rough and shallow I barely recognized my own voice, the animal need throbbing through every limb.

"Skin – yes! Let's come together. I want to feel you burst so bad."

His sharp breath mingled with a low laugh when he heard me whimper the last two words. His cock slowed while his fingers moved faster, and his teeth sank into my neck.

I felt like I had a rocket between my legs, or a dam about to burst. The harsh blood tearing through me became a torrent, something I couldn't hold back, no matter how hard I tried.

My knees started shaking. It didn't stop me from bucking as hard as I could, riding his cock, fucking him just like a whore for the first time in my miserable life.

I'd been forced to sell myself to those other men. I hadn't really enjoyed sex with anyone before Skin. I'd been too self-conscious, too focused on what they could do to me, or too scared, just wanting to get it over with as quickly as possible.

With the biker sinking his teeth into my neck, marking me, all of that faded. It died in the explosive urge to please him, to feel him fused to me in the height of my own pleasure.

I *had* to let go.

"Come the fuck on, Meg. Stop holding back. Your little pussy's gonna soak every damn inch of me when I fill you, right?'

I couldn't answer him at first. I was right on the verge – if only he'd give me something more, add his body pounding strokes to mine, spill his seed inside me.

His hand jerked my hair, pulling my ear to his lips. "I asked you a fucking question. Answer me, babe!"

"Yes," I hissed, barely a whisper.

His cock sped up. Shit.

So. Fucking. Close.

"You feel that fire building between your legs?" He growled. "You're gonna give it all to me. I'm gonna walk you through the damned mountains dripping me when we're done. You're my old lady, my girl forever, and you're coming for me anytime I ask. Got it?"

"Yes!"

"Fuck yeah, you do."

Yeah, I did.

His hold on my body tightened. His cock sped up, hammering into me with the full force of his hips, all the masculine strength he had focused around my clit.

The tension building around my womb went off like dynamite, ripping me in two.

I shuddered, I screamed, I think I blacked out for a few insane seconds in the throbbing inferno consuming me.

My pussy completely lost control, and I could feel myself gushing all over him, adding my wetness to his as he stroked deep, buried himself with a roar, and erupted.

Skin never stopped fucking me through our blinding climax. His cock thrust in and out while he buried his seed, adding more heat than I could handle, making me come so hard my fucking heart stopped.

With other men, there was fucking. Then there was *this,* whatever it was.

No filthy word seemed fit to do justice to the wild cascade he'd ignited in my body, burning me down.

I gasped, desperate to refill my starving lungs, when I finally came down from the frenzy. Skin held me tight and stroked my hair. He hadn't gone soft. He held his cock inside me, enjoying my warmth, our heartbeats dancing as one.

"You believe in destiny, babe?"

Jesus. He asked me a question that deep when my head was still buzzing from the sex? I laughed and shook my head.

"Don't think so. I'm a free will kinda girl, or that's what I remember from the philosophy course I took freshman year."

"Too bad. Stick with me, and I'll make a believer outta you. I knew we were meant to be from the second I gave you my ring." Skin grinned, but his eyes were deadly serious.

They poured a little more crazed, masculine energy into me every time I looked at him.

I grabbed his fingers, feeling the precious hand-me-down I'd kept while I waited for my rescue. It was so warm, holding a little of his heat. I missed having it on my hand.

"I know you like that shit," he growled, stopping to kiss the fresh hickeys he'd left on my neck. "Hang on just a little longer. You think my ring felt good on you before, I'll have to give you CPR to make sure you don't die on me when I give you a pretty new one."

My body jolted. Was he talking about marriage?

It didn't surprise me. This old lady branding thing felt like I'd taken on something deeper than a proposal, crazier than ordinary wedding vows.

I'd told him I was ready, and I meant it. My whole body jerked, mad excitement rushing through me. We kissed again, and my hips started to move, stroking up and down on the hardness still in me.

I didn't believe in destiny. Not yet. I could back out if I wanted to, I didn't have to be an outlaw's bride.

But by the time I began moaning and clenching on his length all over again, I couldn't imagine anything else.

I couldn't wear him down. My legs burned like fire by the time we were heading back to his cabin that evening, and not just from all the hiking.

The man brought a whole new meaning to *insatiable.*

He'd fucked me two more times out in the forest clearing, and he was already giving me that look like he wanted me naked as soon as we got home. I should've been drained, but my traitorous pussy tingled anyway, horny for more of what he'd left inside me.

God. At this rate, he'd knock me up whether I was on birth control or not.

Everything was moving too fast, and he was in the lead. He took my hand whenever I slowed down, pulled me forward, helping me through the woods just like he'd drawn me through life.

"Think I'll fuck you on the porch tonight," he said, squeezing my fingers. "We're damned lucky we've got another clear night. You saw those stars last night, didn't you?"

"Yup. Better make the most of it. It's our last night

here for a little while."

The nervousness building in the back of my brain started to seep out. I worried about how I'd go out with him again, much less get moved in.

My parents would want me dragged off to therapy with a court order if I told them I'd decided to hitch up with some man I'd only met weeks ago. And if Daddy didn't keep the pressure on Detective Harlow, he might come looking for more evidence about the dead men.

If he found out about Skin, he'd have *a lot* to dig through, too. I couldn't let it happen.

"Babe, what's wrong?" My man stopped, pulled me close, scanning my eyes with his.

I couldn't hide anything. "I'm worried," I said.

"Tell me what's behind it, and I'll make it right."

It sounded so easy, and I wanted to believe him. I smiled, wiggled my fingers in his, and looked past him at the wild fall colors lighting up the trees.

"It's not that simple. I don't know what I'm going to tell my parents, Skin. They're expecting me to come home and shove off to this place in Georgia for a few weeks so I can get some help. Mentally, I mean."

"Bullshit. I'll talk to your old man, face to face. Call him up right now."

I laughed at how ridiculous it sounded. But the biker reached into my bag, found my phone, and jerked it out, pushing it into my hand.

"Tell him the truth. Tell him about us. You're welcome to see a shrink on the side, Meg, I ain't gonna stop you. But when I look into your eyes, I don't see a broken, beat down woman. I was afraid that's what you'd be, even after I blew the pimp's fucking brains out, but I was wrong. You're stronger than that. You've got everything you need to get your life back on track right here."

He thumped his chest, then narrowed his eyes, giving me that killer look he'd used all through the rescue. "Call him. Tell him."

"This is crazy!" My eyes were about to pop out of my head. "Skin, come on, can't we figure something else out?"

"No."

One word, like thunder in his voice. Amazing how he could melt everything else inside me as easily as he melted my panties. I couldn't think of a good argument against his idea either, however insane it seemed.

I wasn't going to tell him about the detective unless I needed to. He'd saved my life and I'd given him and his club a second chance. I meant to keep on giving it too, even if I had to handle everything on that end myself.

I had a lot to learn about this lifestyle I'd taken on, but I knew my old man deserved better than having more problems dumped in his lap. Daddy had the pull to put this to rest once and for all.

Maybe Skin was right. I'd lied to my parents enough. Hell, my father *knew* I'd done as much.

Muddying the truth wasn't going to bring us closer.

With a heavy sigh, I tapped my dad's cell on my screen and held it up to my ear.

"Jesus, Megan! Where the hell have you been? I was about to call the police."

"What?" My heart went into overdrive. "Why?"

"Had a little chat with Becky this morning to see how she's getting along with the car business. She told me she'd seen you leave a few hours ago, but I know a girl who's tongue tied. It took her three times to get her story straight!"

Shit. I almost died on the spot between Dad's angry disappointment growling in my ear, and Skin's stern eyes fixed on me, turning me to stone.

"I'm sorry I lied to you." Bitterness crept into my voice. The truth always stung, but it was the only thing that could save me now.

"My God, honey. You don't know the damage you've done." He let out a long sigh. "Where are you, then? Are you on drugs? Did the man who took you away get you hooked?"

"No, Daddy, no." I cringed, turning away from Skin. "Nothing like that."

"I don't understand. You'd better start talking."

"There's someone else. I've met a man. He helped me get away from the whorehouse alive, and I think I'm falling for him."

My ears buzzed as I waited through the long, awkward pause.

"Now, honey, you listen to me. Very carefully. I know you mean well and I'm sure you believe this man is on your side. But you're in no condition to see *anyone* until you get your head straight. Come home. We'll sort all this out, and maybe someday you can visit this...*gentleman* after you're healed."

Gentleman was the last thing Daddy believed about my love. And he wasn't completely wrong. But the contempt in his voice hurt.

I definitely couldn't go back. He'd drag me off to the clinic kicking and screaming, anything to spare the family more embarrassment.

"I can't do that yet," I said softly. "I'm telling you the truth, but I think we both need time to process. You don't understand, Daddy. I wish you did. I'm happy when I'm with Skin. I'm me again."

Crap. I let his name slip before I could catch myself. If only I'd used Parker, something normal, maybe I wouldn't have had another pause twice as long, before he exploded.

"Skin? Skin!? Jesus Christ, Megan, you've got to be kidding me. Where's the punchline? What kind of disgusting low life are you spending your time with? What kind of drugs is he giving you to tear you away from your own family, your mother and father who love and support you?"

"I told you, I'm not on any fucking drugs!" I broke, hot tears falling down my face.

How could he think I was lying now? Sure, I'd done it once or twice, but now I was telling him the stark, cold truth. I'd tell him everything else, even if he disowned me and cut me out of the family fortune, if only he'd shut up and listen for a change.

"I'm only going to say it one more time, honey." Rage sizzled in Dad's voice. "Come home. Let us get you some help. Forget all about this Skin, and everything that happened to you before. I've turned away reports and gotten the cops off your back for more than a week, and you'd better hope to high heaven *they* never find out about these lies. You owe us, Megan."

My heart stopped cold, along with my tears. Hot anger hissed through my blood, slowing the heartbreak, an indignation I hadn't felt since watching the pimp die on Skin's phone.

"I don't owe you anything, Daddy. Don't call me again. I'll call you." I killed the connection and angrily stuffed it into my purse.

Skin's strong arms curled around me before I could take another breath. "You okay, babe? Heard it didn't go so well."

"It's going to take time." I rubbed his arm, clutched it desperately. I couldn't fit in with my own family anymore, but I could as his woman, his old lady. "I don't care what he says anymore, Skin. Everything I need today is right here."

"You're damned right. Now, dry those eyes and kiss me again."

His lips took away the pain, just like they always did.

I had to be patient. I had to keep my wits.

We'd survived so much in such a short time, and this was just one more fiery hoop to climb through. But we'd do it, together, no matter how hot it burned.

I hadn't met anything that would keep me away from this man, and God willing, I never would.

The night passed like a dream. Skin kept me on his lap around the fire pit outside his cabin. We slow roasted steaks we'd picked up in town, shared a couple beers, and just enjoyed each other's warmth underneath the sprawling starlight.

It was a simple, but filling dinner with a complicated man I knew I'd remember for the rest of my life.

His hands were all over me before the moon peaked in the sky. I knew he was serious about the porch thing when he dragged a thick blanket outside. He wrapped it around us near the fire when my clothes came off.

Skin's mouth moved across my body, slowly at first, taking my heat from a glowing spark to a scalding roar. His muscles covered me, bare, inked, and beautiful.

Please fuck me, Skin. Please. Please!

Begging wasn't even a question when his mouth sucked my hard nipples, and he lodged his cock between my folds, holding it against my wetness, teasing me until I thrashed against him.

I needed him inside me. No matter how many times he gave it to me, it would never be enough.

Every tease, every kiss, every lick reminded me who owned me now. As the fire inside me crackled hotter than the blaze in the pit next to us, hotter than the bright white stars above us, I never wanted him to stop.

Never.

I just wanted to fuck him. So badly. Tonight, tomorrow, and forever.

We rolled together, wrestling in the blanket. His cock brushed my clit, forcing my arms and legs around him. My nails raked down the stripes tattooed on his back, digging into his power, pleading for what I needed most.

Just before he pushed inside me with a savage grunt, he looked me in the eyes like a wolf on the hunt. "I fucking love you, babe. Whatever ends up happening, however rough it gets, just remember that. I'll love you, keep you, and fuck you like you're mine 'til the day I die."

"Skin…"

He covered my mouth with his, suffocating me in another steamy kiss as his cock plunged into me.

We fucked long and hard. I lost track of how many times I came while he moved like a piston, growling into my mouth, thrashing his tongue against mine to match the energy in his hips.

"Wrap your legs tight, woman. I'm gonna flood you again, and I don't want you to lose a damned drop."

Yes, sir. I did exactly what he asked. He fucked me so hard the wooden porch creaked underneath us. He fucked me like the animal he was, the beast I'd fallen in love with.

I'd fallen so hard, too.

So hard it hurt. So hard it pleased. So hard it let me know that he meant every single word he'd said today, everything he'd had stamped on my skin, everything about being his forever.

I came like a madwoman. His hands clasped my ass

with a snarl, pulling me deeper onto his cock, roaring as he came inside me.

I'd say it was too much, but then, it always was.

This outlaw's pleasure was a crime itself, so forbidden it only made me come harder on his length while he pumped his seed inside me. I cried out again and again as he fucked me straight through it, the fire in my belly becoming lava again.

When he finally pulled out, the sweet relief lasted all of about five minutes before he started stroking my pussy again, holding his come inside me.

I shifted, climbed over him, drew him into my mouth. His taste, his scent, his strength enveloped me on the longest night of my life, but also the best.

We kissed, sucked, and fucked ourselves hoarse for what seemed like hours. I wasn't sure when my body finally collapsed into sleep. But when I woke up the next morning tangled with him, eyeing the fog drifting over the lake and blanketing the colorful mountains, I knew I'd found paradise.

There wasn't any question. If I'd been crazy to do this old lady thing without really knowing what I was getting myself into, then it was the very best way a woman could lose her mind.

I started coffee back inside the cabin. Skin lingered for a little while, cleaning up, told me he'd be inside in a little bit to help with the food.

Humming to myself, I watched the sweet black stuff

brew in the pot. I hurt like hell, and I smiled, knowing I'd be feeling last night all day. The bathroom mirror showed several new deep purple marks around my throat.

I'd thought the branding ended back at the clubhouse, and of course, I was wrong. Part of me wanted to punch him. The rest of me adored it, secretly loved having a man who wanted to mark me up.

Thank God for winter, right around the bend. I'd be stocking up on turtlenecks for all the long, cold nights we'd undoubtedly have together.

I was fishing eggs and bacon out of the fridge when the screen door slammed open. Skin stepped into the kitchen with his eyes dark and serious.

"Get your shit together and throw the food back, babe. We have to go. Now."

Fear shot through my heart. "What's wrong? What happened?"

"Club's in trouble. Firefly took a bullet in the shoulder less than a block away from the clubhouse. The guys have been patrolling all morning and it looks like the area's secure. This shit's a message from the Deads. I've got to get you the fuck outta here."

For a second, I froze, cold blood running through me. "What do they want? Are they finally back to fight over the dead men?"

"Don't know, that's for us to figure out. My only worry's keeping you safe 'til I get you somewhere secure. I'd prefer that be the clubhouse, but if you wanna swallow the poison yesterday and go back to your family for this,

I'll understand."

"No way." I shook my head. "There's nowhere I'd rather be than with you. I know you'll keep me safe, Skin. You always have."

"Good." He looked at the stuff behind me on the counter. "Let's hurry the hell up. We've got a long run back, and then you're going in the vault. Safest room in the clubhouse. Nobody breaches that shit without a nuclear warhead."

"Whatever it takes, Skin. I'm yours." I said the last word in a hurry, right before I desperately began throwing food into the refrigerator and dumping the coffee.

A spatter caught my skin as I watched the hot, black liquid hiss down the sink. It should've burned, but it was the only thing keeping me from turning into solid ice.

X: All Hell (Skin)

She clung tighter to me than usual on my bike. I wished like hell I could grab her little arms and hold 'em even closer, whatever it took to wipe away the fear and remind her that I'd never let her hurt again.

Easier said than done now that we had a dragon breathing down our necks, but damn if I wasn't gonna try. We'd just gotten outside Knoxville on the isolated highway, about ten minutes from the clubhouse, when I heard the convoy.

They came up fast, taking the mountain curves like raging chariots.

"Skin!" Meg screamed my name as they surrounded us.

Four bikes. Two trucks. More than half a dozen bastards, all wearing Deadhands' patches on their cuts, and those mean motherfuckers meant business.

"Hold on as tight as you can, baby." I wouldn't let the worry creep into my voice and spook her more.

Just throttled my bike as hard as it would go, taking the next curve around the mountain so fast it felt like we were on a fucking rocket. She leaned into me. I could feel the poor girl's breath catching in her throat, the terror running through her blood.

Bastards. I'd find a way to make them all pay for scaring her like this. They'd give me their miserable, fucked up lives, and then some.

I took the first side road where it was too narrow for them to surround us, blazing toward the trees. I had to get ahead. We had to run.

It was our only hope. There were too many of them to outrun on the long stretches of open road, and we were too far away from HQ to risk it.

My eyes focused on a little stretch of road near a cliff overlooking the forest, an old scenic overlook next to a crumbling stone wall and battered stairway. It had just enough space to roar into it and jump the hell off.

"Babe, as soon as this bike stops, you run," I growled back at her, preparing to slam on the brakes. "Forget about your helmet, forget about the shit on the bike, just go!"

Ten seconds later, the bike screeched to a stop on the cracked pavement, nearly running off the damned cliff. I threw myself off it and grabbed her hand. She raced with me into the brush, struggling to navigate the steep cliff.

This part of the mountains was rugged as all hell. I'd been here a few times before. The boulders were our saving grace, and we headed for the first large crop we saw. I shoved her against the rocks and then pressed her to the ground, hiding her under me for extra safety and support. I also needed to muffle everything coming out of her mouth.

If she broke and whimpered while they were combing the area, we'd be dead for sure.

The Deads weren't giving up just because we'd quit the road chase. Shit, I could hear them now, swearing and trundling down the same overgrown path we'd taken, crashing through the trees, fanning out to search.

It wouldn't take them long. I had to delay. I had to put in a call to the boys, get them the fuck out here, or at least let them know that we were about to be whipped.

I ripped out my phone in one hand, and my nine millimeter in the other. I let my shit dial while I peered up over the rocks, looking for our pursuers. Hellfire tingled in my fingers, the need to put bullets through their skulls, even though we were past outnumbered.

"Skin? Where the fuck are you, boy?" Joker answered in his usual sharp, dead voice.

"We're in trouble, Veep," I growled in a hoarse whisper, feeling Meg tremble. "Deads here, a whole lot of 'em, just off the old stonewall overlook. I gotta go."

"Fuck. I'm on it."

The line went dead. We'd said everything we needed to, and the guys would be on their way soon, minus poor Firefly, who'd taken a shot I hadn't even seen yet.

One man down. Not good when the Deads came in force, and there might be more on the way, ready to hit the clubhouse while they came after my ass.

Another murmur. Some bastard coughed, and my trigger finger tensed. I saw his shadow climbing through the torn brush just past our rocky hiding place.

The rules of war were off. I had to shoot first. These assholes weren't going to show us any mercy, and the only hope we had was delaying them with a couple spilled brains, before it was our blood spattered all over the cool Smoky Mountain soil.

"Stay down, babe," I said in the softest voice I had.

One more second, and the Dead would be in my sights. I raised my gun, ready to watch his brains shoot out his skull.

I never got the chance to pull the trigger. Cold metal pressed into my spine.

"Don't."

I spun, planting my gun in another motherfucker's chest. I knew I was fucked when I heard the man I'd been aiming at, coming through the brush. Now, he had his gun trained on my head. I didn't even need to turn to see it.

"What the fuck? You're her only bodyguard? You got any idea how much this bitch is worth?" A big man in a Deadhands cut with a bald head and a satanic goatee smiled.

Fuck. Of course. The cold realization they were after Meg hit so hard I had to struggle not to shoot the asshole right through the heart and feel a hail of bullets slice me in two.

"You're not taking her," I growled. "You bastards are making a big mistake, showing your ugly faces in our territory."

Baldie tipped his head back and laughed. I glanced at the patches on his front, and saw V. PRESIDENT, then the bastard's name, BIG VIC.

"Shame you're not as good at protecting this cunt as you are making me laugh. Step outta the way, little man, and maybe we'll give you a fighting chance by putting lead in your kneecaps instead of your guts."

"Skin..." Meg fumbled up behind me, clutching my shoulder, desperate to diffuse the bomb already exploding in slow motion. "Don't risk your life. Not again."

"Ha, the bitch has balls, Veep," the man behind us said, right before he cleared his throat and spat on the ground. "Sure gonna be fun making her squeal for her folks. I bet she'll hiss and yowl through the whole fucking thing while we're holding her down."

Instinct took over. I pushed my gun deeper into Big Vic's chest, baring my teeth. Several more men emerged from the clearing, cocking their guns. I heard a shotgun pump, and a big one by the sounds of it, perfectly capable of cutting me to pieces several times over.

Fuck.

"Easy, boy." The Deads Veep looked at my name patch. "Skin, huh? A name like that gives me some ideas, especially if you're one of the fucks who took out our brothers a couple weeks ago."

"If that's what you're here for, then you need to talk to the Prez," I snarled, my words barely coherent through the rage spilling out my teeth.

"Careful. Please." Meg's grip on my shoulder

tightened.

She sounded so scared, like she was turning to stone. Goddamn it. The urge to pull her into my chest was almost as bad as the rush to kill, the demon need to watch this bald sonofabitch and every last man in his crew die beneath my gun.

But that shit was pure fantasy. I hated to admit my woman was right. I had to keep my cool, or they'd snuff me out like a fucking June bug, and maybe Meg too as collateral damage.

"Yeah, boy, *careful.*" Big Vic laughed, before his face went dead serious and he pushed his gun into my chest hard, wedging me between it and the one on my spine. "I'm gonna give you to the count of three, and you'll both drop to your knees. Put the gun down. Let me and Snappy do our thing, and you'll get to breathe a few more minutes while we decide what to do with you."

Several men chuckled. I wanted to make them all choke on their own fucking blood.

The boys are on their way, I thought. *Gotta delay. Gotta stay sane. Gotta keep these motherfuckers occupied before they can hurt her, or put me out of action before the cavalry shows up.*

"Whatever." I let my gun drop to the ground and hit my knees.

Meg did the same a second later. The skinny man with the long greasy hair behind me grabbed her, shoved her wrists together behind her back, and fixed something around her hands.

I couldn't fucking look at her. I was on the verge of failing the only woman I'd ever cared about. The only man here who deserved to be gutted more than the Deads was me for letting her down.

"Don't hurt her," I growled, staring up at Big Vic.

He looked down, his face half-shadowed, looking more like the devil himself than before. His lips curled up in a nasty grin.

"Sorry, bub. Gotta let her folks know we're fucking serious before we pass her off for ransom. Here, let me make sure you don't get too stir crazy while we're ramming our big cocks up her tight little ass."

"Fuck no!" Two words. "I swear, if you even think that shit again, I'll tear your fucking throats out with my bare hands."

If only it were as easy as the demon rage boiling over inside me made it feel.

Those words were all I managed before I noticed the heavy, round object swaying in his hand, bigger than his handgun. A split second later, the big rock crashed across my skull, and the world went instantly black.

I woke up seeing red. It took me a second to realize it wasn't just the blood caked all over my face – the fucks hit me so hard my vision blurred to bright red stars. I counted myself lucky they hadn't cracked my head completely open.

"Shut the fuck up and look into the camera, cunt!" Big Vic's command ended in a loud slap. "I already explained to you exactly what to say, and I'm not gonna do it again."

I forced my eyes to focus, and saw Meg sprawled on the forest floor, next to some shitty little hollow. They'd dragged us deeper into the forest.

Her face snapped back when he hit her. Adrenaline flooded my heart, turned it into a fucking grenade. I jerked up, and found a shotgun in my face, the bug-eyed twig boy they called Snappy holding it.

"Careful, Pistol. Wouldn't wanna have to blow your fucking jaw off before the Veep tells me too." His boot crashed into my chest.

I hit the ground and rolled, imitating more pain than his weak ass kick really brought to my ribs. I'd learned a long time ago to play weak when somebody had you by the balls. If a man managed to fool 'em, then they'd be too damned busy planning to rip off yours before you took theirs clean off.

Only, this time, I wasn't sure I'd get the chance to tear their worthless nuts off, and it fucking killed me.

Meg, Meg, beautiful Meg. My Meg. Suffering in front of me because I'd fucked up and failed to protect her.

I pressed my cheek into the dirt and leaves, turned my head, and saw her crying. Big Vic had her cornered, holding a small camera in her face, swearing up a storm.

The bastard's face was beet red. I couldn't figure out how long he'd been screaming at her, but it must've been awhile. She'd obviously tried to fight him.

God help her, the woman was brave, doing the last fucking thing in the world she should to stay alive.

"I can't do it!" she barked back, holding herself up on her hands and knees. "I won't! You'll have to kill me first if you hurt him or try to make me lie to my parents. I don't care what you do to me. I've seen it all before."

"Bullshit!" Big Vic roared, so hard I saw spit fly outta his mouth. "I know that piece of shit, Ricky, was easy on you, and the Pistols are pussies too. You ain't never been properly fucked 'til you bleed. Fuck, I'd have done it that night you sucked me off in that shitty condom, but I had to be happy making you gag instead because I thought you'd bring the club some goddamned money."

Her eyes went wide. Big Vic smiled, his teeth as big as tombstones.

"That's right, bitch. You remember now. You were crying or going to your happy place or some shit when I rammed my cock down your throat. Made you turn blue in the fucking face." He stood up and turned around, slapping the flat edge of his switchblade on his thigh. "Shit, what the fuck am I saying? We don't need you to follow script. We can send mommy and daddy a message plenty of other ways. How 'bout I show 'em what me and the boys'll do to you if they don't cough up a cool million?"

The motherfucker's nasty smile said it all.

"No!" I bolted up, staggering to my feet, ignoring the shotgun barrel jabbed between my ribs. "You fucking piece of shit, let her go before I kill every last one of you."

I screamed it 'til I nearly passed out a second time, going outta my damned mind. Big Vic heard my shouting before Snappy slammed the barrel into my guts, hard enough to wind me. I got in one good blow, cracking the fuckhead's jaw, before he clubbed me over the head.

I went down easy. That fucking wound they'd given me with the rock was still open, oozing blood. Took everything I had to fight the blaze of pain threatening to drag me under.

"What do you think, Snappy? Maybe I hit this asshole a little too hard, yeah?" Big Vic planted his boot on my chest, pressing down 'til I suffocated, and smiled. "Listen here, jackoff, the only ones here who oughta be talking about any killing are *us.* Not you. Have to say, you've given me one fuck of an idea, though."

"Sure hope it involves us getting this rich slut naked." Snappy laughed, rubbing his hands together like a damned raccoon. The other bastards circling Meg like sharks chuckled too.

"Here, K-Man, hold the fucking camera for a second." Big Vic handed off the camera to another henchman with a potbelly and pock marks all over his face. "Tell you what, Skin, since I bruised that shit in your head so hard, I'm gonna make it up to you. I'll let you help us decide what happens here."

Oh, fuck. I wanted to puke before he finally lifted his leg, easing the savage pressure off my chest.

Big Vic took his sweet time. He looked at Meg, huddled on the ground with hatred in her bright blue eyes, and winked, before he turned his ugly face back to me.

"Bring the two love birds over. I need that damned

brush cutter too." He gave another greasy Dead a dark look as the man walked over and retrieved a big machete.

He waited while several Deads pulled Meg over, kicking and screaming, and dumped her off next to me. We were completely surrounded. Big Vic stepped in front of us, his evil fucking smile getting bigger all the time.

Christ, I couldn't wait to shoot him in the throat.

"You've got two choices, kids. In another minute, we're gonna roll some beautiful footage to send to Megan's folks. They're not gonna hesitate to drop a cool million off in the next twenty-four hours if they ever wanna see their bitch alive again. It's gotta be bad to make 'em do that."

"Fuck, yes!" Snappy growled, grinding his teeth like he'd gone into rapture.

Animals. All of them. Sick fucking animals I've got to put down.

"First you, darlin'." Snarling, he grabbed her by the chin, holding her face in his hand as she tried to struggle. "Option A – we record you taking our dicks in every hole, slapping your ass raw, choking you 'til you're blue in your face, all for mommy and daddy to see we mean fucking business."

"You're already dead, and you don't even know it yet," I growled. Every word stuck like heartbreak in my throat, bitter and full of blood, but I'd never meant anything more in my entire goddamned life.

Big Vic looked at me and grinned. "Yeah, I thought you'd say that, boy. So, here's Option B – we hand this bitch the machete and put a shotgun to her head. You put your hand out on the ground so she can give it a nice, clean cut. We watch her lose her fucking mind while she sees your miserable ass bleed out on the sweet Tennessee ground. If you live, you'll never ride a bike or grip a beer again. Sound good?"

Meg gasped. Her eyes went huge, filling with tears, but she still managed to look at me.

My eyes never wavered. I gave her a grim nod, knowing these motherfuckers would probably choose both options. But if I could get them to pick the one that prevented her from being totally destroyed, that bought us time, precious time, then I'd accomplish something here today.

"Do it," I said.

"No, Skin. No, no, no, no, no…" she sobbed and turned beet red.

Poor baby girl. Asking her to fucking kill me to buy time wasn't easy, but I was ready to die if it'd keep their wicked hands off her for a few more seconds.

"It's okay, babe. Really. You have to do this. I won't even feel it."

Total fucking lie. I didn't give a shit. I'd feel myself tortured for a thousand years before I let any devil stick his dick in her again, tear her to pieces, hurt her.

"Aw, shit." Big Vic sighed, breaking the last intense look I'd ever share with my old lady. "Here I thought you might keep us in suspense, Skin, but I figured you were a pussy. All right, I'm a man of my word. Let's get this shit show on the road."

Big Vic nodded. Meg shook while the thug holding her untied her, pushed her arm out, clawed her hand open, and pressed the machete handle into her palm. He forced her fist closed around it, then jerked her arm toward me, moving her like a weeping puppet.

I didn't even hesitate. My hand went out, more than ready for the blinding pain, the final, best sacrifice I could make for this woman I loved.

I'd given her my heart the second I claimed her. What the fuck did my hand, my blood, matter after that?

The sharp, sandpaper squeal leaving her mouth shook the whole forest as the bastard behind her lifted her arm, holding it up above my hand.

"It's okay, baby. It's okay. Everything's gonna be all right."

I said it like a mantra. My heart slammed against my ribs on overdrive.

I thought about my parents, wondering if my old man felt anything while he bled out on the side of the road. He'd suffered less than ma, surely, taking her last breaths in that shitty cot at the hospital, eaten up with cancer.

I thought about my brothers, tearing down the highway, too little too late to save my ass. But at least they could save her if they showed up in the next five minutes while the life went outta me.

I thought about the brand on her back, something she'd always have, the best memory I could leave her. I'd given her a second chance, dammit, and now it was up to the universe to do the rest.

God forgive me, Meg, baby. I love you.

"No!"

All hell broke loose at once.

She screamed. The machete hit the earth just an inch from my wrist. The asshole holding the shotgun fired, spooked himself into blasting his shells straight into the ground.

Shrapnel and dirt flew everywhere. Big Vic and his boys cursed.

By some miracle, she'd jerked herself hard enough to miss before they took my hand, and set off the fucking dominoes that gave us a fighting chance. I kicked like a mule, slamming my boots into the motherfucker behind me, holding me down.

I pulled on Meg's hand, jerked her away from Snappy, and we ran by Big Vic while the assholes were all dazed and confused. I reached for my belt, pulled out a stun grenade, and ripped the pin with my teeth as more bullets hit the dirt next to us.

I hurled it behind me and pinched my eyes shut.

The motherfuckers screamed bloody murder when the flash burned their eyes. Unfortunately, the shit must've blinded Meg too. She stumbled. All the signal I needed to lift her into my arms and carry her uphill, digging my boots in fast as I could go, ignoring the hellfire tearing through my head, making the world spin, threatening to drag me back into the blackness.

"Go, go, go, you stupid sonsofbitches! Don't let 'em get away!" The Deadhands' Veep roared behind us.

His voice was fading, but the bastard was still way too close. They'd catch up to us sooner or later, as soon as their vision cleared, assuming one of the fuckheads still firing aimlessly didn't catch a lucky shot.

There wasn't time to worry about that shit now. We had to keep going, odds be fucked, no matter the cost.

I ran, carrying her, zoning out as the fire lapped hotter in my muscles, burning me straight down. I'd crawl through hell itself for this woman, anything to keep her safe.

We'd done all we could, and I staggered up to the old stone wall, listening to their angry boots stampeding toward us.

"Over the wall, baby. Just roll, get up, and go. Run!" I told her, dropping her over the wall in front of me, before staggering over it myself.

My heart got a jolt when I hit the ground and looked up. Tinman and Lion were roaring into the parking lot, right behind all the other brothers, who'd just switched off their bikes.

"Skin? What the fuck?" Dust instantly drew his gun, pointed it behind me, sensing hell coming before I grabbed my piece and pushed Meg flat on the ground.

"The woods – they're coming!" All I had time to scream.

I started firing with the rest of the guys, who hit the dirt behind their bikes, dropping the first sick fucks running into the clearing. I saw two Deads filled with holes, but the guys behind 'em fired back, alerted to our ambush.

Meg whimpered underneath me. I kept her down, anything to protect her as I peaked over the wall and fired, ducking every time the Deads shot back.

The firefight lasted a cool minute before Sixty charged and rolled next to me at the wall. His magnum blasted right through a skinny tree, hit one of the fucks hiding in the brush.

My ears rang with his satisfying scream. The other two retreated, falling back into the forest, probably on Big Vic's orders. I could hear the asshole screaming behind 'em.

They were fucked. Our prospects circled their bikes, cutting off their only escape.

Soon as the return fire stopped, Dust waved us toward the forest, the only signal we needed to go after 'em.

Fucking finally. I'd never been so goddamned happy to see the tables turned.

Meg clasped my arm, trying to stop me from going in. I tore myself away from her with a grunt, shaking my head.

"I've got to do this, babe. It'll be over fast. I promise."

I'd make it up to her later. I sure as shit wasn't gonna let the Prez and the rest of my brothers take down Big Vic and the rest of his guys.

That sonofabitch had to die by my hand, just like I swore.

I always kept my word, ever since I'd put on this patch. *Always.*

We chased the fuckers deep, crawling over tangled brush. Caught the greasy haired shit, Snappy, first, found him hiding behind a stump. He got off a few more shots, but the asshole was blinded with pain.

Joker got him from behind, close combat, stabbing a knife through his throat while the little hyena was too busy trying to shoot us. He died with his other hand still pressed to the nasty wound on his thigh, a jagged wound too messy to be one of ours.

I nodded to myself, satisfied that Meg had fucked a few of them up by making that dumb bastard blow his shotgun. He'd caught a piece of his own shrapnel, and now the devil had his soul. We pressed on.

The raging pain in my head stopped. I hit a second wind, running ahead of my boys, Sixty and Crawl at my side.

We found their guns before we found them. The last two Deads dropped everything, trying to run in a headlong panic. Crawl stopped for a second, picked up their shitty camera, and I took the machete laying next to it.

They'd followed a stream, probably hoping it'd lead them somewhere to hide, when we dropped 'em. Me and my best two brothers shot Big Vic and his boy in their calves from behind. They went down screaming like rats.

The Prez and the rest of the guys had just enough time to catch up as we approached.

"Goddamn, we got ourselves an officer." He pointed his gun at Big Vic's name patch, ready to dispatch him at any time.

I grabbed his arm and shoved his gun down with a growl. The Deadhands' Veep blubbered like a baby, begging for his miserable life. I'd seen his type before – big, ugly bullies who always shit their pants when they were fresh outta bullets and guts.

The Prez walked up and kicked him in the ribs before he turned around and looked at me.

"He's mine, Prez. Let me do him. He tried to kill me and fuck my old lady. Asshole was planning to film it all for ransom from her folks."

"No arguments," Dust said coldly. "What about this other piece of shit?"

He gestured to the pot bellied biker with the pockmarked face. I shook my head. I didn't have a personal beef with this asshole like I did their VP. He was just another faceless soldier in the wrong place, wrong time, wrong club.

"Joker?" Dust smiled as he looked at our crazy ass Veep.

The boy was finally wearing a ghost of a smile as he pulled his knife out. Sixty and Crawl grinned, holding the bastard down. Joker sliced his shirt open and started carving the ink off his chest, stuffing the scrap of dirty fabric in the asshole's mouth to drown out his screams.

Ironic how he ended up suffering longer for Big Vic's sins. I wasn't interested in tolerating that bad motherfucker tainting more air on this planet for a second longer.

He tried to crab crawl away from me with his shot up leg when he saw me coming, machete in hand. "Oh, fuck. Oh, fuck. Oh, fuck."

Normally, I gave assholes a chance to say some final words.

Not today.

I stepped ahead of him to the creek's river bed and took off his arm with one quick, clean cut. Then the other. The bastard howled so loud he would've gotten our asses in trouble, assuming there was anybody to hear.

Lucky for us, that wasn't a concern when I swung the blade again. His ugly fucking head came off and rolled like a rotten pumpkin, right to the edge of the stream, stopping against a jagged rock with his eyes frozen open in shock.

I looked at his sick face one more time. Asshole's mouth hung open like he died surprised, and I grunted. Sweet, sweet satisfaction.

He'd need a lot more than fresh mountain water to purify his black soul down in hell for what he'd done to my woman.

Two hours later, I was back at the clubhouse, Meg at my side while Dust's ma, Laynie, checked me over.

She had her work cut out for her today as a former nurse. First, Firefly, and now me.

"You should really go down to the hospital and get a brain scan, son." She shined the bright light into my eyes one more time, turning everything brilliant white. "I'm not seeing any obvious signs of damage, but you took a terrible blow to the head. I don't have the right equipment to rule out the worst."

"I'll be fine," I grunted, feeling a tiredness coming over me, nothing but the burning drive to curl up with my old lady and go the fuck to sleep.

"Skin, I want one of your friends to take us on a drive. I'm going to get you some help." Meg stood up, pulling the rag she'd used to help clean the blood off my face out of its water, and wiped a spot she'd missed.

Fuck, that shit stung when she grazed my cuts. But it wasn't half as bad as having to get used to these people buzzing around, all concerned about me passing out.

We'd cleaned up the dead weight in the woods and taken off earlier that night. The prospects and Joker split to head deeper into the mountains, taking the motherfuckers we'd finished out to our usual burial sites.

"Forget about it, babe. I just need to sleep this shit off, I'll be fine by morning."

Yeah, right. The way the roar in my temples deepened every time I tried to talk told me I was kidding myself and everybody else here with me.

"Bullshit, Skin." The Prez barked, leaning against the frame in the open doorway. "You need to listen to my ma, and your old lady. I won't have this club's brains getting scrambled for good. I've heard enough. I'm getting Crawl and Sixty together and having them take ya'll in to medical."

Fuck. So much for getting a luxury condo, as soon as I

saw the medical bill I'd wrack up after they did half a million scans on my skull.

"I can't afford that shit, and neither can the club treasury. We're just barely getting back on our feet. I'm not gonna burden the brothers, taking away from this club and the profit share for the guys when we've all risked our asses."

"You risked yours the most, Skin. It's my choice – or did you forget what this patch means?" Dust stepped forward, sharing a quick glance with his ma, and tapped the PRESIDENT patch on his cut.

"Yeah, I remember. Your way, Prez. No backtalk."

"Guys, let me do this," Meg said, speaking up. "I have an idea."

"Start talking, baby doll," Dust growled. "I'm not letting this boy close his eyes for a goddamned cat nap 'til he's had his head looked at good and proper."

Meg sat down with a nervous smile, and began to explain. By the end of it, I wasn't sure whose eyes were bugging out harder – mine or the Prez's. That was when I knew beyond any doubt I'd hitched up with the craftiest girl this side of the mountains, and maybe the craziest too.

"This is it?" Sixty pulled a smoke from his mouth and flicked it out the truck's window.

"Yup. I'll walk him over and buzz the gate. Just wait for us out here." Meg tugged on my arm. "Come on, old man. It won't be as bad as you think."

My brothers nodded. They watched me stagger out of

the passenger seat with my girl on my arm. The fucks probably thought I was heading for death row.

Her daddy didn't say much when she buzzed the gate. The big, iron bars I'd only seen from the outside slid open. It was a long walk to the double-wide front door between the roman columns, a country mansion like something outta Civil War times.

A tall, wiry man with spectacles came out to meet us, looking like a damned owl. He took one look at me and twisted his face.

"Honey, what the hell is this? Some kind of joke? My God, you brought *him* here."

"Of course I did, Daddy. Are you telling me the man who saved my life isn't welcome in our home?"

Pain roared in my temples. Didn't distract me from fixing eyes on her father, watching the hard, venomous look he gave me soften the longer his daughter looked at him.

Finally, he let out a heavy sigh. "No. We're civilized here. Assuming you have no weapons…Mister Skin, you're welcome to come inside for some water."

I narrowed my eyes, staring at him, and decided to do the only thing that made any damned sense. "I'd like that. It's a pleasure to meet you too, Mister Wilder. Call me Parker."

"What's going on here, Eric? Who is this man, and what's he doing in our house so late?" An elegant looking older lady in a thick burgundy robe sashayed into the kitchen, heading right for us.

We'd barely even sat down and gotten started. Meg squeezed my hand and smiled. I clenched my jaw, holding in a big fat *whatever*.

If she wanted to introduce me to her old man, then she'd might as well do the entire family.

"This is Megan's friend, Parker. She's come back to us."

"Oh, baby, I'm so glad you're finally going to get the help you need." Meg's ma slipped past me, hung over her, and kissed her on the forehead.

Finally, she looked up, staring into my eyes. The chick must've been in her fifties, but she'd aged well. I could see the resemblance in her chestnut hair and high cheeks. She must've been a total fucking knockout in her heyday, a perfect trophy for a rich businessman.

"Parker, huh?" she sniffed. "And how do you know my Megan?"

"He's the man I'm moving in with, Mom. I love him."

The old lady's jaw dropped. I would've laughed if it wasn't for the bison stampede in my head, the aftershock of that motherfucker slamming his rock into my skull hours ago.

"You. Can't. Be. Serious." Her mother pulled away from her, folding her arms.

"I am. Like I tried to tell Daddy over the phone, this man is the missing piece of the last six months of my life. He's the only reason I'm home, and not chained up in some dark, musty basement, being forced to service a man who wanted to buy me from my pimp."

The color drained outta her ma's face. Hubby stood up and took her hand, pulling her onto his lap so she wouldn't fall.

"Megan, please, we don't need to talk about all that. We've rehashed it enough with the police." Her father looked up angrily. "The detective, mind you, who I lied to repeatedly for you. Apparently, that wasn't good enough. You've still decided to throw your own family under the bus to protect this – this biker."

Fuck this shit. I stood up, feeling hot blood rushing to my face, listening to the heavy chair squeak across their perfectly polished tile.

"We done here yet?" I growled.

Meg looked at me, her eyes big and pleading. Then she turned her gaze on her parents, and it was a lot more ruthless.

"You really don't get it, do you? I'd be dead, if not worse, right now, if it wasn't for Skin. Parker. Go ahead, call him whatever you want. Treat him like trash." She reached out, took my hand, and jerked it against her cheek, brushing against me like a kitten. "It doesn't change the fact that he saved my life, or that we're in love. And nothing's ever going to change it."

Damn if her touch didn't smolder the fuse inside me. It always did. This woman's skin was magic against mine, and I could almost forgive the haughty fucks who'd raised her.

"But it doesn't change the fact that you'd be making

my funeral arrangements right now if he hadn't gotten me away from that whorehouse. If you want, I'll leave this house with him, and you'll never see me again. Keep the rest of my trust, I don't care. There's just one more favor I'm after – we're here tonight because he's taken a terrible blow to the head. You're both decent people, even if you don't like my man. I have to believe you'll give me my own money one more time to help the man who's kept me breathing."

"We'll have to discuss this privately," her dad snapped. "Here, sit tight, let me get you some water, dear."

Just as he sat her mother down in the chair and got up, she grabbed his hand, as if she'd been struck by lightning. "Don't. Eric, she's right. I believe her. Whatever she said before, I know our baby's only with us now because of this man. We can't just kick him out and leave him to suffer."

The whole damned world froze over in my woman's eyes, and melted like a steaming glacier. She nodded softly, gratitude on her lips.

"Thank you. Somebody finally understands."

"All right, all right," her dad growled at last, giving me a sharp look. "Parker, Skin, whoever you are, I don't know if I'll ever be happy about this situation you've created with my daughter, but I'll listen to the women in my life. I'm going to go downstairs and get the account information so my little girl can get you checked out."

"I appreciate it. Whatever the hell I look like to you, I take good care of her. That's never, ever gonna change." I said it like I was swearing on my life, ignoring the sirens in my head, calling me to look her daddy dead in his eyes.

"I need your word on that." He stepped closer, flattening his hands on the table, accepting the challenge in my eyes. "Because if I ever find out she's gotten hurt thanks to you, I know what club you belong to. I'll have the National Guard out there dismembering it."

"Save the fucking call to the Governor," I said. "I'll die before I ever let anything happen to this woman."

"He's telling you the truth," Meg said, running her hand gingerly through my hair. "Please, guys, can't we put the egos on hold until he's better? I promise we can work this through. He's saved me more times than I can count, and now it's my turn to return the favor."

Satisfied, her dad nodded. Her ma served us some water and made small talk while he retrieved the paperwork. Then, folder in her hands, we headed back to my brothers in the truck, waiting behind the gate.

I waited 'til we were out by the gate, where the high floodlights didn't reach, before I grabbed her and pressed her to my lips.

"You're supposed to be sick," she laughed, giving me that smile that made me want to fuck her through the pavement.

"Yeah, whatever, babe. You know I love you. I'm gonna get my shit checked out, and then it's gonna be a whirlwind moving you in. I'm not living one more night without you in my bed."

"Oh, Skin," she whimpered, all she could manage before she pushed her hot little lips against mine.

Oh was right. I'd be hearing her make that noise over and over, clenching on my cock. Whatever the fuck happened to me or the club, I'd be reminding her she was mine for the rest of my life.

One Month Later

It was a frosty day, a couple weeks past Halloween. I'd closed up the cabin a couple days ago for winter, the place we'd been sharing for the last month, while I got all our shit together.

My head hadn't fucked me over too bad. A few days rest and a follow-up said it hadn't done permanent damage, and I hit everything hard as hell as soon as they let me off bed rest.

I let Meg off at work that morning. She was back at her dad's company, taking it more seriously than before, talking about following me into accounting or some shit. I didn't give a damn what she did, as long as she was happy and wearing my brand.

I couldn't wait for evening. It was finally moving day. We'd be hauling our junk into the new place we'd picked out, this cozy apartment just outside the city, overlooking the mountains.

Today was the first day of the rest of my life with this woman. Just had to get through church first.

I met up with Sixty and Crawl at the bar. We filed into the big meeting room, with all the brothers waiting.

Dust twirled the gavel in his hand, staring through the wall like usual. Or, at least, that's what he wanted everybody to believe. I knew he was looking at the club relics on the wall, all the photos and things that belonged to the guys who were gone, perched forever beneath our big black DEADLY PISTOLS MC flag.

Bit by bit, the Prez was fixing up the club into something his old man would've been proud of. Shit, today I could say the same about myself, knowing my dad's eyes would've popped if he could see me with the woman I'd claimed.

And it was all fireworks from here. I'd have a ring on her finger before New Year's, and then we'd be working hard and long on our family.

My dick jerked when I thought about all the fucking we'd do to make our baby. Sweet, merciful Christ.

If I didn't strap her to the bed 'til she was knocked up, I'd lose my damned mind.

"Okay, boys, let's keep this short and sweet because some of you got other business." He looked at me knowingly. "We've got girls to interview next week for the new skin shop in Knoxville. The place has got its pink lights and a liquor license, and it's all set to go. We just need some girls before we can open the floodgates to some serious money."

Joker grunted. "Fuck, Prez, you know that ain't the real reason we'll be bringing in bank. Do we really need to spend so much time interviewing some chicks?"

"Damned right we do. The Deads are a few men short,

but God knows the bastards aren't beneath using anybody as spies, even women. Hell, if we hadn't stopped 'em, they'd have sold Skin's old lady to some twisted fucker looking for a bitch to hide under his bed."

My eyes darkened. I looked at the Prez and nodded, trying not to imagine the hellish fate that would've been on the line for my woman if I hadn't come along.

I'd saved her. And she'd done the same to me. That woman didn't owe me anything except her heart, and now that I had it, I was gonna keep it 'til we were both ashes.

"Let me put it out there now – who wants to screen the girls?"

Half a dozen hands with shit-eating grins behind them shot up like lightning. Everybody's except for me, Joker, and the Prez.

"Damn, Prez, just say the word. I'll have a fucking classified up on the web by nightfall if it gets us hiring pussy sooner." Firefly grinned wide enough to chew the world up, his big biceps flexing as he slapped the table.

He'd been outta commission riding for a week or two with his torn up shoulder. But the bullet hadn't set him back much. I'd seen him in the bar last week, another hot blonde on his lap, sucking the horny bastard off while he sucked down the closest bottle of Jim.

"The sooner things are looking legit, the better." Dust said, moving his eyes across us, and stopping on me again. "Skin, you've got all the financials together for our order up north, right?"

I nodded. "Fifty big. That'll get us lots of shiny new

toys from the Prairie Devils. I talked to Throttle's man last week to work out the specifics. All cash, locked up tight. They'll bring everything we want down to Kentucky. It'll be good to start building a relationship with those boys now, before we clear a trade route to the Carolina beaches."

Dust grinned. I'd never seen the Prez look so determined, as if he was already seeing the clubhouse plated with gold.

"That's what I wanna hear. We'll work on the battle plans and make sure we've got some residual money coming in to keep us afloat. Then, when the trap is set, we'll swing it shut on the Deads' balls so fucking hard they scream."

The boys laughed. Even I couldn't resist a bloodthirsty grin. I'd never give their club enough payback for what the motherfuckers tried to do to Meg and me.

"You heard the Prez." Firefly looked around, still wearing his smug grin. "Let's party harder and hire the hottest sluts we can get for the new bar. We're gonna have a route punched clean through Deadhands' territory to the ocean by spring. And then this club'll be so fucking rich we'll make every man wearing different colors cry like a jealous bitch."

"Firefly said it. A year from now, half of you won't even recognize this clubhouse, and the rest of you'll be blinded by the glory. One year." Dust's voice went stern, hushed, and he lifted a finger. "We'll make the whole continent shake. Everybody's gonna know the Smokies are home to the biggest, baddest MC around, one that will fuck anybody who fucks with us straight into oblivion."

Fists hit the table. Men jeered. I believed he was right, all except one thing – I already had the hottest pussy in the world waiting for me at home. I was already overflowing with wealth, rich beyond my wildest dreams, as long as I put my lips on hers every night.

Didn't blame any of my brothers for getting all excited about heaps of money and hot new girls. Shit, a couple months ago, and I'd have done the same.

The Prez had a lot to be crazy about, and so did all the boys. But my life was shining like a second sun, all thanks to her.

What the hell use did I have for more bloodlust when the only thing I had on my mind was getting home and fucking my girl?

XI: Old Lady's Way (Megan)

I stood in front of the mirror, doing a spin to check the skintight stockings clinging to my thighs. We'd fucked so many times by now it was second nature, but something about today made me flush like a virgin.

I couldn't believe we were really moving in together. Heck, I couldn't believe I was going to survive watching him unloading all those heavy boxes, everything the movers I'd hired brought to our doorstep.

Work could wait. I needed to keep my sanity, and so, I planned a surprise, the best way I knew to bring my man into bed and wear me out. The boxes could wait until tomorrow. Tonight, it was all about us, and I couldn't wait to christen our empty new place with cries of our pleasure.

I heard his bike pull into the garage just as I slid beneath the sheets. The screen banged shut half a minute later.

"Babe?" he called, his heavy boots thudding on the hardwood floors, gradually weaving through the maze of boxes and furniture, making his way to the bedroom.

"I'm in here," I said softly, once I knew he was in the hall.

He froze in the doorway the second he saw me. "Fucking shit."

I grinned, turning on my side, feeling like something out of an old 1960s movie where women went all out to seduce their men. Of course, none of the men in those black and white flicks had a thing on Skin. Not with their suits, their ties, their sharp waxed mustaches.

The man holding himself in the frame looked like a bull about to charge. "What's this? I thought you wanted to get started setting up? You must need my cock like crazy."

"You know I do," I moaned, pushing my legs together.

Jesus, my panties were already soaked. He stepped loudly into the room, his hands working on his belt, dragging it out through the loops and fisting it in one hand.

"I oughta spank you silly for teasing me like this," he growled, his eyes dark and serious enough to do it.

"You know I'm not a tease," I cooed. "Well, not much, anyway. Come on, old man. Take what's yours. I know you can't get enough of me. I'm yours, all yours, forever."

I still couldn't say those words without my voice shaking near the end. Several months ago, I couldn't have imagined this.

When Ricky and his Johns had me under lock and key, I never thought I'd willingly give myself to a man again.

I never thought I'd give it all up so easily.

Never thought I'd crave a masculine touch.

Never thought I'd stamp something like PROPERTY OF SKIN into my very flesh.

But I did. I did it all for him, as surely as my pussy burned to feel him in me, slick and hot and wanting.

"Shit, woman, there goes the whole night." His belt dropped, banging its buckle on the floor.

His clothes weren't far behind. I sucked my bottom lip as I saw his cut fall, and then the shirt he wore under it. He rolled it off over his head to reveal the dark tattoos I loved to scratch, kiss, and bite.

We always started slow, but ended so rough. Fucking Skin was like a slow moving heat storm, a tempest that made me wet with sweat and desire. One that didn't let up until I was completely exhausted, shaken, and wanting him all over again.

His pants dropped and he kicked off his boots, saving his boxers for last. His cock sprang out, angry and ready, pulling him toward the bed like a magnet, eager to fill me hard and deep.

Two more steps, and his hand shot out. He stopped near my belly, grabbing at the sheet, and ripped it off in one vicious yank. It went flying over his shoulder across the room, and there was nothing else between us.

"Fuck me outta my mind," he growled.

I swooned as his hungry eyes crawled over me, slowly feeding our lust. He saw everything I had for him, the creamy lingerie I'd picked out. White stockings, white panties, white bra.

White, just like something I'd wear walking down the aisle, or maybe on my honeymoon.

I'd decided that morning I wasn't waiting for a wedding to dress like his whore, his wife.

I ached to feel every inch of him slamming me senseless in our brand new home. It had been the longest morning of my life at Daddy's office, like torture, waiting to trade my long business dress for this lingerie I'd picked out as his old lady.

"You're damned lucky I'm gonna make you come your brains out before I shove my cock inside you, woman. It'll make it easier when I shred that white lace you're wearing like fucking confetti."

He pounced, covering me with his massive, beautiful body. I moaned when I felt his cock press against my panties, nothing but sopping wet lace between us. Skin's lips pulsed along my neck, kissing down my throat.

His hand moved aggressively, pulling my bra aside. I whimpered and shook when he took my nipple in his mouth. It only caused him to growl, and pin me down harder.

Holy shit. Holy Skin. Holy Parker!

Yes, everything was holy when his wicked mouth went to work. His free hand slipped down the waistband to my panties and he circled my clit, faster and faster as his tongue moved like clockwork over my nipples.

I feared I'd come on the spot. My hands scratched at his powerful wrist, but he held me down so easily, dominating me completely.

This man never lied. He always lived by his word, doing exactly what he promised, whether he was killing monsters on the street or taking over every inch of me.

That meant I could never hide, never hold back, never stop the waves of pleasure from crashing over me and sweeping me away.

When a man possesses you so much, seizes every molecule with his energy, hiding isn't even an option.

"Fuck, Parker…I can't!"

Oh, but I could. His tongue moved to my opposite breast just as his thumb found my clit, running over it again and again. His rough fingers stroked my pussy to heaven.

I could take anything and everything with this man.

I came hard, right on his hand, feeling my cunt tense up and gush. He lifted his head off my breasts and crushed his lips over my mouth, stifling my breathless gasps, swallowing every scream.

"Beautiful, babe, just fuckin' beautiful. You know you come like a rocket a little more every time we do this, yeah?"

I squinted through the ecstasy, regrouping my senses. "Light me up again."

He stared down at me with those dark brown eyes and grinned. "Baby, you don't need to ask me twice. You're a kept woman now that we're sharing a bed every night. We're gonna ruin these sheets with scorch marks by the end of the week."

He took my hands, jerked me up like a ragdoll, and

flipped me over on the bed. Before I even knew what was happening, my panties snapped down to my knees so fast I swore he really did rip them in two.

His growl pressed against my thighs, vibrating through his lips, moving into my skin like a slow moving storm.

Even after all this time, he still scared me in the best ways. I finally had a man who'd *never* let anyone disrespect me, not even myself. He'd fight for me, bleed for me, kill for me. He'd already done it.

I couldn't imagine how possessive he'd get someday when we were hitched and I had a baby in my arms. The thought made my knees tremble, and so did his tongue, his stubble, both sliding deliciously up, up, up, dangerously close to my aching pussy.

"Skin – please! Let me feel you. No teasing, not today. You know what I'm dying for…"

Wish granted. Without a word, his thick hands shoved my legs apart, and his tongue caught the cream leaking out of me. He licked my entire slit like it was the sweetest thing he'd ever tasted.

Long, greedy, pussy clenching licks. *Fuck!*

I almost lost it again. With him, I turned into every cliché in romance, a sticky, breathless mess of a woman whose mind blanked on everything except the primal need to have him buried in me.

His tongue was so, so good, but it was never enough. I started panting like an animal in heat as he buried his face between my legs.

Sucking, fucking, tonguing me until my core tightened

like the world's hottest coil. He held me down the more I shook, a force of nature teasing my most tender flesh, his pressure quickening by the second.

Oh.

Oh, fuck.

Heaven. Help. Me.

But the only man I ever needed help from pushed me into the blinding fire when his tongue landed on my clit one more time. I nearly scratched a hole through the new mattress, clawing at the bed for support, feeling his strength holding me up as I came.

Harder than before. Always, always harder.

Hot, wet, fiery bliss consumed me.

I rocked against his face while he rumbled pleasure in his throat, fucking his tongue into me, everywhere seemingly all at once. I'd never understand how he did it. He was only human, but he put me into a zone nobody else ever would, a place so secure and sexy I wanted to stay forever.

Skin held me gently for a moment when I finally stopped screaming.

I struggled to catch my breath, loving his fingers running through my hair, stroking me back to soft awareness.

His hot, feral whisper helped too. "You've got thirty seconds to fill your lungs, baby girl. Then I'm filling you. We're fucking all night, and I'm not gonna stop 'til the sun comes up."

"Oh, God."

"Yeah, that's the only thing that'll save you from this dick, babe. What were you expecting here? Did you really think I wouldn't fuck you stupid after seeing you dolled up like my goddamned bride? Did you really think I'd just drop my load and crash without leaving you spent to the whole fucking world?"

His hand slipped down to my ass and struck me hard. I whimpered and jerked forward, but he caught me by the hair, shoving me into place, making me feel the hard-on raging against my ass cheeks.

I still pretended I didn't like being spanked and ordered around. But we both knew better. My little white lie only seemed to turn him on more, and soon he nipped at my ear, growling raw desire into me again.

"Bullshit, Meg. I love you so fucking much I could die. You ain't stupid. Don't you ever play coy with me. You're as smart as you are beautiful. You know what lovers do."

I did. Oh, how I did, and I learned a little more every night I was with him. I had a feeling my education was about to swell a hundred times faster now that we finally had a home together, a new bed to wear down every sultry night.

The cabin was only permanent, fickle, as lovely as it could be. Here, we'd forge a future, in the bedroom and out.

"I know, Skin. Trust me, I do."

"Yeah, you'd fucking better, beautiful." He pulled on my hair, twisting me to the side, pointing out the window with the pale gray light streaming in. "Winter's coming soon, sweet babe, and that means you're gonna spend those long, dark nights coming every way I tell you to. We've got to stay warm. We've got to light a fire. And I'm gonna make this town echo with the sounds of my cock making you scream."

"I love you!" I shouted it just as he spread my legs and pushed inside me.

It wasn't tender. It sounded like a curse on my lips, and it only made his hips piston when he went to work, anchoring his angry tip deep inside me, stroking me in hard, fast, aggressive waves. His balls slapped my pussy harder as he pinned me to the bed.

No surprise, our first fuck here hit harder than lightning. Just like the way I'd fallen for this man. He bent me to him in a flash of fire, heat, insatiable lust.

Whatever spell he'd worked on me today, it was stronger than ever.

He couldn't have fucked me for more than a couple minutes before I felt my pussy tightening again, burning for release, begging me to beg him for what I needed more than anything else.

"Come with me, Skin. Come inside me!" I panted, I moaned, I surrendered as my eyelids fluttered shut.

"Fuck, no. Not 'til I feel your little pussy squeeze this cock like you're losing your mind. You're hot, babe, but you're not burning down yet. I want to fuck a fireball before I let you feel my come."

Sweat hissed out my pores. He slowed his strokes. I could've turned around and killed him, if only he didn't have me hog-tied with his arms, pinned down like his personal fuck toy.

He stopped me right when I was on the brink. My hips shook. I fought to fuck him back, slam my ass into him, make him lose control until he filled me with his smoldering seed.

"You're a bastard!" I whimpered. "I love you, but I hate you right now. Please let me come. *Please.*"

"Fuck, yeah, woman, you always knew I was. Lucky for both of us you love it like this, don't you? You love all the new ways I find to make you come harder."

Bastard. Angel. Old man.

Whatever he was just then, he was absolutely right. I'd never felt so alive as my heart pounded, sending fire through every vein, awakening a need in my body like I'd barely known before.

"You want it harder, don't you?"

Was he serious? Like he couldn't feel the raw ache pouring out of me in every gasp, every buck of my hips, every plea filling every molecule?

"Fuck me!" I grunted through my teeth, practically spitting like a lioness in heat. "Harder!"

"Nah, not yet. You've gotta make me believe you deserve it, babe. I oughta have a damned straitjacket on you to hold you down. I want you to fight for this. Remember it. I want you coming so hard on this cock you never, ever forget our first night together, even when we're both too old and senile to fuck like mad."

"I will! How could I ever forget, Skin?" His cock sped

up, slamming into me, and he pulled on my hair. "How?"

The only answer was in his hips. That was when I knew he was right – I was so wound up, so ready to explore in a shower of ecstasy, that I'd remember this until the day I died.

"Because I just might fuck you so hard you lose your damned mind."

And he did. One hand tore at my hair, holding me up while his other hand grabbed my ass, all the better to jerk me into him with so much force I knew I'd be sore for days.

This was fucking. *This* was love.

This was him and I, tangled together on levels I could barely comprehend, thrashing our bodies raw. His cock slammed into me so fast and hard I was sure he'd break, and I didn't fucking care.

Not when the pleasure hit. It throttled me like a nuke going off in my belly.

Slow. Dense. Delicious.

Skin roared when he pushed himself deep one more time, and added his explosion to my clenching, sucking cunt. The hot come I'd learned to crave hurled into me at last.

"Skin! Skin! Skin!"

I came harder than I ever thought possible, screaming his name like a mantra until I couldn't even move my jaw. The whole world froze, locked in this unforgettable instant, this fire so hot it turned to ice.

There was nothing here but me, him, and the flames

twirling inside of me. I lost myself in the dizzying pleasure and the sound of his rough grunts, stretching out forever, emptying everything he had inside me.

Or at least getting started.

I knew we weren't finished. Not by half. When this badass told me he was going to fuck me all night, he meant every word. I thanked my lucky stars I'd taken a few days off for the big move.

"Come on, baby. Walk with me." He jerked me up and pulled me to his chest when we were done, grabbing my old lady jacket off the chair.

I loved the little coat. It had PROPERTY OF SKIN patched on the backside, just like my brand. It made me believe I could be the world's baddest bitch every time I slipped it on, or at least one fit for him, the only man whose opinion mattered anymore.

He wrapped it around my shoulders. He wouldn't let me wear anything else, nor did I want to. Then he led me out to our new porch, stained old world brown, a color that reminded me of my dad's library.

The cool autumn air brushed my legs. He pulled me close to his heat when he felt the first shiver running through my body. I rubbed his arms, remembering how much I loved them.

As if I could ever forget. These were the arms that saved me, loved me, dark and devilish with their inks as they were delightful.

He let me lift his hand to my face and I kissed it. I still wanted to worship every inch of him.

"What're we doing out here?" I asked, as if in a dream.

"Having a moment, babe. Just you and me. I told you before, you're gonna remember tonight for the rest of your damned life."

It was his turn to take my hand. He pushed it against the bottom pocket. My eyebrows flicked up when I touched the hard little box there. Without another word, he grabbed my hand and pushed it inside, pulling it out a second later with –

"Oh my God."

The little black box sat neatly in my palm. Amazing how something so small could hold the key to the rest of my life.

"Skin…"

"No, baby. Don't talk. Not yet." He pushed a stiff finger against my lips.

His other hand circled to the black box in my hand, and he flicked it open. The world's most beautiful gold ring sat there inside it, a tiny silver dagger molded on the loop, with diamond in the middle.

"When I told you I wanted you to remember today forever, it's not because we're moved in. It's not even because we're fucking like wild animals. We've been living together for weeks back at my cabin before we landed this place, and I cherish every damned day with you. But you're gonna remember tonight because it's the night you became my wife. All you've gotta give me is one simple word." He paused, tense and dramatic. "What do you say, Megan Wilder?"

I could barely think. There wasn't time when it all came rushing out.

"Yes!" I whispered, turning toward him, pushing my lips against his.

At some point we stopped kissing long enough for him to take the ring out and shove it on my finger. Its coolness surrounded my finger, but more importantly, it was *right.*

"Don't ever forget I loved you before you just made me the happiest outlaw in the whole damned world." He grinned, gazing into my eyes.

I eyed the scar running down his face and smiled, a beautiful imperfection as beautifully imperfect as all of this.

Fuck perfect. Fuck the man with the trust fund and the job with a suit and tie. Fuck everything I'd thought was grand, what I'd feared had been stolen from me forever by the pimp.

I had the only man I'd ever want right here, the one who'd shown me there was more life on the back of a motorcycle than a lifetime in a stuffy mansion.

"I'm not sure about that, Skin. I think I can make you a whole lot happier before the night's through." I reached down, feeling his muscular thighs, rounding my fingers to his cock, hard again and pulsing for attention.

"Fuck, you know I love a challenge, babe. Show me. I already know my old lady gives good head, and now I wanna feel my fiance's tongue on every inch of me."

Smiling, I dropped to my knees. I worshiped his body all night, the same way I knew I would for the rest of my life.

Alive, loved, and finally free.

I never thought I'd love an outlaw, much less marry one. Now, I couldn't imagine being happy with anything less.

Thanks!

Want more Nicole Snow? Sign up for my newsletter to hear about new releases, subscriber only goodies, and other fun stuff!

JOIN THE NICOLE SNOW NEWSLETTER! - http://eepurl.com/HwFW1

Thank you so much for buying this book. I hope my romances will brighten your mornings and darken your evenings with total pleasure. Sensuality makes everything more vivid, doesn't it?

If you liked this book, please consider leaving a review and checking out my other erotic romance tales.

Got a comment on my work? Email me at nicolesnowerotica@gmail.com. I love hearing from my fans!

Kisses,
Nicole Snow

More Erotic Romance by Nicole Snow

FIGHT FOR HER HEART

BIG BAD DARE: TATTOOS AND SUBMISSION

MERCILESS LOVE: A DARK ROMANCE

LOVE SCARS: BAD BOY'S BRIDE

RECKLESSLY HIS: A BAD BOY MAFIA ROMANCE

STEPBROTHER CHARMING: A BILLIONAIRE BAD BOY ROMANCE

STEPBROTHER UNSEALED: A BAD BOY MILITARY ROMANCE

Outlaw Love/Prairie Devils MC Books

OUTLAW KIND OF LOVE

NOMAD KIND OF LOVE

SAVAGE KIND OF LOVE

WICKED KIND OF LOVE

BITTER KIND OF LOVE

Outlaw Love/ Grizzlies MC Books

OUTLAW'S KISS

OUTLAW'S OBSESSION

OUTLAW'S BRIDE

SEXY SAMPLES: OUTLAW'S KISS

I: Cursed Bones (Missy)

"It won't be long now," the nurse said, checking dad's IV bag. "Breathing getting shallower…pulse is slowing…don't worry, girls. He won't feel a thing. That's what the morphine's for."

I had to squeeze his hand to make sure he wasn't dead yet. Jesus, he was so cold. I swore there was a ten degree difference between dad's fingers in one hand, and my little sister's in the other. I blinked back tears, trying to be brave for Jackie, who watched helplessly, trembling and shaking at my side.

We'd already said our goodbyes. We'd been doing that for the last hour, right before he slipped into unconsciousness for what I guessed was the last time.

I turned to my sister. "It'll be okay. He's going to a better place. No more suffering. The cancer, all the pain…it dies with him. Dad's finally getting better."

"Missy…" Jackie squeaked, ripping her hand away from me and covering her face.

The nurse gave me a sympathetic look. It took so much effort to push down the lump in my throat without cracking up. I choked on my grief, holding it in, cold and sharp as death looming large.

I threw an arm around my sister, pulling her close.

Lying like this was a bitch.

I wasn't really sure what I believed anymore, but I had to say something. Jackie was the one who needed all my support now. Dad's long, painful dying days were about to be over.

Not that it made anything easy. But I was grown up, and I could handle it. Losing him at twenty-one was hard, but if I was fourteen, like the small trembling girl next to me?

"Melissa." Thin, weak fingers tightened on my wrist with surprising strength.

I jumped, drawing my arm off Jackie, looking at the sick man in the bed. His eyes were wide open and his lips were moving. The sickly sheen on his forehead glowed, one last light before it burned out forever.

"Daddy? What is it?" I leaned in close, wondering if I'd imagined him saying my name.

"Forgive me," he hissed. "I…I fucked up bad. But I did it for a good reason. I just wish I could've done it different, baby…"

His eyelids fluttered. I squeezed his fingers as tight as I could, moving closer to his gray lips. What the hell was he saying? Was this about Mom again?

She'd been gone for ten years in a car accident, waiting for him on the other side. "Daddy? Hey!"

I grabbed his bony shoulder and gently shook him. He was still there, fighting the black wave pulling him lower, insistent and overpowering.

"It's the only way…I couldn't do it with hard work.

Honest work. That never paid shit." He blinked, running his tongue over his lips. "Just look in the basement, baby. There's a palate…roofing tiles. Everything I ever wanted to leave my girls is there. It was worth it…I promised her I'd do anything for you and Jackie…and I did. I did it, Carol. Our girls are set. I'm ready to burn if I need to…"

Hearing him say mom's name, and then talk about burning? I blinked back tears and shook my head.

What the hell was this? Some kinda death fever making him talk nonsense?

Dad started to slump into the mattress, a harsh rattle in his throat, the tiny splash of color left in his face becoming pale ash. I backed away as the machines howled. The nurse looked at me and nodded. She rushed to his free side, intently watching his heartbeat jerk on the monitor.

The machine released an earsplitting wail as the line went flat.

Jackie completely lost it. I grabbed her tight, holding onto her, turning away until the mechanical screaming stopped. I wanted to cover my ears, but I wanted hers closed more.

I held my little sister and rocked her to my chest. We didn't move until the nurse finally touched my shoulder, nudging us into the waiting room outside.

We sat and waited for all the official business of death to finish up. My brain couldn't stop going back to his last words, the best distraction I had to keep my sanity.

What was he talking about? His last words sounded so strange, so sure. So repentant, and that truly frightened me.

I didn't dare get my hopes up, as much as I wanted to believe we wouldn't lose everything and end up living in the car next week. The medical bills snatched up the last few pennies left over from his pension and disability – the same fate waiting for our house as soon as his funeral was done.

Delirious, I thought. *His dying wish was for us, hoping and praying we'd be okay. He went out selflessly, just like a good father should.*

That was it. Had to be.

He was dying, after all…pumped full of drugs, driven crazy in his last moments. But I couldn't let go of what he said about the basement.

We'd have to scour the house anyway before the state kicked us out. If there was anything more to his words besides crazy talk, we'd find out soon enough, right?

I looked at Jackie, biting my lip. I tried not to hope off a dead man's words. But damn it, I did.

If he'd tucked away some spare cash or some silver to pawn, I wouldn't turn it down. Anything would help us live another day without facing the gaping void left by his brutal end.

My sister was tipped back in her chair, one tissue pressed tight to her eyes. I reached for her hand and squeezed, careful not to set her off all over again.

"We're going to figure this out," I promised. "Don't worry about anything except mourning him, Jackie. You're not going anywhere. I'm going to do my damnedest to find us a place and pay the bills while you stay in school."

She straightened up, clearing her throat, shooting me a nasty look. "Stop talking to me like I'm a stupid kid!"

I blinked. Jackie leaned in, showing me her bloodshot eyes. "I'm not as old as you, sis, but I'm not retarded. We're out of money. I get that. I know you won't find a job in this shitty town with half a degree and no experience…we'll end up homeless, and then the state'll get involved. They'll take me away from you, stick me with some freaky foster parents. But I won't forget you, Missy. I'll be okay. I'll survive."

Rage shot through me. Rage against the world, myself, maybe even dad's ghost for putting us in this fucked up position.

I clenched my jaw. "That's *not* going to happen, Jackie. Don't even go there. I won't let –"

"Whatever. It's not like it matters. I just hope there's a way for us to keep in touch when the hammer falls." She was quiet for a couple minutes before she finally looked up, her eyes redder than before. "I heard what he said while I was crying. Daddy didn't have crap after he got sick and left the force – nothing but those measly checks. He didn't earn a dime while he was sick. He died the same way he lived, Missy – sorry, and completely full of shit."

Anger howled through me. I wanted to grab her, shake her, tell her to get a fucking grip and stop obsessing on disaster. But I knew she didn't mean it.

Lashing out wouldn't do any good. Rage was all part of

grief, wasn't it? I kept waiting for mine to bubble to the surface, toxic as the crap they'd pumped into our father to prolong his life by a few weeks towards the end.

I settled back in my chair and closed my eyes. I'd find some way to keep my promise to Jackie, whether there was a lucky break waiting for us in the basement or just more junk, more wreckage from our lives.

Daddy wasn't ready to be a single father when Mom got killed, but he'd managed. He did the best he could before he had to deal with the shit hand dealt to him by this merciless life. I closed my eyes, vowing I'd do the same.

No demons waiting for us on the road ahead would stop me. Making sure neither of us died with dad was my new religion, and I swore I'd never, ever lose my faith.

A week passed. A lonely, bitter week in late winter with a meager funeral. Daddy's estranged brother sent us some money to have him cremated and buried with a bare bones headstone.

I wouldn't ask Uncle Ken for a nickel more, even if he'd been man enough to show his face at the funeral. Thankfully, it wasn't something to worry about. He kept his distance several states away, the same 'ostrich asshole' daddy always said he was since they'd fallen out over my grandparent's miniscule inheritance.

All it did was confirm the whole family was fucked. I had no one now except Jackie, and it was her and I against the world, the last of the Thomas girls against the curse turning our lives to pure hell over the last decade.

A short trip to the attorney's office told me what I already knew about dad's assets. What little he had was going into state hands. Medicare was determined to claw back a tiny fraction of what they'd spent on his care. And because I was now Jackie's legal guardian, his pension and disability was as good as buried with him.

The older lawyer asked me if I'd made arrangements with extended family, almost as an afterthought. Of course I had, I lied. I made sure to straighten up and smile real big when I said it.

I was a responsible adult. I could make money sprout from weeds. What did the truth matter in a world that wasn't wired to give us an ounce of help?

Whatever shit was waiting for us up ahead needed to be fed, nourished with lies if I wanted to keep it from burying us. I was ready for that, ready to throw on as many fake smiles and twisted truths as I needed to keep Jackie safe and happy.

Whatever wiggle room we'd had for innocent mistakes slammed shut the instant daddy's heart stopped in the sharp white room.

I was so busy dealing with sadness and red tape that I'd nearly forgotten about his last words. Finishing up his affairs and making sure Jackie still got some sleep and decent food in her belly took all week, stealing away the meager energy I had left.

It was late one night after she'd gone to bed when I finally remembered. It hit me while I was watching a bad spy movie on late night TV, halfway paying attention to the story as my stomach twisted in knots, steeling itself for the frantic job hunt I had to start tomorrow.

I got up from my chair and padded over to the basement door. Dust teased my nose, dead little flecks suspended in the dim light. The basement stank like mildew, tinged with rubbing alcohol and all the spare medicine we'd stored down here while dad suffered at home.

I held my breath descending the stairs, knowing it would only get worse when I finally had to inhale. Our small basement was dark and creepy as any. I looked around, trying not to fixate on his old work bench. Seeing the old husks of half-finished RC planes he used to build in better times would definitely bring tears.

Roofing tiles, he'd said. Okay, but where?

It took more than a minute just scanning back and forth before I noticed the big blue tarp. It was wedged in the narrow slit between the furnace and the hot water tank.

My heart ticked faster. So, he wasn't totally delusional on his death bed. There really were roofing tiles there – and what else?

It was even stranger because the thing hadn't been here when I was down in the basement last week – and daddy had been in hospice for three weeks. He couldn't have crawled back and hidden the unknown package here. Jackie definitely couldn't have done it and kept her mouth shut.

That left one disturbing possibility – someone had broken into our house and left it here.

Ice ran through my veins. I shook off wild thoughts about intruders, kneeling down next to the blue plastic and running my hands over it.

Yup, it felt like a roofing palate. Not that I'd handled many to know, but whatever was beneath it was jagged, sandy, and square.

Screw it. Let's see what's really in here, I thought.

Clenching my teeth, I dragged the stack out. It was lighter than I expected, and it didn't take long to find the ropey ties holding it together. One pull and it came off easy. A thick slab of shingles slid out and thudded on the beaten concrete, kicking up more dust lodged in the utilities.

I covered my mouth and coughed. Disappointment settled in my stomach, heavy as the construction crap in front of me. I prepared myself for a big fat nothing hidden in the cracks.

"Damn it," I whispered, shaking my head. My hands dove for the shingles and started to tug, desperate to get this shit over with and say goodbye to the last hope humming in my stomach.

The shingles didn't come up easy. Planting my feet on both sides and tugging didn't pull the stack apart like I expected. Grunting, I pulled harder, taking my rage and frustration out on this joke at my feet.

There was a ripping sound much different than I expected. I tumbled backward and hit the dryer, looking at the square block in my hands. When I turned it over, I saw the back was a mess of glue and cardboard.

Hope beat in my chest again, however faint. This was no ordinary stack of shingles. My arms were shaking as I dropped the flap and walked back to the pile, looking down at the torn cardboard center hidden by the layer I'd peeled off. Someone went through some serious trouble camouflaging the box underneath.

I walked to dad's old bench for a box cutter, too stunned with the weird discovery to dwell on his mementos. The blade went in and tore through in a neat slice. I quickly carved out an opening, totally unprepared for the thick leafy pile that came falling out.

My jaw dropped along with the box cutter. I hit the ground, resting my knees on the piles of cash, and tore into the rest of the box.

Hundreds – no, thousands – came out in huge piles. I tore through the package and turned it upside down, showering myself in more cash than I'd seen in my life, hundreds bound together in crisp rolls with red rubber bands.

Had to cover my mouth to stifle the insane laughter tearing at my lungs. I couldn't let Jackie hear me and come running downstairs. If I was all alone, I would've laughed like a psycho, mad with the unexpected light streaking to life in our darkness.

Jesus, I barely knew how to handle the mystery fortune myself, let alone involve my little sis. I collapsed on the floor, feeling hot tears running down my cheeks. The stupid grin pulling at my face lingered.

Somehow, someway, he'd done it. Daddy had really done it.

He'd left us everything we'd need to survive. Hell, all we'd need to *thrive.* Feeling the cool million crunching underneath my jeans like leaves proved it.

"Shit!" I swore, realizing I was rolling around in the money like a demented celebrity.

Panicking, I kicked my legs, careful to check every nook around me for anything I'd kicked away in shock. When I saw it was all there, I grabbed an old laundry basket and started piling the stacks in it. I pulled one out and took off the rubber band. Rifling my fingers through several fistfuls of cash told me everything was separated in neat bundles of twenty-five hundred dollars.

I piled them in, feverishly counting. I had to stop around the half million mark. There was at least double that on the floor. Eventually, I'd settle down and inventory it to the dime, but for now I was looking at somewhere between one to two million, easy.

It was magnitudes greater than anything this family had seen in its best years, before everything went to shit. I smoothed my fingers over my face, loving the unmistakable money scent clinging to my hands.

No shock – sweet freedom smelled exactly like cold hard cash.

An hour later, I'd stuffed it into an old black suitcase, something discreet I could keep with me. My stomach gurgled. One burden lifted, and another one landed on my shoulders.

I wasn't stupid. I'd heard plenty about what daddy did for the Redding PD's investigations to know spending too much mystery money at once brought serious consequences. Wherever this money came from, it sure as hell wasn't clean.

I'd have to keep one eye glued to the cash for…months? Years?

Shit. Grim responsibility burned in my brain, and it made my bones hurt like they were locked in quicksand. Dirty money wasn't easy to spend.

I'd have to risk a few bigger chunks up front on groceries, a tune-up for our ancient Ford LTD, and then a down payment on a new place for Jackie and I.

It wouldn't buy us a luxury condo – not if we wanted to save ourselves a Federal investigation. But this cash was plenty to make a greedy landlord's eyes light up and take a few months' worth of rent without any uncomfortable questions. It was more than enough to give us food plus a roof over our heads while I figured out the rest.

Survival was still the name of the game, even if it had gotten unexpectedly easier.

Once our needs were secure, then I could figure out the rest. Maybe I'd find a way to finagle my way back into school so I could finish the accounting program I'd been forced to drop when dad's cancer went terminal.

It felt like hours passed while I finished filling up the suitcase and triple checked the basement for runaway money. When I was finally satisfied I'd secured everything,

I grabbed the suitcases and marched upstairs, turning out the light behind me. I switched off the TV and headed straight for bed.

I sighed, knowing I was in for a long, restless night, even with the miracle cash safe beneath my bed. Or maybe because of it.

I couldn't tell if my heart or my head was more drained. They'd both been absolutely ripped out and shot to the moon these past two weeks.

I closed my eyes and tried to sleep. Tomorrow, I'd be hunting for a brand new place instead of a job while Jackie caught up on schoolwork. That happy fact alone should've made it easier to sleep.

But nothing about this was simple or joyful. It wasn't a lottery win.

Dwelling on the gaping canyon left in our lives by both our dead parents was a constant brutal temptation, especially when it was dark, cold, and quiet. So was avoiding the question that kept boiling in my head – how had he gotten it?

What the *fuck* had daddy done to make this much money from nothing? Life insurance payouts and stock dividends didn't get dropped off in mysterious packages downstairs.

He'd asked for forgiveness before his body gave out. My lips trembled and I pinched my eyes shut, praying he hadn't done something terrible – not directly, anyway. He was too sick for too long to kill anyone. He'd been off the force for a few years too.

I lost minutes – maybe hours – thinking about how he'd earned the dirty little secret underneath my bed. Whatever he'd done, it was bad. But at the end of the day, how much did I care?

And no matter how much blood the cash was soaked in, we needed it. I wasn't about to latch onto fantasy ethics and flush his dying legacy down the toilet. Blood money or not, we *needed* it. No fucking way was I going to burn the one thing that would keep us fed, clothed, sheltered, and sane.

Jackie never had to know where our miracle came from. Neither did I. Maybe years from now I'd have time for soul searching, time to worry about what kind of sick sins I'd branded onto my conscience by profiting off this freak inheritance.

Fretting about murder and corruption right now wouldn't keep the state from taking Jackie away when we were homeless. I had to keep my mouth shut and my mind more closed than ever. I had to treat it like a lottery win I could never tell anyone about.

Besides, it was all just temporary. I'd use the fortune to pay the rent and put food in our fridge until I finished school and got myself a job. Then I'd slowly feed the rest into something useful for Jackie's college – something that wouldn't get us busted.

It must've been after three o'clock when I finally fell asleep. If only I had a crystal ball, or stayed awake just an hour or two longer.

I would've seen the hurricane coming, the pitch black

storm that always comes in when a girl takes the hand the devil's offered.

An earsplitting scream woke me first, but it was really the door slamming a second later that convinced me I wasn't dreaming.

Jackie!

I threw my blanket off and sat up, reaching for my phone on the nightstand. My hand slid across the smooth wood, and adrenaline dumped in my blood when I realized there was nothing there.

Too dark. I didn't realize the stranger was standing right over me until I tried to bolt up, slamming into his vice-like grip instead. Before I could even scream, his hand was over my mouth. Scratchy stubble prickled my cheek as his lips parted against my ear.

"Don't. You fucking scream, I'll have to put a bullet in your spine." Cold metal pushed up beneath my shirt, a gun barrel, proof he wasn't making an empty threat.

Not that I'd have doubted it. His tight, sinister embrace stayed locked around my waist as he turned me around and nudged his legs against mine, forcing me to move toward the hall.

"Just go where I tell you, and this'll all be over nice and quick. Nobody has to get hurt."

I listened. When we got to the basement door, he flung it open and lightened his grip, knowing it was a one way trip downstairs with no hope for escape.

Jackie was already down there against the wall, and so

were four more large, brutal men like the one who'd held me. I blinked when I got to the foot of the stairs and took in the bizarre scene. They all wore matching leather vests with GRIZZLIES MC, CALIFORNIA emblazoned up their sides and on their backs.

I'd seen bikers traveling the roads for years, but never anything like these guys. Their jackets looked a lot like the ones veterans wore when they went out riding, but the symbols were all different. Bloody, strange, and very dangerous looking.

The men themselves matched the snarling bears on their leather. Four of them were younger, tattooed, spanning the spectrum from lean and wiry to pure muscle. The guy who'd walked me down the stairs moved where I could see him. He might've been the youngest, but I wasn't really sure.

Scary didn't begin to describe him. He looked at me with his arms folded, piercing green eyes going right through my soul, set in a stern cold face. He exuded a strength and severity that only came naturally – a born badass. A predator completely fixed on me.

An older man with long gray hair seemed to be in charge. He looked at the man holding my sister, another hard faced man with barbed wire ropes tattooed across his face. Jackie's eyes were bulging, shimmering like wide, frantic pools, pulling me in.

I'm sorry, I hissed in my head, breaking eye contact. One more second and I might've lost it. The only thing worse than being down here at their mercy was showing them I was already weak, broken, helpless.

They had my little sister, my whole world, everything I'd sworn to protect. No, this wasn't the time to freak out and cry. I had to keep it together if we were going to get out of this alive.

"Well? Any sign of the haul upstairs, or do we need to make these bitches sing?" Gray hair reached into his pocket, retrieving a cigarette and a lighter, as casually as if he was at work on a smoke break.

Shit, for all I knew, he probably was.

"Nothing up there, Blackjack." The man who'd taken me downstairs stepped forward, leaving the basement echoing with his smoky voice, older and more commanding than I'd expected. It hadn't just been the rough whisper flowing into my ear.

"Fuck," the psycho holding Jackie growled. "I like it the fun way, but I'm not a fan when these bitches scream. Makes my ears ring for days. Can't we gag these cunts first?"

Nobody answered him. The older man narrowed his eyes, looking at his goon, taking a long pull on the cigarette. My head was spinning, making it feel like the ground had softened up, ready to suck me under and bury me alive.

Oh, God. I knew this had to be about the mystery money the moment those rough hands went around me, but I hadn't really thought we were about to die until he said that.

Gray hair turned to face me, scowling. "You heard the

man, love. We can do this the easy way or the hard way. I, for one, don't like spilling blood when there's no good reason, but some of the brothers feel differently. Now, we know your loot's not where it was supposed to be – found this shit all torn up myself."

Blowing his smoke, he pointed at the mess on the ground. I could've choked myself for being too stupid to clean up the mess earlier.

"You've got it somewhere. It couldn't have gotten far," he said, striding forward. "Look we both know me and my boys are gonna find it. Only question left is – are you gonna make this scavenger hunt easy-peasy-punkin-squeezy? Or are you gonna make all our fucking ears ring while we choke it out of you?"

I didn't answer. My eyes floated above his shoulder, fixing on the man across from me, stoic green eyes.

"Well?" The older asshole was getting impatient.

Strange. If Green Eyes wasn't so busy hanging out with these creeps and taking hostages, he would've been handsome. No, downright sexy was a better word.

My weeping, broken brain was still fixed on the stupid idea when Gray Hair grunted, pulled the light out of his mouth, and reached for my throat…

Look for Outlaw's Kiss at your favorite retailer!